THE ELVES OF ANDROMEDA

THE IMPERIUM CHRONICLES
BOOK FIVE

W. H. MITCHELL

Cover design: Steven Novak (NovakIllustration.com)

Published by: Willbot Books, 2023

ISBN-13: 978-1-7351189-4-9

Works by W. H. Mitchell

The Imperium Chronicles Series

The Arks of Andromeda, Book 1 (2017)

The Dragons of Andromeda, Book 2 (2018)

The Robots of Andromeda, Book 3 (2020)

The Dreams of Andromeda, Book 4 (2021)

The Elves of Andromeda, Book 5 (2023)

Humor

A Little of Me Goes a Long Way (2015)

To my wonderful wife, who's always willing to lower her expectations of me.

Special thanks to Brad Snyder and
Patron of the Arts, Judy Veatch.

Additional thanks to my beta readers:

Chris Buckland

Mary Hanover

A character list and glossary are located at the back of the book.

CHAPTER ONE

A new era had dawned on the Imperium. After the abdication of the previous emperor, the Imperial Conclave had selected Jack Groen as the new ruler. Since Jack was still too young, the Conclave had also picked Lady Veber, matriarch of the Veber family, as regent until the boy emperor came of age.

On the planet Aldorus, in the capital city of Regalis, Lady Veber browsed through documents on her datapad, deciding which emergency took precedence over the others. Her office, adjacent to the Imperial throne room, overlooked the palace gardens through towering windows.

Still in her forties, with a wide face and blue eyes, Lady Veber wore her blond hair in an intricate braid. Her turquoise dress, covered in a shell motif, was tucked beneath the intricately carved, walnut desk.

A door opened and a young man in his late teens entered. His tunic and pants were green, denoting his family's colors, while a gold ringlet over his short, blond hair denoted his status as Emperor of the Imperium.

"Your majesty!" Lady Veber said with a smile.

Jack Groen rolled his eyes as if embarrassed by the title.

"You don't have to call me that," he said, his face faintly blushing.

Lady Veber set the datapad down.

"You'll need to get used to it," she replied.

"Well, I'm not," he said. "Not yet anyway."

The boy emperor approached the desk and surveyed the various pads and papers littering the surface. "Busy?"

She laughed.

"If I knew I'd be imprisoned in this office," she replied, "I wouldn't have accepted the position."

"That bad?"

"Well," Lady Veber conceded, "I have time for a walk, I suppose..."

Jack flashed a grin.

"Come on then!" he said.

In the Imperial gardens, Lady Veber's office windows visible behind them, the emperor and his regent strolled between hedges shaped like animals while pea gravel crunched beneath their shoes.

"I'm sorry you're shouldering so much work for my sake," Jack said.

Lady Veber lifted her dress slightly, careful the taffeta wouldn't drag across the gravel.

"It's only my responsibility for another year," she replied. "Then it's *your* problem."

Lines appeared between Jack's eyes. "Right."

"Sorry, your majesty," she said. "I'm only joking. Anyway, I have no doubt you'll do very well. That's why I voted for you during the Conclave..."

"Thanks for that," Jack replied sardonically.

"Are you worried?"

"A little."

"Well, you won't be alone," Lady Veber said. "Your ministers will help, and you'll always have me after all."

"Thank you," he replied, and then after a pause asked, "What's the biggest danger right now?"

"Now? Oh, the same as always," she said. "The Magna Supremacy remains poised on our borders, waiting for the first sign of weakness. I'm sure they're eager to see how you do once you're in charge."

The Magna were the historic enemies of the Imperium, just as ruthless and expansionist as the humans themselves. However, after multiple interstellar wars, neither side had emerged dominant.

"And, of course," she went on, "there's the other royal houses. The Five Families will try to manipulate you every chance they get."

"Except yours and mine..." Jack said hopefully.

Lady Veber chuckled. "Don't bet on it."

"Great," he said dejectedly.

"Don't worry," Lady Veber assured him. "You'll do just fine. Anyway, I should get back to my cell..." She turned, her dress swishing. "Thank you for the fresh air," she said.

"Don't mention it," the boy emperor replied, his voice trailing off behind her.

Still on the planet Aldorus, but miles from the capital of Regalis, the Dharmesh Monastery rose from the peaks of the Palatine Mountains like a granite ghost. Lit with torches, the otherwise darkened hallways hosted the sounds of young acolytes practicing their psionic mind powers and the monks admonishing them to do better. Down one of these corridors, away from the rest, a heavy door barred the entrance to the Abbot's study. Inside, the elderly Dahl was perched behind a desk like a bird nesting in a clutter of tomes, tablets, and loose papers.

Dressed in the amber robes of his order, the Abbot stared at a book of Dahlvish history while wisps of his gray hair dangled around his pointed ears. He was so enthralled with what he was reading, the Abbot failed to notice the shimmering blue image of a female Dahl hanging in the air in front of him.

"Ahem," the apparition said, clearing her throat.

The Abbot glanced up and felt his heart skip a beat.

"Blynora!" he exclaimed.

"That's *Elder* Blynora," she corrected him.

"My apologies, *Elder*," the Abbot replied. "I wasn't expecting a psionic projection this morning..."

The ghostly image of the Elder, projected by Blynora's mind all the way from the Dahlvish home world, wore pale robes of white to match her long, silver hair. An intricate headpiece, made of platinum with a sapphire at the center, adorned her forehead.

"One wonders if you've lived too long among the humans," she remarked acerbically.

"I keep my distance as much as possible," the Abbot assured her.

"Yet, you have a continuing mentorship with *one* of them. What was her name?"

"Miss Doric," the Abbot said. "Jessica Doric."

"Exactly."

"As a matter of fact," the elderly monk went on, "Miss Doric has shown a true appreciation of our culture. I see no harm in fostering her enlightenment."

"Is that why you have failed to retrieve the artifact in their possession?" Blynora asked.

"I assume you're referring to the beacon?" the Abbot replied. "Although they call it the *Singing Lantern* as I recall..."

"It is a powerful relic of our people's past. Far *too* powerful to remain in human hands."

"There's not much *they* can do with it," the Abbot said, "and they've taken safeguards to prevent anyone with psionic powers from using it either."

The shimmering image flickered with irritation.

"Regardless," Blynora said, "it should be studied by our scholars, not sitting in a rich human's display case. To that end, Prenwyn University has once again requested access to the artifact."

With some embarrassment on his face, the Abbot hesitated.

"As you say," he replied, "Lord Maycare has been reluctant to part with it..."

"If this human woman is indeed your protégé," Blynora said, "perhaps she could use her influence with Lord Maycare. She is, after all, his *paramour.*"

The Abbot nearly swallowed his tongue.

"No, no!" he replied, coughing. "Their relationship is purely platonic."

"Really? With Maycare's reputation as a playboy? I just assumed..."

"Miss Doric leads the Maycare Institute of Xeno Studies," the Abbot said. "She's a consummate professional."

"I see," Blynora replied. "Well, perhaps she can appeal to Lord Maycare by some other means?"

The Abbot nodded. "I'll see what I can do."

"Thank you."

Without saying goodbye, the projection faded, leaving the Abbot again alone in his study.

"Bother," the old Dahl said with a sigh. "I'm sure this will end well..."

The private library on the Maycare estate was a long room full of shelves, with polished oak tables in the center and a fireplace on either end. Jessica Doric sat at one of the tables, poring over a tome of Dahlvish love sonnets.

She brushed away the dishwater blond hair hanging in front of her pale brown eyes, careful not to spill a cup of tea perched precariously on a stack of other books. More essential to her work at the Institute of Xeno Studies, these books included publications about history and lore, and anything that might mention the whereabouts of ancient artifacts.

Although the Maycare library was extensive, Doric often wished she had more access to the Pool of Memory at the Dharmesh Monastery. The pool was a liquid computer containing the sum of all Dahlvish knowledge, but only the Dahl were permitted its use except in the rarest of cases. Even her mentor, the Abbot at the monastery, had refused all but the occasional visit.

Beside the teacup, a datapad began buzzing with a photo of the Abbot on the screen. Doric quickly closed the poetry book and slipped it between the other tomes before answering the call.

She touched the screen and the Abbot's real face smiled back at her.

"What a surprise!" Doric said.

"Miss Doric," the Abbot replied warmly. "So good to see you. I thought about projecting myself psionically, but humans usually act as if they've seen a ghost!"

"I suppose that's true," Doric admitted, "although I personally don't believe in ghosts."

"Well, wait until you meet one!"

Doric wasn't sure if the Abbot was being serious or not, so she merely nodded.

"What can I do for you?" she asked.

"Funny you should ask," the Abbot replied. "I need a favor..."

"Of course. Whatever you need."

"It's about the Singing Lantern," the old monk said, "apparently Prenwyn University on my home planet wants to study it."

"Oh," Doric replied. "I don't know if that's possible..."

The Abbot waved his hand. "Yes, yes, I realize Lord Maycare keeps a tight grip on his trophies, but I was hoping you might have a word with him."

"I've tried," Doric said, "but you know how he can be."

"Quite right, but—" the Abbot said before hesitating, "you see, Elder Blynora made the request herself."

"The head of the Elder Council?" Doric replied, suddenly aware her mouth was hanging open. "What an honor!"

"If you say so," the Abbot said, "although I've always found her unduly demanding..."

"But why now? We've had the artifact for over five years."

"I really couldn't say," the Abbot replied, "but Elder Blynora made clear she would feel more comfortable with it in Dahlvish hands."

"I'm sorry, Abbot," Doric said, "I just don't think Lord Maycare will change his mind."

The monk's expression became thoughtful.

"You know, Miss Doric," he said, "if you were to accompany the artifact on the journey to Gwlad Ard'un, it's possible you could take part in the study."

Doric's eyes widened. "Really?"

"After all," the Abbot continued, "it would be a great opportunity to see my home planet."

Doric felt her pulse quicken.

"I've never been there," she admitted.

"But it's a shame that someone with such a short attention span as Lord Maycare can't be persuaded to part with his toy, even though he's surrounded by newer trinkets I'm sure..."

"I'll talk to him," Doric said, straightening in her chair. "Maybe he *can* see reason."

"Maybe he can!" the Abbot replied cheerfully. "I have every confidence in you!"

Saying goodbye, Doric ended the call, the screen on the datapad going dark. Breathing deeply, she felt a surge of excitement flowing through her petite frame. Then, with a thump in her heart, Doric realized she had no idea how she would convince Maycare to give her the artifact, let alone take it all the way to Gwlad Ard'un.

"Shit," she said.

Henry Riff's apartment was poorly lit, the drapes drawn across the single window, but this only made the television screen brighter as a result. Henry's goldfish, Finneus Finnegan, watched the TV from his bowl without comprehending the words on the screen:

ENJOY MIASMA MIST!
THE NEWEST PURPLE FLAVOR
OF SPASTIC COLA!
ANOTHER FINE PRODUCT FROM MOFOCO!

From looking at the television, the goldfish's bulging eyes meandered to the floor where fast food wrappers and other trash cluttered the carpet. One item, a soda bottle, lay empty except for a few drops of purple cola.

The door to the bathroom opened and Henry emerged, his face even paler than usual. Holding his stomach with one hand, he steadied himself against the door frame with the other. His hair was uncombed, and his rumpled clothing gave him the appearance of someone younger, perhaps living in a college dorm or under a bridge.

Henry dragged himself over to the couch, collapsing onto the cushions while Finneus looked on.

Henry moaned when he felt something vibrating beneath him. Thinking he needed to rush to the bathroom again, he stood up only to realize it was a call on his datapad. Henry lifted one of the cushions and retrieved the pad underneath, swiping the screen to reveal his boss's face staring disapprovingly back at him.

"Henry?" Jessica Doric said.

"Yes?" Henry replied weakly.

"Have you been drinking Spastic Cola again?"

"I had a coupon..." he said.

Doric rolled her eyes. "I need you at the Maycare estate."

"Now?"

"Are you busy?" she asked.

Henry glanced at the various things he should be cleaning in his apartment.

"No," he said.

An hour later, he arrived in the West End, the exclusive district of Regalis where most of the nobles lived and much of the Imperial government was located. The Maycare estate was there as well, built like a castle with turrets and stone walls. Henry let himself in and found Jessica Doric in her office.

Henry had managed to comb his hair somewhat and exchanged one set of shabby clothing for another, slightly less shabby set. Doric didn't seem to notice.

"We have a problem," she said.

"Oh?" Henry replied.

"The Abbot called me—"

"How is he doing?" Henry asked.

"Focus, Henry!"

"Sorry..."

"The Abbot called me," Doric went on, "and he really wants us to hand over the Singing Lantern."

"The Lantern?"

"Yes."

"But Lord Maycare doesn't want to do that..."

"I'm aware of that, Henry," Doric replied. "Any ideas?"

Henry scratched behind his ear. "I dunno."

Doric groaned.

"The Abbot said Prenwyn University wants to study the relic on Gwlad Ard'un," she said, "and I could bring it there myself."

"Wow," Henry remarked.

"I could probably bring you too," Doric added.

"Really?"

"Yes, so it's a real opportunity for *both* of us."

"Okay," Henry replied, and then after a pause, "Maybe we could appeal to Lord Maycare's selfless nature?"

Henry and Doric both snickered.

"Well," Henry corrected himself, "we'll think of something..."

Down the hallways of the Maycare estate, artifacts of Lord Devlin Maycare's journeys were on display in all their glory. Maycare had always contended that he was saving these relics from falling into the hands of Warlock Industries or other nefarious entities. Ostensibly, that was the reason he founded his Institute of Xeno Studies and hired Jessica Doric to run it. Doric was thankful for the job, especially since she had just been laid off from Regalis University at the time, but she remained skeptical of Maycare's true intentions. He was an egotist, and Doric secretly suspected he was more interested in adding extra trophies to the ones he had won as a sportsman.

In fact, it was in his trophy room where Doric, with Henry in tow, found Lord Maycare, his deep, masculine voice emanating from inside while they still remained in the corridor. Beside them in the hall stood a display case labeled *The Singing Lantern*, the glass surrounded by a shimmering force field. Behind the glass, the relic's concentric crystal disks, roughly in the shape of a lantern, had a dull luster, but Doric knew psionics would make it glow. It was a powerful artifact in the wrong hands, and Doric had insisted that Maycare install the force field to keep it safe and prevent anyone from accessing its powers.

Maycare's voice drifted into the hallway. "Maybe over there..."

"I don't think it will fit," the voice of Benson, Maycare's butlerbot, replied.

Doric motioned for Henry to follow as she went inside the room where awards, both big and small, were crammed on shelves reaching from floor to ceiling. Benson was holding a particularly large cup forged from silver and engraved with names, presumably one of them being *Lord Devlin Maycare*.

"I bet that would hold a lot of cereal," Henry remarked.

Maycare turned around. "What?"

"Nothing..." Henry muttered.

In his late forties, Maycare was a tall, muscular man with broad shoulders and warm, brown eyes. His tailored shirt was perfectly starched and his family's crest, a white stallion, was embroidered with golden thread just above his heart.

"Are you busy, Lord Maycare?" Doric asked.

"Jess!" he replied with a jolt of energy. "Help me find a place for this, would you? Benson is no help at all!"

Benson focused his eyes on the ceiling as if he would rather be somewhere else. He offered the heavy cup to Doric who waved it off.

"No, thanks," she said.

"Come on, Jess," Maycare pleaded. "I've run out of room!"

"What's this one for anyway?" she asked.

"Yacht racing, I think," Maycare said, casting an eye at Benson who nodded. "I was victorious... apparently."

Doric surveyed the collection of shiny objects on the shelves. "Why do you need all of these?"

"What do you mean?" Maycare asked.

"At some point," she went on, "don't you have *enough*?"

Maycare took a moment to digest the question before laughing. "No, of course not!"

Doric's shoulders slumped.

"How silly of me," she said.

"I see your point though," Maycare admitted. "Why should I keep winning if I've nowhere to put the evidence?"

"That's not exactly what I—"

"Unless there's a trophy for *most trophies*..." Maycare said, again his eyes falling on Benson who shook his mechanical head.

From behind Doric, his voice tiny in comparison to Maycare's, Henry spoke up, "Maybe if you took out this wall?"

"What's that?" Maycare asked.

Doric stepped out of the way while Henry did his best to seem bigger.

"If you took down this wall," he said meekly, "you could extend the room into the hallway."

Everyone, including the butlerbot, stared at him.

"That's brilliant!" Maycare shouted at last. "Why didn't *you* think of that, Benson?"

The robot shrugged.

"But what about whatever's in the hallway now?" Maycare asked.

"The Singing Lantern is just outside the door," Henry said.

"Actually," Doric said, "they've been asking to study the Lantern on Gwlad Ard'un and wondered if they could borrow it for a while."

Maycare rubbed his expansive chin. "I don't know, Jess..."

"If it's under my supervision," she replied, "I'm sure it'll be alright."

"Think of all the extra space you'll have with that bulky display case out of the way," Henry said. "You could fit another ten trophies for *sure*."

"Hmmm," Maycare murmured. "I hadn't considered that..."

Benson set the cup on the floor with a clunk. "Just say *yes*."

"Alright!" Maycare replied, turning to Doric. "But I expect you to take good care of it, Jess."

"I will!" she said, her eyes brightening. "You won't even miss it."

"That reminds me," Maycare said, addressing Benson. "Enter me in another ten races next week. I've got more trophies to win!"

Above a dead planet orbiting a burned-out star, a Magna vessel floated on the Imperial side of the border with the Magna Supremacy. A Daemon-class commerce raider, the ship had short, curved wings along a stubby body. Normally, such a warship would be attacking merchant shipping, but now it was silent as if waiting for something.

After several minutes, a flash split the curtain of stars and a ship emerged from hyperspace. Of ancient Dahlvish design, this craft was more bird-like with a long fuselage and swept wings. It gracefully came to rest beside the Magna ship.

On the bridge of the raider, the Magna captain sat in the command chair among the rest of his crew. On either side of the captain's bald head, horns curled above his emerald-green skin.

"The ship is hailing us, Captain," one of the crew said.

"Put him on screen," the Magna replied, his voice a deep growl.

The windows at the front changed from a view of the dead planet below to the crimson face of a Sarkan named Enrion.

The Sarkans were an offshoot of the Dahl race with the same pointed ears, but dark red hair and vermilion skin, not to mention an overly aggressive disposition.

"Captain Ra-Gor," the Sarkan said. "My apologizes for being late."

"I don't like waiting," Ra-Gor replied.

"You should have picked a less remote rendezvous point then," Enrion remarked.

The Magna scoffed.

"Secrecy is paramount," he replied. "Imperial ships rarely patrol here."

"Very well. What do you want?"

Ra-Gor scowled, displeased with the Sarkan's tone.

"Your masters wish to test the new Emperor," he said through clenched teeth. "We want to see how the Regency reacts."

"The Magna are not my masters," Enrion replied, his eyes narrowed. "The Sarkans are not lapdogs like the Dahl are to their human conquerors."

"You are *all* inferior!" the Magna captain replied. "None of you are worthy to lick my boots!"

Enrion sighed.

"This was a mistake," Enrion said. "I'm leaving—"

"You will stay!" Ra-Gor commanded, curling his hand into a fist. "Or my ship will blast you from the sky."

"Fine," the Sarkan said. "What do you want *exactly?*"

Ra-Gor attempted to regain his composure. "As the humans would say, you are an *agent provocateur*, yes?"

"Yes."

"Then *provoke!*"

Enrion thought for a moment before his mouth curled into a grin.

"As a matter of fact," he said, "I may have a few ideas..."

"Good," the Magna captain replied. "We will monitor the usual channels for your reports. Do not disappoint us."

"I'll do my *best*," Enrion said, his voice steeped with contempt.

The Sarkan's face vanished from the screen, replaced by the image of Enrion's ship firing its thrusters and banking away. In a few moments, the ship disappeared back into hyperspace.

Watching from his command chair, the Magna captain couldn't decide whether he wished the Sarkan to succeed or fail.

Arrogant fool, he thought, confident in his own superiority.

CHAPTER TWO

On the planet Eudora Prime, Melinda Freck burst from the forest riding a gravbike. Mel, as most people called her, had built the bike mostly from spare parts salvaged from junk yards and whatever she could procure, legally or otherwise, from the businesses of Technotown.

She had spent most of the day working on a generator in the Sylvan town of Gowyn. The Sylva, otherwise known as Woodland Dahl, were another sub-race of the Dahl. Although it was a long trip there and back, Mel was happy for the work since jobs had been scarce for quite some time.

Mel leaned into the handlebars as the wind pressed her pink hair tight against her head. A Gnomi, she was no more than three feet tall, making the gravbike seem massive beneath her.

In the distance, Technotown rose out of the evening gloom, the city lights beginning to waken. Five years ago, an invasion by the robots of the Cyber Collective had destroyed much of Technotown. Filled with humans at the time, those who didn't escape were either killed or thrown into internment camps. After the war, when the warbots had withdrawn, few humans remained and fewer still returned to the planet, leaving Technotown in ruins.

Before the invasion, non-humans like Mel lived below ground in a place called the Underdelve. Their subterranean bazaar rivaled the shops in the city above. Once the warbots and humans left, however, the non-humans moved to the surface and rebuilt Technotown. Since then, the streets had teemed with those who had previously lived out of sight.

Mel nudged the accelerator as the gravbike dropped a few hundred feet until she was skimming across the ground. She reminded herself to check the propulsion unit, which had been giving her trouble. She might need to "liberate" a new one if she couldn't fix this one.

Entering Technotown, even at high speed, Mel could still make out the signs in the shop windows: *No Tinks Allowed!*

Her eyes narrowed.

These were stores owned by non-humans, people who had lived with her in the Underdelve before the war. Now, they acted as if Gnomi like her, disparagingly called *tinks* or *tinkers*, were nothing more than thieves.

If I steal from you, it's because you have the best parts, Mel thought. *It's a compliment!*

Mel parked the gravbike near a culvert and disappeared into the darkness. At the end of a long tunnel, she came out into a chamber once part of the sewer system decades ago. Beneath pipes running along the ceiling, old market stalls of wood and tattered cloth were all that remained of the bazaar that had once rivaled Technotown above. This had been the heart of the Underdelve, but Mel was one of the few who remained.

She came to a rusty steel door with the words *Freck's Gizmos & Gadgets* welded into the metal. It creaked as she pushed it open and went inside.

Her shop, such as it was, contained boxes of loose wires and broken machinery, scattered around a work bench. Actually, it had always looked this way, but the lack of work of late made Mel even less inclined to clean it up. Rent was cheap, as in zero, but a Gnomi still needed to eat. Also, she was growing increasingly bored with every passing day.

Tired, she headed toward the cot at the back of the shop where a red light on her computer caught her attention. Flicking on the screen, she found a message waiting for her. It had come all the way from the Imperial capital Regalis on the planet Aldorus:

DEAR MELINDA,
I'M WORKING ON A NEW PROJECT
AND I NEED YOUR HELP!
COME TO ALDORUS ASAP!
YOUR FAVORITE RELATIVE,
UNCLE ARTIE

For the first time in quite a while, Mel laughed out loud. Then, just as quickly, her smile turned to a frown.

"How the hell am I going to get to Aldorus?" she asked.

The coffee maker in the galley aboard the *Wanderer* hadn't worked for a week and Captain Rowan Ramus was losing his patience. He stared into his empty coffee mug and wondered if he should have had tea instead like some kind of animal.

Ramus wore a leather jacket over a red t-shirt and a pair of leather pants. His hair was also a bright crimson. He was a Dahl, but the silver rings in his pointed ears suggested he was not like most Dahl people would meet.

"Fugg!" he shouted.

"What?" a harsh voice yelled back from down the corridor.

"Get in here!" Ramus ordered.

Orkney Fugg, the chief engineer, ambled through the doorway without a sense of urgency, followed by a robot.

Fugg was a Gordian, short and stocky, with a pair of tusks protruding from his mouth and a boar-like pig nose. He wore loose-fitting cargo pants and a black tank top exposing a tattoo on his meaty right biceps. The tattoo was like a pirate flag except with a pair of crossed wrenches below the skull instead of bones.

"I was doing something!" Fugg protested. "I'm teaching Gen how to fix stuff..."

"Hi, Captain," Gen the General-Purpose Robot said. She smiled at Ramus with big blue eyes, matching the rest of her largely plastic and metallic frame.

Ramus scowled at the engineer while simultaneously giving Gen an encouraging nod.

"How can you keep the *Wanderer* in shipshape when you can't even fix a coffee maker?" the captain asked.

"I've got priorities!" Fugg replied, waving a thick finger in the air.

"We've been sitting on the ground for a week," Ramus said. "What else have you been doing?"

Fugg's eyes darted left and right. "Things!"

"I could try fixing the coffee maker," Gen suggested.

Ramus took a long breath.

"Sure," he said, exhaling. "Go ahead, Gen. At least *somebody* around here is working."

"What about *you?*" Fugg asked the captain. "We've only been sittin' here because you haven't found us any *work!*"

Now it was Ramus' turn to be defensive.

"It's been slow!" he yelled.

"Like a tortoise in a tar pit!" Fugg replied, crossing his arms.

"It's fixed," Gen said.

"What?" both the captain and chief engineer replied, turning to the robot now standing beside the coffee maker.

"It was just a loose wire," Gen said.

"That was quick," Fugg muttered.

"Sorry," the robot replied with an embarrassed shrug.

Ramus cleared his throat, raw from too much yelling.

"No reason to apologize," he said. "Good work."

Gen smiled. "Thanks!"

Fugg raised an eyebrow. "Do you hear something?"

Ramus became aware of a faint pounding from somewhere on the ship. It had a steady cadence, stopped, and then began again.

"You've had a week to fix this ship..." he said, staring accusingly at Fugg.

"It's not my fault!" the engineer replied. "It's coming from outside!"

The crew of the *Wanderer* made their way to the outer hull where Ramus punched the button for the cargo ramp. With a hiss, the hydraulics lurched into motion, lowering the ramp. Through the open walkway, standing beside one of the landing gear, Mel Freck was holding a length of pipe.

"Are you people deaf?" she shouted. "I've been banging on this forever!"

Ta Demona liked the dark. Countless times, she would lay in the silent darkness, listening to the thoughts of others in an adjoining room. This was how she gathered intelligence for the Psi Lords, her employer, who would sell that information to the highest bidder. The Psi Lords were a data cartel and knowledge was their currency. Ta Demona was one of their agents with skills they found extremely useful.

In a dimly lit operating room deep within the Psi Lord headquarters, Demona examined her handiwork while still wearing the black robes of her former sisterhood, the Augmentors, who worshipped technology. Like her, the man in the surgical chair was bald with circuitry running along his head. However, he was human while Demona's skin was green.

The patient grinned. "Well?" he asked.

Her mouth beneath a respirator mask, Demona could not return the smile. Her eyes merely surveyed the man approvingly.

"You'll live," she replied.

Kanet Solan reached up and touched the fresh scar on his scalp. A slight bump was visible just under the skin.

I can already feel the improvement, he said directly into Demona's mind. *My psi power has grown tenfold!*

Let the graft take hold before testing it too much, she warned. *We wouldn't want your head to explode.*

"Indeed," Solan said aloud.

"Although some might celebrate that happening..." she added.

Crossing the operating room, Demona organized some of her tools while Solan pulled a hooded robe over his body. Unlike the sisterhood, Solan worshiped no one except himself. In that way, he was a true believer.

"When I recruited you on Technas Delphi," he said, "I never dreamt how useful you would become. You're my most valuable asset."

"You flatter me!" Demona scoffed.

"Now, now," Solan replied. "Don't tell me you regret leaving the sisterhood?"

She turned to face him.

"Not at all!" she said. "I've gained more since leaving there than I could have by staying. To them, I was a freak, but to you... I'm an *asset.*"

"Keep that in mind," Solan said. "You'll always remain one of us as long as you remain useful."

"Let's hope I continue to do so."

Solan changed the subject. "How long before the implant is fully integrated into my body?"

"A day or two," Demona replied matter-of-factly.

"Good," he said, "but it's still not enough..."

"No?"

"I must show the Dahl just how powerful I can become," Solan said, clenching his fist. "But for that, I'll need *additional* augmentation."

"Your skull may run out of room," Demona remarked.

He nodded.

"Perhaps," Solan replied, "but I have *other ideas*."

Inside the *Wanderer*, Mel dropped her heavy, leather satchel at the top of the loading ramp.

"Make yourself at home," Fugg remarked sarcastically.

Mel ignored the engineer, focusing her attention on Ramus along with Gen a few steps behind him.

"I heard you guys were in town," Mel said.

"So, you brought us your laundry?" Fugg asked. "Not that we couldn't use the work..."

"I need a lift," the Gnomi replied.

"Where to?" Ramus asked.

Mel ran her fingers through her messy, pink hair. "The capital..."

"That's halfway 'cross the Imperium!" Fugg grunted with a snort. "You got money?"

"My uncle sent me a message," Mel said, still avoiding eye contact with the engineer. "He needs my help with a big project he's working on."

"I didn't know you had an uncle," Ramus said coolly.

"Arthur Freck!" Mel replied as if insulted. "The most famous Gnomi tinker there ever was!"

"Oh!" Gen the robot exclaimed, duly impressed. "He sounds important!"

"You're damn right!" Mel replied.

Fugg crossed his chubby arms.

"If he's so great," he asked, "why's he need *your* help?"

For the first time, Mel gave the engineer the full benefit of her glaring eyes. "What's that supposed to mean?"

"You couldn't tink your way out of a Faraday cage!" Fugg said.

Mel made a quick charge at the engineer, only to find Ramus' arm blocking her way.

"That's enough," the captain said and then added, "Fugg has a point. Why does your uncle need your help anyway?"

Mel stopped and considered the question, which had apparently not occurred to her up until that moment.

"I dunno," she admitted.

"Perhaps he just misses his niece?" Gen offered. "Family is important..."

"Maybe," Ramus replied skeptically. "And not to side with Fugg twice in one day, but do you have any money to pay for the trip?"

"Well—" Mel hesitated.

"I knew it!" the chief engineer shouted, throwing up his hands.

"Shut up, Fugg!" Mel replied. "I'm good for it!"

"Aldorus is a long way," Ramus went on, "and fuel isn't cheap."

"My uncle can pay you when we get there," Mel said.

Ramus shook his head. "I'm sorry, no."

"I'll pay you a quarter now and my uncle will pay the rest on Aldorus," she replied.

"No."

Mel stomped her foot. "Business has been slow for everybody! Fugg just said you needed the *work*!"

The captain paused. "A *third* now."

Mel groaned but nodded.

"Fine, but you have to feed me," she said.

"Do you like ramen?" Gen asked.

"I guess..."

"Then it's a deal," the captain said.

Gen clapped her hands, making a metallic noise. "You can bunk with *me*!"

"Well she ain't stayin' in *my* cabin!" Fugg said, scowling.

"You wish!" Mel replied.

Ramus slapped the button at the top of the ramp, which slowly rose with enough clatter to drown out Mel and Fugg's bickering.

Mel slung the heavy satchel over her shoulder and followed Gen down a passageway into the heart of the *Wanderer*. They came to a door that slid to one side, revealing a small cabin with a bunk bed and a desk in the corner.

"Top or bottom?" Gen asked, pointing at the bed.

"Bottom would be better," Mel said, realizing there wasn't a ladder to the upper bunk.

"You bet!" the robot replied.

Mel kicked the bag underneath the bed and gave the room another look. Several posters were taped to the walls, including one with a robot with metal horns protruding from a curly, black wig. His face was painted with a white skull and the name *Diode* was written above his head.

"Do you like Diode?" Gen asked.

"Who's that?"

"A heavy metal singer from the Cyber Collective," Gen replied. "He plays at a frequency most humans can't hear, but I wasn't sure about Gnomi."

"We don't get a lot of Cyber music on Eudora Prime," Mel admitted. "Not since they invaded and killed a bunch of people..."

Gen's eyes widened.

"I'm so sorry!" she said, cringing.

"Don't worry about it," Mel replied. "Not all robots are killbots."

"Did you lose anyone you knew?"

"Some, but most of my non-human friends survived... not that they *act* like friends anymore."

"Fleshlings can be difficult," Gen remarked.

"So, you like Diode?" Mel asked, desperate to change the subject.

The robot gave an embarrassed laugh.

"I used to!" she said. "I even painted my face with a skull for a while, but Fugg said the music gave him migraines. Anyway, I'm into K-bots now! I love their choreography!"

"Uh-huh," Mel replied with added determination to talk about something else. "How are Fugg and Captain Ramus treating you?"

"Oh, fine," Gen said.

"To be honest, I'm a little surprised you're still with them."

"Why?" the robot asked.

"When they passed that Cyber Civil Liberties Bill, I thought for sure you'd get a job somewhere else," Mel replied.

Gen sat on the edge of the desk, her head tilted to one side.

"Oh, voting is nice," she said, "but I like it on the *Wanderer*. Captain Ramus started paying me a real salary and everything."

"How did Fugg take that?"

Gen cast her large eyes at the ceiling. "I don't remember..."

"Really?" Mel asked.

"He might've said something about robots being property, but the Captain talked to him about that. He made him watch a sensitivity video about robo-racism."

"Did that help?"

"Not really."

"Then why the hell did you stay?"

"Well, because..." Gen replied, her voice growing soft. "I mean, I know the Captain isn't perfect and Fugg threatens to throw me out of the airlock sometimes, but we're like a *family*."

Mel paused. "I guess I wouldn't know about that."

"Oh, did they die in the invasion?"

"No, no," Mel replied. "I never knew my parents. I was abandoned when I was a baby and Uncle Artie raised me. He's not my real uncle I guess, but he's probably the closest I had to a father."

"I'm sorry," the robot replied.

"It's fine."

"How come you aren't living with *him*?" Gen asked.

"I wanted to be on my own," Mel replied. "Sometimes I can be a little rebellious..."

"I hadn't noticed," Gen replied.

"Robots aren't very good liars," Mel remarked.

"No, I guess not."

The evenings were Arthur Freck's favorite time of the day, when the garbage gravbarges would float in from all over the city of Regalis and dump their trash on the *Boneyards*. For years, Regalis had used this corner of the Ashetown district as its main dumping ground.

Like his niece Mel, Uncle Artie was a Gnomi and, as such, smaller than most other races. A cap covering his bald head, Uncle Artie wore a brown boilersuit coated in decades of oil and grease. Wrinkles sagged beneath his purplish eyes, and his nose was shaped like a baby potato.

Uncle Artie smiled, showing off the gaps between his yellowing teeth.

In the distance, the bottom of a gravbarge opened, sending several tons of garbage onto the pile immediately below. Although he felt an eagerness to see what the city had disposed of for that day, Uncle Artie was keen on returning home. It was getting late and he was getting hungry.

I'll go through that pile tomorrow, Uncle Artie thought.

He wound his way between the mountains of junk until he came to the rear hatch of an old gravtruck sticking out from one of the peaks. Pulling the hatch open and closing it behind him, Uncle Artie found himself at the entrance to a tunnel that burrowed deep into the refuse. He hung his cap on a peg beside the door and walked down the passage until it opened into a larger room lit with lights strung from the ceiling.

"Welcome home!" a mechanical voice said.

Practically camouflaged against a wall of trash, a robot took a few steps forward, his body made from a mishmash of discarded items.

"Evenin', Zat," Uncle Artie replied. "What's for dinner?"

"Possum soup," the robot said. "Unless you found something better?"

"Nope, possum will have to do."

The robot went to a stove and began stirring a boiling pot. He had two eyes, one an integral part of his head while the other was welded to the side. The designation *Z-4T* was written on the chest plate in faded paint.

Zat's legs were two different sizes, one slightly shorter than the other, giving him an uneven gait as he brought a bowl of the soup over to the table where Uncle Artie was waiting. With a plastic spork, the Gnomi gave it a taste.

"Delicious!" Uncle Artie declared. "You got out most of the gristle this time!"

Although they didn't move in unison, Zat's eyes beamed with pride.

"I'm so glad," the robot said.

Uncle Artie went about finishing the meal, careful to fish out any bones. It was only when he noticed a shimmering reflection in the soup that Uncle Artie realized he had a visitor. Glancing up, he saw a bluish ghost hovering over him.

"Crap on a cracker!" Uncle Artie yelled, clutching his heart. "Why can't you just *call* like a *normal* person?"

The translucent specter lowered the hood he was wearing, uncovering the face of Kanet Solan from the Psi Lords.

"Because psionic projection is more secure," Solan replied. "Believe me, I *know*."

Uncle Artie grunted. "I suppose you've got every comm bugged from here to the Magna border."

"Oh, and *beyond*," the Psi Lord said with pride.

"Well, what do you want?"

"You know perfectly well," Solan replied. "I want an update on the device. You've had ample time to build the prototype."

"Of course I have," Uncle Artie said. "It's coming along quite nicely!"

"When can I see it then?"

"Soon enough," Uncle Artie replied. "There's still a few adjustments I need to make and then we can start testing it."

"You haven't started testing yet?"

"In good time!" Uncle Artie protested. "You can't rush a new invention. Everybody knows that!"

The hovering image heaved a sigh before pulling the hood back over his head.

"Very well," Solan said. "But don't try my patience. I don't like to be kept waiting..."

The ghost faded away, prompting Zat to ask, "What device was he talking about?"

"The Psi Lords want me to build a prototype for them," Uncle Artie said.

"I don't remember seeing you working on something like that," Zat said.

"Well, there's a perfectly good reason for that," Uncle Artie replied. "I haven't started yet."

CHAPTER THREE

Jessica Doric had packed everything she needed without knowing how long she would be gone. In two large suitcases, she had stowed enough tweed skirts for at least a week, several white blouses, and an appropriate number of unmentionables. She had neatly organized toiletries into smaller containers within the larger bags, as well as a collection of books dedicated to Dahlvish history. She had stored many more books on her datapad which she intended to read along the way.

Henry Riff's personal effects were entirely stuffed into a single gym bag, although Henry had never been to the gym in his life. He had momentarily considered using a trash bag instead, but Doric had been very insistent that he should use something that at least *resembled* actual luggage.

Henry also carried a glass bowl containing his goldfish.

"Why didn't you leave that at home?" Doric asked, the two standing in Maycare's foyer with Lord Maycare and his butlerbot. "I'm sure Benson would feed your fish."

"I would not," Benson the butlerbot replied. "My duties do not include *pets*."

"It's fine," Henry said. "Finneus only ever sees the inside of my apartment. I thought it would be nice to let him stretch his legs."

"Fish don't have legs, Henry," Doric said.

Lord Maycare puffed out his chest, preparing to speak.

"Jess, I don't see why you don't have *me* fly you to the Dahl home world," he said.

Doric gave him a courteous if somewhat triumphant smile.

"The Dahl sent me a ship," she said proudly. "It would be rude to turn them down."

"Suit yourself," he replied, shrugging his sizable shoulders. "Just make sure they don't drop my artifact..."

Everyone's eyes fell on a container the size of a steamer trunk sitting to one side. Like Pandora's Box, it was sealed, but beckoned someone to open it.

"It's locked, right?" Henry asked.

"It has a numeric code lock," Doric replied. "I'm the only one with the combination."

"Good!" Maycare said and glanced at Benson. "You're giving them a ride to the starport?"

"Indeed," the butlerbot said.

Returning his gaze to Doric and Henry, Maycare asked, "Sure you don't want me to come along?"

"Yes!" both of them replied.

"Huh," he said, poorly concealing his bruised ego. "Off you go then, apparently..."

Benson loaded the luggage, including the Singing Lantern, into the trunk of Maycare's gravcar while Doric and Henry loaded themselves into the backseat. Getting into the front, the butlerbot soon had the vehicle in the air where he entered the destination into the nav controls. The city's traffic control then automatically merged the car into the closest artery of other grav vehicles making their way across Regalis in invisible lanes.

Benson kept his hands on the wheel, however, just to keep up appearances.

With the fishbowl in his lap, Henry stared out the window. From a few hundred feet off the ground, he had a good view of the West End as they approached the Regalis River running north to south. Across the water, the Middleton district with its skyscrapers was visible on the left and the slums of Ashetown could be seen on the right.

Nearly an hour later, they reached the starport northeast of the city. A sprawling hive of activity in its own right, the port consisted of several buildings surrounded by miles of flat concrete slab where ships of all sizes were sitting like hunkered down animals.

Benson regained control of the gravcar and set it beside one of the ships. The main fuselage had a long, leaf-like shape with a slender, recurved belly in the middle. At the back, a pair of stubby wings protruded, ending in a hilt-like engine section. The hull was white with gold stripes painted along its length as well as the ship's name, the *Blaenwaun Bay*.

"It's beautiful," Doric remarked as she stepped out of the car.

"Is it Dahl?" Henry asked, joining her with the fishbowl in his hands.

"Dahlvish design, surely," she replied.

"It looks like a goose," Henry said.

"No, it *doesn't*."

"But with the long neck—"

Doric stopped him. "Don't embarrass me, Henry!"

"Sorry," he muttered.

One of the crew, a male Dahl dressed in robes of white with blue trim, came out of the ship and helped Benson unload the luggage onto a gravsled, which the Dahl then pushed back to be loaded into the hold.

"If everything is in order," the butlerbot said, addressing Doric, "I'll take my leave."

"Thank you, Benson," Doric said, prompting a short bow from the robot.

"Will you miss us?" Henry asked.

"Why, yes," Benson replied. "Bringing you coffee and tea has always been the highlight of my day."

Henry, unaware of the robot's sarcasm, waved goodbye as the gravcar lifted off and flew away.

"We should get aboard," Doric said.

When they reached the main airlock, they found the same crew member as before waiting for them at the foot of the ladder.

"Welcome aboard!" he said grandly.

Once everyone was inside, the Dahl showed Doric and Henry to their cabins and then the lounge where they sat while the ship prepared for takeoff.

"This *is* nice," Henry said, rubbing his hands on the velvet upholstery.

Doric motioned to the bowl in Henry's lap. "Why didn't you leave that in the cabin?"

"Finneus?" Henry replied. "I thought he could watch the takeoff through the window."

In fact, a long window stretched the length of the lounge, giving them, including Finneus, an excellent view of the ship lifting off the tarmac. Henry felt the artificial gravity activate, compensating for the g-forces. He glanced worriedly at his fish, but if Finneus was uncomfortable, his inscrutable expression gave nothing away.

What a trouper! Henry thought.

After the *Blaenwaun Bay* had made the jump to hyperspace, the crew served Doric and Henry a lavish meal before the two retired to their respective cabins. Compared to the rooms on Lord Maycare's yacht, these were smaller but better decorated, with ornate furniture painted white with blue and gold trim.

Henry set Finneus and his bowl on a dresser that had graceful curves inlaid with gold. Shaped like a leaf with bronze branches sprouting from the sides, a large mirror hung above it.

Hours later, Henry woke from a nightmare that he immediately forgot. A general sense of dread, however, kept him from falling back to sleep. He wandered out into the dimly lit lounge where he found Doric reading a book.

"Couldn't sleep?" Henry asked.

Doric looked up and squinted at him, her eyes adjusting.

"Yes," she replied. "I'm too excited about tomorrow."

"I bet," Henry remarked. "This must be like a dream come true!"

Henry took the seat beside her while trying to flatten down his bed-headed hair. "Why do you like the Dahl so much?"

"I don't know," she replied with a thoughtful expression. "I guess because they're life-long learners. I mean, I've always been an academic at heart, but the Dahl have dedicated their lives to gathering information and trying to make sense of it all. It's like we're kindred spirits."

"I see," Henry replied, but it was clear he did not.

Doric took a long breath before exhaling. "How much do you know about the Dahl?"

"They're like space elves, aren't they?" Henry said.

Doric's eyes widened before tightening into narrow lines. Henry felt the back of his neck grow hot.

"No, Henry!" Doric scolded. "They're *nothing* like that!"

"Sorry..."

"They're an ancient civilization," Doric went on, "with a rich heritage of art and culture."

This sounded suspiciously like elves to him, but Henry had enough sense not to say so out loud.

"They had an empire once," Doric said, "but they realized that learning about the universe was more important than ruling it."

"I thought the Pool of Memory was cool," Henry said.

"And it holds all of their collected knowledge," Doric replied. "A liquid computer like that is a technological marvel."

"But," Henry said, hesitating to upset his former teacher further, "their mind powers are kinda scary..."

Doric's face softened, much to Henry's surprise.

"Don't worry," she said. "The Dahl have committed themselves to *helping* humans, not harming them."

"I guess," Henry replied. "I've never understood *why* they help us."

"Because they want us to be better," she said. "It's part of their philosophy."

"What is?"

"Learn, understand, teach," Doric replied. "It's the three pillars the Dahl live by. You know, *see one, do one, teach one.*"

"Oh!" Henry replied. "I've heard of that!"

She opened her book again. "Good night, Henry."

When the *Blaenwaun Bay* dropped out of hyperspace, the planet of Gwlad Ard'un presented itself like a shining jewel of blue and green as if a sapphire and emerald had somehow melted together. The Dahl ship entered the atmosphere in a fiery glow before setting down beside Prenwyn University. While Doric and Henry waited for the crew to unload their luggage and the box holding the Singing Lantern, the two humans marveled at the Dahlvish architecture.

"Wow," Henry murmured, his eyes bulging.

The university was like a walled city surrounded by battlements of white marble thirty feet high. Slender towers rose from inside, the tall structures decorated with vine-like tendrils of gold.

From an arched gate, a Dahl approached. He appeared older than the crew of the *Blaenwaun Bay*, but younger than the Abbot. Doric had trouble gauging Dahlvish ages since their lifespans were so much greater than humans'.

Wearing brown robes, the Dahl smiled as he reached them, extending his hand to neither of them specifically.

"Are you Jessica Doric and her assistant?" he asked.

"Yes," Doric replied, taking his hand and giving it a tentative shake.

"Good!" he said. "I'm Professor Rhun of the Archeology department. Such a pleasure to meet you!"

"Likewise," Doric said. "I'm thrilled to be here!"

Professor Rhun eyed their bags. "I trust you brought the artifact with you?"

"Absolutely," Doric replied. "It's in the locked container."

"Locked?" he asked.

"You can't be too careful with something so valuable," she said.

He bowed slightly. "Indeed."

The crew had finished placing everything on a gravsled when Professor Rhun said, "Shall we proceed inside?"

"Yes," Doric replied, and turned toward Henry. "Can you handle the bags?"

Eager to please, Henry nodded energetically and got behind the sled, pushing it forward while Doric and the professor walked in front. Passing through the arched gate, the humans got a better look at the university. Most of the structures were tall and slender, with long, narrow windows set into curved frames of gold. Like the outer walls, the buildings were also white marble and carved with sinuous, organic lines.

At the center of an open courtyard, a three-tiered fountain filled the air with the sounds of splashing water, while trees with pink blossoms surrounded the edges of the open space.

"Is it Spring right now?" Henry asked, referring to the trees.

"Actually," Professor Rhun replied, "the trees on Gwlad Ard'un remain in bloom throughout the year."

"Beautiful!" Doric said, her eyes and mouth equally wide.

"I suppose one just grows accustomed to such things," the professor said. "I can't say I even notice them most of the time."

Doric regained her composure.

"Of course," she said matter-of-factly.

"So, where are we going to stay?" Henry asked.

"The university will see to that," Professor Rhun said, gesturing toward a structure Doric assumed was the administration building. "Meanwhile, I'll bring the artifact to my department."

"I'll meet you there once I get settled," Doric said. "I'll need to unlock the crate for you."

"Very good," the professor replied. "I'm eager to begin studying it..."

The university assigned Doric one of the houses usually reserved for visiting academics and dignitaries. Henry, on the other hand, ended up getting a shared room in one of the dormitories.

Reaching the door marked *Number 312* and with his luggage and Finneus in hand, Henry turned the old-fashioned key they had given him and went inside. The small room was divided in two, with a bed and desk on either side, and a window in the middle. The sides were identical except for the heavy-set Dahl sitting at the desk on the right, who gawked at Henry like he was a hobgoblin bursting into the room.

"What's the meaning of this?" the Dahl asked.

"I'm Henry," he replied. "I'm your new roommate."

"What are you looking at?"

"Well," Henry stammered, "I've never seen an *overweight* Dahl before."

In fact, the Dahl were known for being slender with elegant features and long, silky hair. This one, to Henry's amazement, was none of those things. The Dahl had a bowl cut and a round face. His robes were typical, but poorly fitting as if two sizes too small, and his belly poked out from under his vest.

"I'm sorry," Henry said. "I didn't mean to stare."

The Dahl frowned, glancing at the floor. "Nobody ever does..."

"What's your name?" Henry asked.

"Pwmpen."

"*Pumpkin?*"

"It's pronounced *pum pen!*"Pwmpen replied.

"Oh," Henry said. "Sorry."

Pwmpen's attention was suddenly fixated on the glass container under Henry's arm. "What's that?"

"This?" Henry replied. "It's my goldfish, Finneus Finnegan."

"A goldfish?" the Dahl asked. "Is it dangerous?"

"No, of course not!" Henry replied with a laugh.

"Well, it's beautiful," Pwmpen remarked, his demeanor softening. "Why don't you come in then, I guess."

Henry closed the door behind him and set the fishbowl down on the desk to the left.

"I apologize for my manners," Pwmpen said. "I didn't mean to be rude, but I've never had a roommate before, let alone a human."

"You've had this whole room to yourself?" Henry asked.

The Dahl looked away from the fish and gave the floor a hard stare. "Nobody wanted to room with me."

"Why?"

"Why do you think?" Pwmpen said tersely, motioning at his rounded figure. "Nobody wants to room with the *fat elf.*"

"The Dahl aren't elves," Henry replied. "Everybody knows that!"

"True, but when you're a freak, you get called all kinds of things."

"Well," Henry said, "I'm not exactly normal either, at least as far as humans go."

"Really?"

"A normal person would've left his goldfish at home, apparently."

Pwmpen looked up, this time setting his eyes on Henry instead of the fishbowl.

"I'm glad that you did, Henry," the Dahl said. "It's very nice to meet you."

Henry spent over an hour getting to know his new roommate before remembering Doric wanted him to meet her at Professor Rhun's office. After Pwmpen drew him a map, Henry set off and immediately got hopelessly lost among the interconnecting hallways and adjoining buildings.

For the most part, the Dahl students who Henry passed along the way were aloof to his plight despite giving him the side-eye. Even to Henry, it was clear the local inhabitants were not used to humans on the loose.

In one of the corridors, walking while studying his map, Henry collided with what he thought was a bear, knowing full well that bears were probably a rare occurrence in the hallways of Prenwyn University. Sent backwards and landing on his backside, Henry stared at the sizable, clawed feet of what definitely looked like a bear. However, as his eyes traveled up the furry creature's belly, Henry was surprised to find the large beak and golden eyes of an owl staring down at him.

"Who are you?" Henry asked.

"I could ask you the same question," the beast replied.

"I'm Henry."

"I'm Professor Grimfeather," the creature said. "We don't see many of *your* kind around here."

"Well, I've *never* seen *your* kind before either!" Henry replied somewhat defensively.

The professor bristled his feathers. "My people are called *Orubea*."

Now feeling guilty, Henry got back to his feet and tried offering his hand, unsure what the Orubea would do with it. Much to Henry's surprise, a furry paw clasped the hand and gave it a firm shake.

"There aren't many of us on Gwlad Ard'un," the professor went on, his voice low and a bit gruff, "but more than humans, I'm sure."

"We're just visiting."

"Oh?"

"Actually," Henry said, "do you happen to know where Professor Rhun's office is?

The Orubea raised a massive wing and pointed in the opposite direction.

"Go back the way you came," he said, "and take the first right."

Henry glanced at his map, turned it upside down, and nodded.

"Thank you!" he said and hurried away.

When he arrived at the door marked with Rhun's name, Henry found the professor along with Doric inside, staring at the now opened container and the Singing Lantern.

"Where have you been?" Doric asked.

"I got lost," Henry admitted.

"Of course," she said.

Professor Rhun, wearing a pair of thick gloves, lifted the Singing Lantern out of the box and placed it gingerly on a table. At the same time, a robot entered from the adjoining room. Floating above the ground, the robot was a spherical chamber about two feet wide with several mechanical arms hanging loosely below. The sphere was filled with a faintly sparkling liquid.

Henry had never seen a robot model like this before.

"What's that?" he asked.

"It's a Sprite," Professor Rhun said, removing his gloves. "I was just telling Miss Doric about it."

"It's like an extension of the Pool of Memory," Doric replied excitedly. "The liquid inside that ball is connected telepathically to the actual pool."

"The one on Aldorus?" Henry asked.

"No, they have one here as well," Doric said. "They use the Sprites like mobile computers, giving the academics access to the full knowledge of the Pool of Memory."

"Cool," Henry remarked. "By the way, do you know there's a big bear with feathers walking around campus?"

"He's referring to Grimfeather, I assume," Professor Rhun said. "He's a professor in the history department."

"Right, that was the name," Henry said. "He scared me…"

"Oh, Henry," Doric said while rolling her eyes.

"Actually, he frightens many of the students, I'm told," Professor Rhun said.

"Why is that?" Doric asked.

"Besides his towering stature," the professor went on, "he's also an expert in *all* of Dahlvish history, even the parts we'd prefer to forget."

"The Dahl Empire?" Doric asked.

Professor Rhun nodded, his eyes on the Singing Lantern. "Exactly."

Elsewhere on the planet Gwlad Ard'un, in a valley called Dôlgoch, the members of the Elder Council were gathered at the top of a hill. Six members of the council took seats on marble benches arranged in a semi-circle while Elder Blynora stood in the center against a backdrop of red and yellow poppies in the fields behind her.

"I suppose we should begin?" she asked rhetorically, not waiting for a response.

"As you know," she continued, "the beacon has returned home at long last. Against my better judgment, however, I've agreed with the Abbot to allow two humans to accompany the artifact as well…"

"They call it the *Singing Lantern*," an elder sneered, which brought restrained chuckles from everyone except Blynora.

"Regardless," she said, "having the relic back on Gwlad Ard'un is what matters."

"Frankly," a different elder said, "it would have been safer to keep the beacon where it was."

"Why?" Blynora asked.

"Rumors…" the elder replied, his long gray beard lost in the folds of his white robe.

"I have no time for gossip and idle chatter," she said.

"Perhaps you *should*," he replied. "Dangers can fester below the surface before rearing their ugly head. We should be prepared…"

"I'm *always* prepared," Blynora hissed. "Show me *that* much respect at least."

One of the other Dahl, her auburn hair braided into loops, raised an eyebrow. "We're all equals here, Elder Blynora."

"Perhaps," Blynora replied, eyeing the bearded elder, "but one of us has to be the leader."

The others grumbled, but she dismissed the dissent with a wave of her hand.

"No matter," Blynora said. "I'm well aware of those who pine for the days when our people were in command instead of subordinate. Those days are past. Our role now is to teach and advise, not rule and conquer."

"Still," the elder with the auburn braids said, "bringing the humans here is a risk."

"Why?" Blynora asked.

"They may catch wind of the rumors as well. See our, as the humans say, *dirty laundry*."

Blynora scoffed. "Nonsense."

"Belittle the idea all you like," the other elder went on, "but I've heard a name whispered when they think no one is listening."

"What name is that?" Blynora asked.

"*Echuio.*"

CHAPTER FOUR

The robot Z-4T, or *Zat* as Uncle Artie called him, picked his way through the jagged landscape of the Boneyards. Carrying a wire shopping basket, Zat stepped between the rusting body parts of decommissioned robots, dumped there over many decades. His own body was an amalgamate of discarded pieces long abandoned by others, only to be rediscovered by Uncle Artie and reassembled into something resembling a whole being.

Zat bent to snatch a servo, its yellow paint reddened by oxidization, from a pile of trash. From within the jumble, the dead eyes of a servicebot stared back at him.

"You won't be needing this," Zat told him and dropped the part into the basket.

If it wasn't for Uncle Artie, the robot thought, he would be no different than the servicebot in that garbage heap. The Gnomi was like a father to him, at least in Zat's eyes, mismatched as they were.

Zat reached the summit of one of the mountains that dotted the Boneyards. He took a long look at the mounds stretching into the distance in every direction.

For many years, it had only been him and Uncle Artie, alone but together. To make money, the tinker sold devices to those looking for a specific function. Someone had even offered a tidy sum for Zat himself, but Uncle Artie had flatly said *no*.

"I wouldn't sell Zat any more than my own son!" he had said and shooed the customer away.

It had remained that way for a long time, until the day when one of their regular clients brought a bundle wrapped in cloth.

"What's this?" Uncle Artie had asked.

The man unwrapped the top of the bundle, revealing the head of a baby with wisps of pink hair. Uncle Artie was speechless, something Zat had never seen before.

"This was left at my shop," the man said. "It's a Gnomi, I think."

"Any idea whose it is?" Zat had said.

The man shook his head. "I thought maybe you might know."

"No idea," Uncle Artie replied, but took the child and held it carefully in his arms.

After the man had left, the baby began crying, a shrill, shrieking noise the robot found highly unpleasant.

"Are you going to keep that?" Zat asked.

Uncle Artie gave him a stern look. "Of course!"

Uncle Artie laid the baby girl in a basket someone in Regalis had thrown away long before.

"Well, you should name it, I guess," Zat remarked.

Uncle Artie nodded, scratching his belly.

"My mother was called *Melinda*," he said. "I'll call this one *Mel* for short."

"She's *very* short," the robot replied.

"She'll get bigger," the Gnomi said. "Not *much* bigger, but still..."

Now, from his perch on top of the garbage hill, Zat watched while a gravtaxi flew overhead and appeared to land near Uncle

Artie's cave. The robot surveyed the contents of his basket, and then made his way back home.

Landing in a shallow depression between trash heaps, a black and yellow gravtaxi came to rest and three passengers clambered out. In descending order of heights, Captain Ramus, Gen the robot, and Mel watched the taxi leave, disappearing into the dull sky.

"Are you sure this is the right place?" Ramus asked.

"Of course!" Mel replied.

From inside one of the piles, a much older Gnomi emerged and waved vigorously at the newcomers.

"Hello! Hello!" Uncle Artie shouted and nearly fell over a broken water heater.

Mel ran to him, giving him a sizable hug for such a small person.

"Careful," she scolded him.

"Alright, alright," he replied. "*You* haven't changed."

Uncle Artie gazed over at the Dahl and the robot. "Who are they?"

"My ride," Mel said and waved the others over.

Ramus and Gen plodded across the open space of garbage and the captain of the *Wanderer* shook Uncle Artie's hand while Mel introduced them all.

"Nice to meet you," Ramus said.

"Any friends of Mel are friends of mine!" Uncle Artie said. "Come on in."

Once inside, Gen stared with wonder at the collection of parts hanging from the ceiling.

"Amazing," she said.

Another robot entered, its body made from pieces nearly as varied as the ceiling.

"Say hello, Zat," Uncle Artie told the newcomer.

Mel gave the robot a hug as well, although Zat appeared unsure whether to fully fold his arms around her.

"It's been a long time, Mel," the robot said. "Father has missed you..."

"Oh," Mel replied. "I know I should've visited sooner."

Uncle Artie put his hands on his hips.

"Don't mind him," he said. "You're here now, my girl, that's all that matters!"

Gen drew closer, gawking at Zat's frame. This drew a rebuking glare from the other robot.

"Can I *help* you?" Zat asked.

"Sorry," Gen replied. "I've never seen another robot like you before."

Ramus cleared his throat. "I think what Gen is trying to say is that she's used to seeing robots from a single manufacturer..."

"You got that right!" Uncle Artie laughed. "Zat's got Dyson Yost, Big Bots!, and even a little Cyber Collective in him!"

"I assure you it all works," Zat said.

"Damn right!" Mel said, beaming at the other Gnomi. "Uncle Artie is the greatest tinker there ever was!"

"With that in mind," Ramus interjected, "we need to talk about the rest of Mel's payment..."

"Payment?" Uncle Artie asked.

"I agreed to fly her here," Ramus said, "with the understanding the rest of my payment would come from you."

"Me?" Uncle Artie said. "I don't have any money."

Ramus shot Mel a look.

"You're really broke?" Mel asked.

"Times are tough," Uncle Artie said. "That's one of the reasons I took the job I need your help with."

"Does it pay?" Ramus asked.

"I certainly hope so, son!" Uncle Artie replied.

"Then I better get the rest of my money when it does,"

Ramus said, his eyes still focused on Mel. "I have bills to pay *too*."

"You'll get paid," Mel said. "Sooner or later..."

"Come on, Gen," Ramus said. "I need a drink."

"I've got booze here," Uncle Artie offered.

"I need a drink," Ramus went on, "somewhere *else*."

After the Dahl and robot had left, Uncle Artie turned to Mel.

"He seems nice," he said.

Back in a gravtaxi, Ramus called his chief engineer Fugg on his datapad.

"Where are you?" Ramus asked.

The Gordian's face on the screen glared back. "At a bar. Where did you think?"

"Good," Ramus replied. "We'll meet you there."

With directions from Fugg, the taxi landed in the Ashetown district of Regalis, at the corner of Marlowe and Vine. Ramus and Gen took a short set of stairs from the sidewalk down to where the words "Le Sous-Sol" were painted on a red door.

"The Basement?" Gen asked.

"Since when do you know French?" Ramus replied.

"I've been learning all *kinds* of things!" the robot said proudly.

Inside, Ramus could count the patrons on one hand. Most were sitting at tables in the center of the room although there were burgundy leather booths along the wall. The captain of the *Wanderer* knew where Fugg would be, on a stool at the bar, but he didn't expect another Gordian to be serving drinks.

Fugg called them over. "This is Red."

The bartender, who was bald without a strand of red hair on him, grunted at Ramus and the robot while cleaning a glass with a dirty rag.

"What'll you have?" Red asked.

"A whiskey shot," Ramus replied, "and keep them coming."

Fugg stared over the rim of his beer mug. "There a problem?"

"Uncle Artie's broke," Ramus said.

"*And* he lives in a mountain of garbage," Gen added helpfully.

Fugg slammed the mug on the bar. "I told you, tinks can't be trusted!"

"Maybe Mel didn't know…" Gen said.

"She knew!" Fugg scoffed. "I pegged her as a liar from the start…"

"Well, it takes one to know one," Ramus remarked.

Fugg gave a fake laugh and took a swig of beer. "Very funny."

Ramus downed the shot that Red had poured for him. He had scarcely put the glass down before the bartender filled it again. Ramus drank that one as well and became dimly aware that someone was singing. On a small stage at the back of the bar, a woman sang beside a bandbot playing music. The robot was little more than a synthesizer with legs, but from the speakers in his chest, jazz filled the smoky bar.

Ramus focused on the singer and realized she was Dahl.

"Who's that?" he asked the bartender.

"Roxie Blues," Red replied gruffly while refilling the shot glass. "She's been singing here the last few months."

"What's that terrible noise coming from her mouth?" Fugg asked.

"It's called a torch song," Ramus replied.

"It's so sad!" Gen said.

"Yeah," Ramus replied, standing. "You guys stay at the bar. I want to sit closer."

The captain took his shot with him to one of the tables in front of the stage. Ramus watched the woman finish her song and asked her to join him for a drink.

She nodded with a smile.

"Take five, Sam," she told the bandbot over her shoulder and stepped off the stage before taking a seat across from Ramus.

Zat put the kettle on and, after a few minutes, brought a pair of teacups to the table where Mel and her uncle had taken seats. The robot didn't sit but remained next to the table in case he was needed.

"Your friend seemed upset," Uncle Artie remarked.

Mel blew a raspberry. "Ramus will get over it."

"He's not like most Dahl I've seen," her uncle said.

"Not hardly!" Mel replied with a snort. "They exiled him for studying dark psi. He even did some work for the *Psi Lords*, if you can believe that."

Uncle Artie nearly spat out his tea. "Shocking!"

"Yeah, Ramus is full of surprises..."

"But you'll need to pay him back, won't you?" her uncle asked.

"Probably," Mel said. "To be honest, I'm surprised you're busted."

Zat rolled his eyes.

"You've been gone a long time," he said.

Mel gave her uncle a critical look. "Has it really been that bad?"

"Well..." Uncle Artie hesitated, "without you here to help, it's been tough."

Mel frowned, her eyes on her tea. "I didn't know."

"How could you?" Zat replied. "You've barely said a word to us in years!"

"Now, now," Uncle Artie said, "Don't be like that. I'm sure Melinda has been busy finding her way in the universe."

"I have!" Mel protested. "I've been all over..."

"I heard you just had a little shop on Eudora Prime," Zat said. "Not exactly impressive."

Mel scowled. "Nobody asked you!"

"Anyway," Uncle Artie said, "you're here now and I can really use your help."

"I'll do whatever I can…" Mel replied while still glaring at Zat.

Uncle Artie stood and beckoned Mel over to a drafting table wedged between a broken refrigerator and an old stuffed chair bandaged with duct tape. The elder Gnomi pulled some sketches out from beneath a pile of loose papers and stood back.

"What's this?" Mel asked.

"I call it the *Artie Augmenter*," he replied proudly.

Mel leaned over the sketches, which mostly contained rough lines and indecipherable notes. At the center was what appeared to be a cylinder of some kind.

"What does it do?" Mel asked.

"It's a hand-held device that enhances psionic abilities."

Mel rubbed her chin skeptically. "Whose psionic abilities?"

"Anybody's, really," Uncle Artie explained, "but specifically the abilities of my client."

"Is he a Dahl?"

"Ah, no," Uncle Artie said. "He's human, but he's reached the point that his psi implants are no longer good enough. So, he wants something… ah, *more*."

"Psi implants?" Mel asked, her eyes growing wide. "Are you working for the Psi Lords?"

Uncle Artie hemmed and hawed before answering. "Maybe…"

"Are you crazy?" Mel shouted, throwing her hands in the air. "Those guys are dangerous!"

"Yes, but they *pay* well."

"I'm not helping you with something involving them!" she said.

Zat crossed his arms. "What a surprise!"

"Shut up!" she yelled while pointing an accusatory finger at the robot. "And *you* should've stopped him from getting tangled up with them in the first place!"

"I'm just a simple robot," Zat said. "I just do what I'm told..."

"Don't be cross, my dear," Uncle Artie told Mel. "It was a great opportunity."

"If you don't give them what they want," Mel said, "they'll boil your blood inside your body!"

"Oh, my," he replied. "I suppose that means you'll have to help me then?"

Mel was speechless.

"This is why I left!" she said finally. "You were always trying to pull my strings!"

"Never!" he said. "It's just you're a better tinker than I ever was, and now I could really use your assistance."

Her face red, Mel took several deep breaths.

"Fine," she said, "but I expect to get my fair share. I have to pay back Ramus somehow..."

"Of course, of course," Uncle Artie replied.

"Hmm," Mel murmured while taking another look at the sketches. "This was never going to work."

"Why is that?" her uncle asked.

"Well, for one thing there's no way to focus the psi energy," she said. "How can you increase the power if you don't focus it first?"

Uncle Artie bent over the drafting table as well. "But how is that even possible?"

"You'd need something that's especially attuned to psionics," she replied. "Some kind of crystal maybe..."

"Well, I can tell you I've never found anything like that in the Boneyards," her uncle said.

Mel tapped the table a few times.

"No, of course not," she said, "but it just so happens I know somebody with something that might do the trick."

"Can you give him a call?"

"Well, it's been a while, so I should probably go see him in person."

"Who is it?" Uncle Artie asked.

"Lord Devlin Maycare," Mel replied.

Ramus watched Roxie Blues slide her long, purple dress into a chair at his table. The bartender brought her a tall glass of something red and left them while grumbling about not being a waitress.

Roxie pulled back her luxurious, auburn hair that hung well past her shoulders, revealing pointed ears.

"I've never seen a Dahl singing in a bar before," Ramus admitted.

The corners of her lips curled into a wry smile.

"I'm probably the *only* one," she said.

"My name's Rowan Ramus," the captain said. "I'm assuming *Roxie Blues* is a stage name?"

She shrugged one shoulder while taking a drink. "That's showbiz for you."

"How long have you been a lounge singer?"

Roxie's eyes, a darker brown than her hair, grew darker. "A while..."

"I'm the captain of the *Wanderer*," Ramus said. "That's my crew at the bar."

Roxie gave Fugg and Gen a long stare before returning her attention back to the table.

"An odd menagerie," she said.

"Well, we get along," Ramus replied, "*some* of the time..."

"What brings you to town?" Roxie asked.

Ramus grimaced. "Transporting a passenger."

"It didn't go well?"

"Let's say there's a matter of payment," Ramus replied. "We're still working out the details."

They sat at the table with an awkward silence between them. Finally, Ramus asked, "Where did you learn human songs like that?"

"When I was a little girl on Gwlad Ard'un," she said, "a ship's captain came to sell some machinery to my father. He was the first human I had ever met, even though my parents didn't approve of me actually meeting him. Anyway, he played some music for us and I was instantly hooked."

"I bet your parents didn't approve of *that* either," Ramus said.

Roxie shook her head. "No, not at all."

"What did they do?" he asked.

"After the captain left, my father told me never to listen to human music again," she replied. "Of course, that only made me more determined. I searched the archives and found some sheet music and began singing when I thought nobody was around."

Ramus listened, but he could guess where this was going.

"One day," Roxie went on, "somebody heard me and told the authorities. That's when things got ugly."

"I can imagine..." Ramus remarked.

"I was pretty headstrong and kept singing," she said. "I didn't even care if they heard me or not. Eventually, my parents gave me a choice: either stop or face the consequences."

"And I guess you made your choice."

"I did," Roxie replied. "The authorities accused me of impropriety and sentenced me to exile. Then they wiped my existence from the minds of my parents and anyone else who might've known me." She paused and then said, "I was erased."

"*The Forgotten*," Ramus said.

"Yes."

Ramus drank his shot.

"The same thing happened to me," he said. "Although for different reasons..."

"I haven't seen my parents since," Roxie said. "Not that they'd remember me."

"The Dahl only care about appearances," Ramus said bitterly. "They exile anybody who doesn't live up to what they consider acceptable."

Ramus looked up from his glass to see Roxie's brown eyes on him.

"Do you..." she began, "ever think about going back?"

"To Gwlad Ard'un?" Ramus asked.

"Yes."

"No, of course not," he replied. "Why would I?"

"To see your parents," she said.

"They abandoned me," Ramus said. "They had me erased like I was nobody."

"I wish I could go back," Roxie admitted, "to see my parents again…"

She stood up and turned toward the stage.

"Well," she said, "I've got more sad songs to sing."

"Maybe I'll see you again?" Ramus asked.

Roxie stopped and looked over her shoulder.

"Anytime," she said.

The butlerbot met Mel at the door of the Maycare estate.

"How's it goin', Benson?" Mel asked.

"It *goes* satisfactorily, Miss Freck," the robot replied, his blue and silver casing glinting in the mid-afternoon sun.

"I believe Lord Maycare is expecting me," Mel said.

"Indeed," Benson said, "although I'm afraid he's also busy training for his newest event."

"Really? What's that?"

The robot gestured for her to follow him inside. "You'll see."

Benson led Mel through the winding halls of the estate, taking her past numerous display cases along the way. Mel half expected to spot the Singing Lantern but was disappointed. Most of the artifacts were run-of-the-mill heirlooms and relics, probably worth millions to the right buyer. In the back of her mind, Mel considered how easily she could slip one of them into her pocket but thought better of it. She had bigger fish to fry.

The butlerbot brought Mel to a back staircase.

"Where are we going exactly?" she asked.

"The basement," Benson replied.

"I've never been down there before," Mel remarked.

"Very few have."

"It's not some kinda sex dungeon, is it?" Mel asked.

"Surprisingly, no," Benson said without a hint of irony.

At the bottom of the stairs, the robot opened a heavy door leading into a large chamber with stone walls. A curtain of heat slammed into Mel as she crossed the threshold, along with the sound of a sharp, high-pitched pounding.

At the center of the room, Lord Maycare held a length of red-hot metal with a pair of tongs while striking the metal with a hammer. He was also shirtless, his bare chest dripping with sweat.

"The hell?" Mel said.

Maycare stopped, seeing the two enter.

"Mel!" he shouted. "It's been a long time!"

"Well, I'll leave the two of you *alone*," Benson said and turned to go.

"Sure you don't want to stay?" Mel asked pleadingly.

"I'd rather not," the robot replied and quickly disappeared, closing the door behind him.

Maycare took the metal, its color beginning to dull, and shoved it into a long box, flames coming out either end.

"Why do you have a forge in your basement?" Mel asked.

Setting the tongs down, Maycare picked up a towel and rubbed himself down.

"It's for a show I'm training for called *Break My Blade!*," he said gleefully.

"Never heard of it," Mel admitted.

Maycare was dumbfounded.

"It's a competition show," he said, "like *What's in the Basket?* or the *Zinc Saucier.*"

"So, it's a cooking show?"

"No!" he replied. "Four bladesmiths compete by forging blades and then judges test the knives to see if they break."

"Are you going to wear a shirt?" Mel asked.

"Oh, definitely," Maycare replied. "That's a requirement — the contestants tend to be on the husky side..."

"I was expecting to see Jess," Mel said. "Is she around?"

"Actually, she left a few days ago for Gwlad Ard'un."

"Did Henry go with her?"

"Who?" Maycare asked.

"Henry!" Mel replied incredulously. "Jessica's assistant!"

"Right!" Maycare said, his eyes searching around the room. "Can't say I've seen him around lately, so he must have."

"Well, I'm sorry I haven't stayed in touch," Mel said. "Last time I was here, your nephew was in some kind of trouble. How's he been?"

"Great!" Maycare said proudly. "They rebuilt Robby's old ship, the *Baron Lancaster*, and gave him command after the old captain retired."

Mel nodded and did her best to seem nonchalant.

"Say," she started, "didn't you use some kinda artifact to rescue him?"

"Robby? Well of course! We used the Singing Lantern to communicate with him," Maycare said. "That friend of yours, Ramus, knew an Erudite who could harness the psionics of the thing. We couldn't have done it without their help."

"I remember now," Mel lied, and tried to stay coy. "Mind if I take a look at it again?"

"I'm afraid you can't," Maycare said. "Jess took the Lantern with her to Gwlad Ard'un. I gave the Dahl permission to study it for a while."

Mel's face fell. "Oh..."

CHAPTER FIVE

Somewhere in Ashetown, a hooded figure appeared at the entrance to an alleyway. He followed a trail of trash that littered the narrow space until coming to a symbol on the wall, a tribal mask design in purple ink. Pressing his gloved hand against the image, he opened a concealed door, letting him into a darkened corridor that led to a chamber filled with the smell of incense.

Kanet Solan of the Psi Lords was waiting.

"Welcome," Solan said.

The newcomer pulled back his hood, exposing the bright crimson skin of a Sarkan.

"I see you got my message," Enrion replied.

"Of course," Solan said. "The Psi Lords are always seeking new clients, especially if they bring information to sell."

Enrion's yellow eyes darted toward a curtain at the back of the room.

"You can tell your associate to come out," the Sarkan said. "She won't have any luck scanning my thoughts."

Ta Demona showed herself, her green face gloomier than usual.

"He's shielded his mind," she said, which brought a nod from Solan.

"Prudent," Solan replied, "though not particularly *trusting...*"

"I have no reason to trust you," Enrion said. "I'm well aware of your techniques for stealing knowledge."

Solan waved his hand. "Well, we *do* have a data cartel to run."

"That's why I'm here," Enrion said. "I want to set up a meeting with the Dahl resistance."

"The *Echuio*?"

"Yes."

"They're quite the secretive bunch," Solan remarked. "It won't be easy making contact."

"So you can't do it?" Enrion asked with a sneer.

Solan smirked. "I didn't say *that*."

"I assumed you could," Enrion said, his eyes studying the Psi Lord. "I know about your history."

"Do you now?" Solan replied.

"You're obsessed with the Dahl," Enrion went on. "I can see it by the devices implanted in your skull."

Solan ran his fingers over the rough surface of his scalp, riddled with electronics winding along the skin.

"You should see what's on the inside," he replied.

"You've been trying to outdo the Dahl since they refused to teach you psionics," Enrion said.

Solan glanced at Demona.

"When I face an obstacle," Solan said, turning his attention back to the Sarkan. "I find a way around it, or *through* it as the case may be."

"Then I'm sure you know everything worth knowing about your adversaries," Enrion said.

"Indeed," he replied. "For me, the real question is, what do I get in return?"

Enrion pulled a datapad from his robe.

"I can give you a full dossier on my Magna contact," he said.

"Your handler with Magna Intelligence?"

"Yes," Enrion said. "I'm sure the Imperial government would pay handsomely."

Solan puckered his lips to whistle, but no sound came out.

"You're playing a dangerous game," he said, shaking his head.

"That's my concern, not yours," Enrion replied. "Do we have a deal or not?"

Solan grinned like a crocodile.

"Absolutely!" he replied.

Jessica Doric and Henry Riff spent a few days assisting Professor Rhun with his analysis of the Singing Lantern. On the first of those days, Henry knocked over an expensive piece of equipment and on the second day he inexplicably started a small fire. On the third day, after Henry hit his head on the underside of a table, Doric suggested he take some quality time to explore the campus for a while.

Doric felt a palpable calm return to Rhun's demeanor once Henry was gone.

"I'm sorry about my assistant," she said. "Henry can take a little getting used to."

"I've had my share of graduate assistants," the professor admitted.

From the table, Rhun retrieved a scanner sitting beside the Singing Lantern. The beacon appeared inert, the crystal dim and lifeless.

The professor activated the device and ran it over the Lantern.

"I find the structure of the beacon fascinating," he said. He gestured to the robot floating nearby. "Come."

The Sprite glided through the air until it came alongside the table.

"Do you have the information I requested?" Rhun asked the robot.

"Yes," the Sprite said in a woman's voice.

"That's amazing," Doric remarked.

"What is?" the professor asked.

"At the monastery on Aldorus," she replied, "the Naiad that acted as the interface for the Pool of Memory sounded exactly like this Sprite."

"Of course," Rhun said. "They work on the same principle."

"I wish we had one of these in Lord Maycare's library," Doric said. "It would cut our research time in half."

"What do you do for him again?" the professor asked.

"I head the Maycare Institute of Xeno Studies. We find artifacts and try to keep them out of the wrong hands."

"But your hands are the *right* ones?"

"According to Lord Maycare..."

"Well," the professor said, "I appreciate that you guarded the beacon after you found it. A pity it couldn't have been returned to us sooner."

Doric laughed uncomfortably. "Sorry about that."

"No matter," he said and looked at the Sprite. "Continue..."

"From your scans and our historic records," the Sprite replied, "the beacon was indeed used by the Dahl Empire as a communication device. Its range far exceeds that of regular psionic projection."

"That makes sense," Rhun said. "The empire stretched for thousands of light-years. I'm sure it was difficult to stay in contact with their far-flung outposts."

"But how does it have such a long range?" Doric asked.

"The crystalline structure is specifically harmonized with the Dahl mind," the Sprite went on. "It magnifies the frequency at which the psionic energy vibrates."

"But an Erudite used it effectively," Doric said. "He spoke with Lord Maycare's nephew over several hundred light-years."

"Anyone with psionic powers can use the device," the Sprite replied. "However, Dahl minds resonate more perfectly."

"Thank you," Rhun said, ushering the Sprite back into its corner.

"Your ancestors had some remarkable technology," Doric said.

"Indeed," the professor replied. "You know, I've been thinking you might want to visit one of our dig sites."

Doric's eyes lit up like someone was offering her a puppy.

"Are you serious?" she asked.

"Certainly," he said. "There's a graduate student of mine you should meet. He could show you the ruins and, besides, I think you've been cooped up with me long enough."

"When could I go?"

"Would tomorrow be alright?" Rhun asked.

"Absolutely!" Doric replied.

After Jessica Doric had sent him away, Henry began spending more time with his roommate Pwmpen. The portly Dahl eagerly suggested the human sit in on one of his classes.

"What class is it?" Henry had asked.

"Ancient History 101," Pwmpen replied, sprinkling food into Finneus Finnegan's goldfish bowl.

"I thought you wanted to be a hairdresser?" Henry said.

"I do," Pwmpen said, "but they still make me take other classes."

Henry agreed to go, and they took a leisurely stroll across campus to the history building. On the way, Henry once again noticed the Dahlvish students staring at him, although this time he got the distinct impression they were judging Pwmpen as well.

"How much do you know about the Dahl?" Pwmpen wondered as they walked.

"Not much," Henry admitted, slightly embarrassed.

Once at the building, they took a long, winding staircase up to the fourth floor where they rested for a few minutes while Pwmpen caught his breath. By the time they reached the classroom, they were late.

Henry was horrified by who he saw teaching.

"Nice of you to join us, Mr. Pwmpen," Professor Grimfeather growled, his enormous eyes narrowed into menacing slits.

"Sorry, Professor," the Dahl said meekly.

"And who is this?" Grimfeather asked and pointed a taloned paw at Henry.

"I'm Henry," he said. "We met in the hall a few days ago..."

"I know!" Grimfeather replied. "But I'm wondering why you're *here*."

"I thought Henry could sit in," Pwmpen said, shrinking as he spoke.

The professor flapped his wings. "Oh, by all means! Let's have a sit-in and get to know each other!"

"I think your regular class would be fine," Henry suggested.

Professor Grimfeather turned his back with an angry "Chaw!" and began writing a few notes on the board. Meanwhile, Henry and Pwmpen found some seats among the other Dahl, who glared at them while they did so.

When the professor faced the class, he had regained his composure.

"Students," he said, "today we'll be talking about the Dahl Empire."

This brought a few rumbles from the class.

"I realize for some of you," Grimfeather went on, "this may be a controversial subject. However, it's *part* of your history and you should know it!"

Another murmur passed through the students.

"Thousands of years ago," the professor said, "the Dahl Empire spanned across a swath of stars greater than the Imperium and the Magna Supremacy combined. For centuries, the Dahl ruled hundreds of worlds, bringing stability to their inhabitants under the leadership of Elder Brenin the Great."

"Really?" Henry whispered into Pwmpen's pointed ear.

"Shush," he replied.

"But after Elder Brenin was killed by a Magna assassin," Grimfeather continued, "that Empire shrunk from hundreds of worlds to just the one on which we're currently living."

"Why?" Henry asked, regretting it immediately.

"Don't interrupt, human," Grimfeather said, "but to answer your question, the Dahl began questioning the morality of their empire. Their ambitions had led to a vast dominion but not to enlightenment.

"Over several decades," he continued, "the Dahl refocused inward, in search of knowledge and the wisdom that previously eluded them. Eventually, the empire fell into disrepair — more out of disinterest than anything else — and other worlds carved out their own empires from the remnants.

"When the humans arrived with a war fleet of their own, the Dahl did not resist. In fact, they saw an opportunity to advise the invaders, winning the ear of every human Emperor since."

Grimfeather ruffled his wings before drawing them against his body. He gazed directly at Henry. "Any questions?"

"Don't they miss being in charge?" Henry asked and heard his roommate gasp beside him.

The professor's eyes widened.

"Who knows?" Grimfeather replied. "But I doubt the Dahl government would allow it."

"Why?" the human asked.

"Because to return to those days would mean a direct confrontation with *your* people," the professor said. "And that would likely mean the end of Dahlvish society as we know it."

"Oh," Henry replied.

"Yes, *Oh*," Grimfeather parroted him. "*Oh*, indeed!"

The chancellor of Prenwyn University was a busy Dahl. From his office on campus, behind a desk featuring the crest of the university, Chancellor Telyn held court with the academics and dignitaries who entered his domain. Like most

Dahl, he was of slight build but he compensated by wearing golden robes that included stoles like the vestments of a priest, with silver vines and leaves running down the hemline.

His wife considered the stoles a little much.

"Too lavish," her voice said in the back of his mind. "A bit on the gaudy side, dear."

Still, Chancellor Telyn wore them anyway, wanting to show off his power.

Today, he hosted a visit by Elder Blynora and another member of the council, Elder Arwyn. The latter, her auburn hair braided into loops, listened patiently while Blynora spoke.

"It was my understanding," she said, "the arrival of the humans would not be an issue."

Chancellor Telyn's pointed ears, peeking from beneath strands of black hair, flushed slightly.

"That is *not* the case," he replied with displeasure. "Unless you received approval from my office, the visit was not sanctioned by *me*."

"Well, it can't be helped now, I suppose," Blynora said. "What's done is done."

"Do you know how long these humans plan to stay?" the chancellor asked.

"No idea."

Telyn grumbled. "I see."

"Frankly, I think you should be pleased," Blynora added. "This is an opportunity to showcase the university. It's my understanding Miss Doric has some relationship with Lord Maycare. I'm sure anything positive she says about her visit will give Lord Maycare a good impression."

"Perhaps," the chancellor replied begrudgingly.

"Who knows?" she went on. "He might donate a grav ball stadium!"

"Hmmm," Telyn considered. "The anti-grav generators *did* fail during the last game. There were several injuries..."

"Then it's settled," Blynora said with an air of finality in her voice. "Now, I must go but I'll leave Elder Arwyn behind. I'm sure the two of you have a few things to discuss."

Elder Blynora gave the other council member a nod and left the office. Once the other had departed, Elder Arwyn came around the desk and gave the chancellor a small peck on the forehead.

"I see you're wearing your stoles again," she said.

"I'm the chancellor!" Telyn protested.

"That's no excuse for looking gaudy," his wife replied.

He sighed. "Anyway, you could have told me about the humans."

"I was just as surprised as you, dear," Arwyn said.

"There are enough non-Dahl at the university without muddying the waters further."

"Now, now," she said. "Aren't we supposed to educate *everyone*?"

The chancellor glanced at a Sprite robot floating inconspicuously in the corner.

"Knowledge is power," Telyn replied. "It's best if we hold the key to it firmly in our hands. Otherwise, the humans would no longer need us, would they?"

"It's good to be needed," Arwyn said.

The chancellor slipped his hand into hers.

"Yes, it is," he replied.

Jessica Doric got a ride with a gravtruck that was bringing supplies to the dig site Professor Rhun had suggested. The driver wasn't particularly talkative, so Doric had plenty of time to stare at the landscape. Although most of the trees on the Dahl home planet were beautiful and pink, as if eternally in bloom, the forest below seemed almost foreboding. Many of the trees were bare, with branches like the bony fingers of an old man.

Doric was happy when the gravtruck crossed over an open space, clear of the trees. The craft touched down beside a camp of semi-permanent shelters and a pit where Dahl were working. After saying goodbye to the driver, Doric asked around until finding the one she had come to meet, Elisan Mossdale.

"The professor said you were coming," he told her without offering his hand. Doric noticed it was dirty from digging.

"I hope this isn't an inconvenience," she replied.

Mossdale rubbed his hands on his pants. "No, no, it's fine."

The graduate student was a Sylva, or what humans called a *Woodland Dahl*. His hair was a reddish brown and his face had an olive complexion, shaped like an arrowhead with high cheekbones and a sharp chin. His eyes were even greener than the grass surrounding them, at least where the ground hadn't been dug up in places.

"If you don't mind me saying," Doric remarked, "I didn't realize you were a Sylva."

Mossdale laughed politely. "There's a few of us at the university, but not many."

"Why not more?" Doric asked.

"Well, the males of my race aren't psionic — only the females — and most Sylvan women aren't interested in learning the kinds of psi they teach here. They prefer spending their time among the animals in the forest, not cooped up in a classroom."

"Oh," Doric said, not comprehending why anyone *wouldn't* want to spend their days studying.

"Can I show you around?" Mossdale asked.

"Absolutely!" she replied.

The two of them toured the edges of the dig, careful not to disturb the other students. Most of them were using trowels to clear away earth, and brushes to carefully remove any fine soil remaining. The rough outline of a building's foundation was visible.

"What was it?" Doric asked.

"We believe this was a family residence from the Imperial Era," Mossdale replied, taking her to a wooden table covered by a white cloth. He pulled the cloth away, revealing artifacts in the process of being tagged and categorized. "These are some of the items we've discovered so far."

Doric inspected the items on the table but found some of the shapes unrecognizable. One of the relics, however, stood out. She pointed at a round, flat object, apparently of gold. A circle was cast into the center along with rays projecting outward.

"What's that?"

"Good eye," Mossdale said. "That's a medallion from a necklace we found. The design shows the golden sun symbol of the Dahl Empire."

"It's beautiful," Doric replied.

Mossdale nodded.

"Say what you will about the empire," he replied, covering the table with the cloth, "it certainly had a beauty of its own."

Enrion's ship, the *Narwa*, orbited above the planet Aldorus like a sword with a winged hilt. Although the outside of the ship was an ancient Dahlvish design, the Sarkan had decorated the inside to his own liking. War banners hung along the corridors and his living quarters were grandiose, decorated in gold. Enrion stood at the center of the cabin. In his hand, he held a datapad with the coordinates the Psi Lords had given him. Tossing the device to the side, he cleared his mind and concentrated on the location where the Echuio were due to meet him.

Enrion's arms dropped to his side, his palms facing out. A blue aura grew around him as his psionic powers manifested themselves.

He closed his eyes.

Enrion felt the cold metal of the floor fall away. When he opened his eyes again, he was standing in a different room, this one made from stone. In the corners, braziers burned with an unnatural fire of blue and purple. Down the center of the chamber, a group of people in long, silver robes stood on either side, their faces concealed behind masks. Their pointed ears, however, were still visible. A round medallion hung around their necks, with a sun in the center and rays projecting outward.

Opposite Enrion, on the far side of the room, stood another robed person. His mask, unlike the silver ones of the others, was gold with curved lines carved around the cheeks and mouth.

"Hello?" he asked, his psionic projection casting a bluish light on the robes closest to him.

"You're the Echuio, I presume?" Enrion asked, unimpressed by the theatrics.

"Yes," the one with the golden mask said in a male's voice.

"Thank you for meeting me," Enrion replied with a small bow.

"The Sarkan have never been shy about their disdain for the Dahl," the Echuio leader said. "What do you want?"

The translucent image of Enrion straightened defensively.

"If we appear disdainful," he said, "it's only because we were abandoned by the Dahl so long ago."

"The past is in the past."

"But it's not forgotten," Enrion replied. "Anyway, that's not why I'm here."

"What then?" the Dahl in the golden mask asked.

"I believe we have a mutual goal."

"I can't imagine what *that* could be."

Enrion clenched his fists into tight little balls.

"Just listen and I'll tell you!" he hissed, but quickly calmed himself. "The Echuio want the return of the Dahl Empire, yes?

They want to be in power again, instead of being subservient to the humans…"

After a moment of silence, the voice behind the gold mask said, "Yes."

"The humans have ruled us for too long," Enrion continued. "It's about time someone put an end to it!"

"And you think a Sarkan can help us do that?"

"Of course I can!" Enrion shouted. "While *you've* been advising the humans, my people have been *fighting* them."

"As pets of the Magna," the leader remarked.

"The Magna are a means to an end," Enrion replied.

"If you say so..."

"Anyway," Enrion went on, "we can work together to bring down the Imperium. They have a boy as emperor and one of their females as regent. This is the perfect time to strike!"

A low murmur came from the others beneath their masks.

"Quiet!" their leader commanded. After another pause, he said, this time to Enrion, "We will consider your offer."

The Dahl in the golden mask made a swiping motion with his hand and Enrion felt as if he were flying backwards. He opened his eyes, and he was back in his quarters on the *Narwa*.

Enrion grumbled under his breath. "Arrogant *fools*."

CHAPTER SIX

While Uncle Artie was out scavenging among the garbage mounds of the Boneyard, Mel was bent over her uncle's workbench, examining the device she had cobbled together. It consisted of a tube about six inches long and one inch wide. Different materials ran along its length, including brass, copper, and plastic. Toward the middle, Mel had wrapped the shaft with leather for a better grip and sewn it with black thread. On one end of the tube were four empty titanium prongs designed to hold something. Mel had based the device on Uncle Artie's original design while adding a few touches of her own.

She called it the *Psi Wand*.

Mel looked up from her handiwork as Zat appeared nearby. A tiny servo on the robot's face was acting up, causing one of his eyes to blink sporadically.

"I can fix that if you want," Mel offered.

"Uncle Artie can do it," Zat replied tersely.

"Come on," she said, "if you keep blinking like that, I'm going to call you *Winky*."

"Do it and I'll accidentally poison your tea," the robot replied, making air quotes as he said the word *accidentally*.

"You wouldn't!"

Zat feigned ignorance.

"I get confused about what fleshlings can't drink," he said. "Is battery acid toxic? I can never keep that straight..."

"You need a good rebooting," Mel replied, glaring. "Come closer and bend over."

"No thank you."

"You've gotten a lot more attitude since I left," Mel said.

The robot's wonky eye winked more rapidly.

"You left us," Zat grumbled. "More importantly, you left Uncle Artie, the only father you ever knew."

"I wanted to see the universe," Mel said defensively.

"Well, Mel gets what Mel wants," Zat said.

"That's not true."

"Of course it is! Uncle Artie would've given you the world if he could, and you just walked away."

Mel set the device on the workbench and stepped toward the kitchen area of Uncle Artie's cave.

"Where are you going now?" the robot asked.

"I thought I'd make some tea," Mel replied. "Without any battery acid, thank you."

She put a kettle on the stove top and turned on the gas. After a second or two, the gas lit, although Mel thought the old, rickety range was just as likely to explode.

"You know what," Mel continued finally, "I think you're *jealous*."

"Of what?" Zat asked.

"Me, of course."

"Don't be ridiculous!" the robot replied incredulously.

"I'm flesh and blood," she added, "and you're just a bunch of spare parts!"

"Oh, please," Zat said. "You're a foundling somebody threw away!"

"Well, so are you! There's nothing on you anybody wanted to *keep*!"

The two stared at each other in angry silence, although Zat's winking eye made things more awkward than anything.

"For the love of god, please let me fix your eye!" Mel shouted.

"Fine," the robot replied.

Mel retrieved her tool kit and started rooting around in Zat's head.

"Don't break anything," he muttered.

"You're already broken," she replied.

They remained quiet for a while until Zat's good eye stared at the device sitting on the workbench.

"What are you going to do with that?" he asked.

"Nothing," Mel said. "It's not going to work without a focusing crystal."

"Is that what Uncle Artie is out looking for?"

"Pfft," Mel replied. "He won't find it out there. There's only one thing that'll work and it's on another planet apparently."

"Then why don't you go get it?"

"Because Ramus hates me now," she said. "I doubt he'd give me a ride there. Plus, I don't think the Dahl would be happy to see him if he did."

"Typical fleshlings," the robot remarked. "Wallowing in self-pity..."

"No I'm not!" Mel replied, waving her screwdriver.

"If you need Captain Ramus to fly you somewhere," Zat said, "then go and convince him to. Besides, he won't get the rest of his money unless Uncle Artie finishes the device."

Mel's face brightened. "That's true."

"So, maybe instead of fixing my eye," the robot said, "you should be talking to Ramus."

Mel put the screwdriver back into her kit.

"Actually," she replied, "you're fixed."

"I am?" Zat said and blinked his eyes a few times. "Well, it's about time!"

The *Wanderer* sat idly at the Regalis starport while Captain Ramus did much the same in his cabin on board. He lay in his bunk, listening to torch music he had downloaded from the nodesphere. He felt the sadness and longing in the lyrics and the melodies like they were made especially for him. Strange, he thought, how this music by humans on ancient Earth could speak to him so clearly. He imagined Roxie Blues singing in the club...

Metallic knuckles tapped on the door.

"Come in," Ramus said.

The door slid open and Gen peered in. "Hello, Captain."

"What is it?" Ramus asked.

"Mel is here to speak with you," the robot replied.

"Mel? What does *she* want?"

"I don't know," Gen said lightly. "I hope you're not still mad at her..."

Ramus sighed, pulling himself out of the bunk.

"A little," he replied and slipped into his boots.

Mel and Fugg were waiting for them in the galley. The chief engineer was scowling at the Gnomi with his arms crossed over his broad chest. Mel gave him the stink eye in return, mostly out of habit.

"You've got a lot of nerve showing your face around here," Ramus said.

"I know, I know," Mel said, "but I'm here to make it up to you."

"How?" Ramus asked.

Fugg looked especially skeptical. "Yeah, *how?*"

"I want you to fly me to Gwlad Ard'un!" Mel said hopefully.

Ramus took a moment to scrape his jaw off the floor.

"*What?*" he asked. "You still owe me for the *last* trip!"

"It's for my uncle's project," she insisted.

"You've got to be kidding," Ramus said.

"You want to get paid, don't you?" Mel went on. "Well, this is how."

Even Gen, who had remained largely neutral to this point, seemed doubtful.

"Maybe if you explained?" the robot suggested.

"Fine," Mel said. "My uncle is making a device and it needs a focusing crystal."

"So?" Ramus said.

"You remember the Singing Lantern?" she asked. "Well, that's the only crystal I know of that'll work."

"But Maycare has it at his estate," Ramus countered.

"Not anymore," Mel said. "Jessica Doric took it to Gwlad Ard'un for study. We need to go there and chip off a piece."

"Forget it," Ramus said.

"Listen," Mel said, "I know I let you down before, but I promise this'll work. You just have to *trust* me."

Fugg laughed. "Nobody should trust a *tink*!"

"Better than a fat-assed Gordian!" Mel shot back with a raised fist in the air.

"Even if I wanted to take you — and I *don't*," Ramus said, "I'm an exile. They'd arrest me as soon as we landed."

"We could smuggle you planetside," Mel said, "and dress you up like a regular Dahl. You all look alike anyway..."

"Watch it!" Ramus replied.

"Anyway," she went on, "haven't you ever wanted to go back and see your home planet again?"

The image of Roxie Blues appeared in Ramus' mind. The sound of her voice trailed away in his ears. Mel noticed his hesitation.

"I knew it!" she said. "Everybody wants to go home eventually..."

"Not me," the captain said, "but I know somebody who *does*. Anyway, if we do this, I want *double* of what you still owe me."

"Double?" Mel shouted. "That's robbery!"

"Is it a deal or not?" Ramus asked.

Mel spat into her palm and offered it to the captain.

"Deal!" she said and the two shook hands.

The next day, the *Wanderer* made the jump to hyperspace en route to the Dahl home world. Gen was in the galley while Mel, wearing a pair of old overalls, was giving the side eye to Roxie Blues across the table. Roxie was dressed in fashionable culottes and a silk shirt, her hair hanging about her shoulders like a dark and mysterious waterfall.

Roxie began softly humming a song Mel had never heard of before.

"What's that?" Mel asked.

"Just a little tune I sing sometimes," Roxie replied.

"Ramus said you're a lounge singer..." Mel said.

Roxie nodded. "Something like that."

"And you met in a bar?"

"He sat at one of the front tables and heard me sing."

"Would anyone like some tea?" Gen offered, standing beside the cupboard.

Roxie gave her a wry smile. "Got anything stronger?"

"You mean coffee?" the robot asked.

"I think Fugg keeps fungus beer in the fridge," Mel said.

"Oh, I wouldn't drink that!" Gen replied, raising a hand in warning. "Chief Fugg gets very protective of his beer."

"Well, we wouldn't want to upset the chief," Roxie said sarcastically.

"Screw that pig face!" Mel shouted and went directly for the refrigerator. After pulling a pair of bottles out, she returned to the table, giving Roxie one of the beers while keeping one for herself.

Roxie twisted off the top and took a precautionary sniff. Her near-perfect Dahlvish nose wrinkled disapprovingly.

"This is foul," she said.

Mel took a long drink, followed by a belch.

"Tastes bad too!" she said.

They shared a laugh while Gen looked like the room was on fire. Mel ignored her.

"So, why is Ramus flying you all the way to Gwlad Ard'un?"

"Are you familiar with the Forgotten?"

"Yeah," Mel replied.

Roxie's expression turned serious. "He and I are both exiles, so maybe he feels a kinship with me."

"But why go back to your home planet?" Mel asked. "Nobody's going to know you."

"True," Roxie said, "but I miss my parents. They might not remember me, but I don't want to forget *them*. I feel like I'm starting to."

"I've got no memories of *my* parents," Mel said. "I was an orphan…"

"But you seem to have turned out alright," Roxie replied.

"That depends on who you ask!"

They both laughed again, and Gen grinned awkwardly in the background.

"So, do you know Dark Psi too?" Mel asked Roxie. "That's what got Ramus erased…"

"He knows Dark Psi?" Roxie replied in surprise. "I didn't know that."

"Sure," Mel went on. "He worked for the Psi Lords for a while and did all kinds of shady stuff with them."

Roxie looked around the room as if concerned the captain might be listening.

"You don't have to be afraid of him," Mel said. "He doesn't do that kind of thing anymore."

"Good," Roxie replied.

"Although I *did* see him turn into a monster with claws and teeth," Gen added. "Tore a poor man's head off…"

"Yeah, that can be pretty scary," Mel agreed.

Roxie covered her mouth with her hands.

"But he's mostly left that life behind," Mel said.

"Mostly," Gen said.

At that moment, Chief Engineer Fugg entered the galley and noticed the two half-empty fungus beers on the table.

"What in the actual *hell*?" he shouted.

The rest of the way through hyperspace was uneventful and the *Wanderer* entered the Gwlad Ard'un system on the final approach to the planet. In the cargo hold, Mel and Roxie Blues stood beside a stack of containers, along with Captain Ramus and Fugg. The latter was holding a long, metal rod in his pudgy hands.

"When we get close to Gwlad Ard'un," Ramus explained, "they're going to scan the ship." He motioned toward Roxie. "If they detect either of us, they're not going to let us land."

"So, what do we do?" Roxie asked.

Fugg jammed the end of the rod into the floor and pried open a piece of the planking to reveal a small space underneath.

"We use this for smuggling," Ramus went on. "It's shielded from scans, so we need to hide in there until we land on the planet."

"I didn't know you had a secret compartment," Mel remarked.

"Well, it wouldn't be much of a secret if you did!" Fugg grunted.

Mel glared at him.

"Once we get on the surface," Ramus said, "we should be okay if we don't draw too much attention to ourselves."

"Who's going to pose as the captain while you're in there?" Mel asked.

"*Me*, obviously," Fugg replied, poking his chest with the bar.

"Seriously?" Mel remarked.

Fugg growled at the Gnomi while Roxie stared cautiously into the hole.

"We need to get in there?" she asked. "Both of us?"

"Yeah," Ramus replied. "Is that a problem?"

After a pause, the singer said, "No."

Once Ramus and Roxie were in the compartment, Fugg slid the plating back over the top, sealing them in. The captain felt Roxie's body flinch as darkness swallowed them.

"Are you alright?" he asked.

"Is there a light in here?" she replied.

Ramus realized there was not. "Ah, no..."

"You didn't bring a glow stick or something?"

"In retrospect," Ramus said, "that would've been a good idea."

He heard her sigh in the inky blackness, but she was otherwise completely silent. After a few minutes, Ramus had an idea. He slipped out of his flight jacket, with just a sleeveless t-shirt underneath.

He began to concentrate.

At first, a dull glow like the first hints of a chilly sunrise illuminated the small space. Roxie's form became visible, her eyes fixated on the archaic lettering tattooed on Ramus' arms. The tattoos became like blue talismans surrounded by a bright aura. Soon, the entire compartment was bathed in a cold light.

"Is that better?" Ramus asked.

Her knees pulled up against her, Roxie stared at the captain in alarm.

"It's alright," Ramus assured her.

"Mel and Gen told me about why you were exiled," Roxie said.

"Oh..."

"Do you really turn into monster?"

"Not exactly," he said. "I mean, sometimes I can become a little scary but—"

Her visible apprehension did not improve.

"I mean," he corrected himself, "you don't have to worry about me. You're safe."

She stayed silent.

"When I was younger," Ramus said slowly, "I made a lot of bad decisions, and I fell in with the wrong people."

"The Psi Lords?" Roxie asked.

"But that was a long time ago," he added. "I've been trying to make up for things since then. I never want to go back to the way I was."

She managed a weak smile.

"Okay," she said. "I believe you."

"Good," Ramus replied, and then after a while he added, "Did they really say I become a monster?"

"Kinda," she admitted.

"Hmmm," Ramus grumbled in the blue light of his glowing arms.

The bridge of the *Wanderer* was more of a modest cockpit with two chairs facing a set of control panels and a window. While Ramus and Roxie Blues remained hidden away in the shielded compartment, Fugg and Mel went to the bridge where Gen had been looking after the ship's approach to Gwlad Ard'un. With the Dahl home planet prominent in the window, Gen got up to let the Gordian and Gnomi take their seats. The robot stood behind them near the hatch leading to the rest of the ship.

Fugg slipped into the captain's chair and Mel took the co-pilot's seat.

"I don't see why you get to be captain," Mel complained.

"Because I'm the most senior member of the crew, stupid," Fugg replied.

"Nobody's going to believe a Gordian is captain," Mel said.

"Maybe *I* could be captain," Gen suggested.

Both Fugg and Mel turned in their chairs.

"Don't be ridiculous!" they said in unison and turned back to the front.

Gen made a disappointed face and left through the hatch which closed behind her. Fugg reached for the communication panel, opening a channel.

"This is the *Wanderer* to Starport Control," he said. "Requesting permission to land."

A screen came to life, showing a stern Dahl staring back.

"This is Control," he said. "The *Wanderer* is registered to the exile Captain Rowan Ramus. He does not have permission to land."

Fugg leaned forward so his face was more visible.

"This is Captain Orkney Fugg," he said. "Ramus is no longer the captain of this vessel."

"A Gordian?" the controller asked.

"Yes!" Fugg replied defensively. "I won the ship from him in a card game, fair and square!"

The controller frowned. "That seems doubtful."

"I may have cheated slightly..." Fugg said quietly.

"Ah," the controller said, "that seems more likely. Either way, prepare to be scanned."

The screen went black. From an orbiting satellite, waves of energy traveled through the *Wanderer* while an indicator light on the control panel lit up, showing the scan was taking place.

"I hope this works," Mel remarked.

"Shut up," Fugg replied.

After a few tense seconds, the Dahl controller reappeared on the screen.

"The scans were satisfactory," he said. "You may proceed with your landing."

"Well, thank you very much!" Fugg replied and closed the comm channel. "See?"

"Will wonders never cease," Mel said. "But can you actually land this thing?"

Fugg punched another button on the control panel.

"That's what that auto-pilot is for," he said.

Steering jets fired as the *Wanderer* adjusted its trajectory, entering the atmosphere of Gwlad Ard'un. Through the windows, the blue and green of the planet changed to an orange blaze of fire. Mel had to admit that this was not her favorite part of any trip, especially with Fugg at the controls.

However, she put her faith in the ship's automated systems, and within five minutes the flames subsided. The calm, even graceful visage of the planet returned.

"I can't believe how beautiful it is," she said.

The floor plate above the shielded compartment cracked open, letting the light from the cargo hold flood in. Ramus and Roxie Blues stared up at Fugg and Mel.

"I couldn't remember if that compartment was airtight or not," Fugg said, "but I figured we'd find out eventually..."

Roxie nearly jumped out of the small space and began stretching her legs. Ramus, meanwhile, stood up slowly while glaring at his chief engineer.

"Luckily, we're *fine*," the captain said.

Mel helped him up. "We've landed."

"Good," he replied.

"You know you'll never pass as a regular Dahl looking like that," she told him.

"We've got some extra clothes in the storage locker," Ramus said.

For the next hour, both Ramus and Roxie sifted through storage, trying on different sets of clothing until they settled on some traditional Dahlvish robes. Roxie straightened her hair and tied it into braids while Ramus removed his earrings and shut them away in one of the locker drawers.

Roxie gave the captain the once-over.

"You clean up well," she remarked. "You almost look respectable."

Ramus smirked. "I try."

They met Fugg and Mel at the top of the lowered cargo ramp.

"The two of you should stay aboard for now," the captain said.

"What about the Singing Lantern?" Mel asked.

"That can wait until we get back," Ramus replied. "Believe me, I want to get paid as soon as possible, but I don't want Roxie to wait any longer than necessary to see her parents."

Mel grunted. "Whatever you say..."

Unlike the starport on Aldorus, the one on Gwlad Ard'un was much smaller. Although it was not a backwater planet, it received little in the way of interplanetary traffic besides some diplomatic craft and a few trade vessels. Nevertheless, Ramus and Roxie were able to rent a gravcar without any difficulties. The Dahl female behind the counter didn't even give them a second look, which caused Roxie to breathe a sigh of relief once they were back in the sky.

"You worry too much," Ramus remarked, piloting the gravcar.

She laughed. "I suppose I do."

Roxie Blues had grown up in a small city about a hundred miles from the starport. The car covered the distance quickly and they were soon landing near a stately house surrounded by a low wall and trees with pink blossoms.

"Nice place," Ramus remarked as they got out.

"I haven't seen it in years," Roxie replied, "but it's like I never left."

"Do you know what you're going to say?"

She shook her head. "No idea."

"'Hello, Mother,'" he mimicked Roxie's voice. "'Remember me?'"

She smacked him in the arm.

"Maybe not *that*," she said.

They came to the front door and, after standing there uncertainly, Roxie used the silver door knocker. She waited impatiently for the door to open. When it did, a Dahl woman not much older than Roxie stared at her coolly.

"Yes?" the woman asked.

Roxie stammered.

"Go ahead," Ramus said.

"You don't understand," Roxie replied, "I don't recognize this woman."

"Can I help you?" the woman said.

"I'm sorry," Roxie replied. "I used to live in this house. Do you know what happened to the people who used to live here?"

"Do you mean the couple that died?" the woman said.

The blood drained from Roxie's face.

"What happened to them?" Ramus asked.

"There was an accident a few years ago," the woman replied. "Quite tragic, actually."

"Why is that?" Ramus said.

"Oh, it's just so sad," she added, "when a couple dies without having children."

CHAPTER SEVEN

Henry's goldfish, Finneus Finnegan, hadn't expected to be an intergalactic traveler. The sights he had seen through his glass bowl, from the Dahl starship *Blaenwaun Bay* to the campus of Prenwyn University, were more than *anyone* could expect.

Especially Finneus himself, because he was a fish.

For his part, Henry hadn't expected his goldfish would see all these things either. Now, they were off to visit Pwmpen's parents and, at Pwmpen's insistence, Finneus was coming along.

"Have your parents ever met a human before?" Henry asked Pwmpen as the Dahl carried the fishbowl up the street.

"I don't think so," Pwmpen replied after a moment's consideration.

They arrived at the house which Henry thought looked very much like a cottage from the English countryside, at least as far as Henry knew what one looked like. The outer walls were plaster and painted white, and the roof was thatched instead of the usual blue tiles found on the campus buildings. Green ivy with sapphire-colored blossoms grew up the sides, framing the little windows and the oak front door.

"Are they *expecting* to see a human?" Henry asked.

"I told them you're coming," his roommate replied.

"Okay..."

Pwmpen opened the front door and walked in without knocking.

"Hello!" Pwmpen shouted. "We're here!"

Two Dahl, his mother and father presumably, came out of what appeared to be the kitchen. They were dressed conservatively, his father in a tunic with pants and his mother in a long dress. Like most Dahl Henry had encountered, he couldn't tell their ages exactly. They could have been anywhere between fifty and five hundred.

Both parents smiled, but Henry thought the father's expression was strained.

"This is Henry," Pwmpen said.

"Nice to meet you," the mother said before noticing the fishbowl. "And what's this?"

"It's a goldfish," Pwmpen replied.

"Do we cook it?" she asked.

"No!" Pwmpen exclaimed. "It's Henry's pet."

"A fish for a pet?" his father asked. "What for?"

"Because that's what humans do!" Pwmpen replied.

The father shook his head.

"Alright then," he said doubtfully.

"Would you like to see the house?" the mother asked Henry.

"Sure!" Henry replied.

The tour was brief. The cottage had only one floor which included a dining room, a kitchen, a bedroom, and back to the entryway again where Pwmpen and his father stood in stoic silence.

"We're so happy Pwmpen is making friends," the mother said, rubbing her son's head and messing up his bowl cut.

"Mom!" he protested.

"A few Dahlvish friends would be nice," his father added.

"Dad!"

"I didn't know anybody when I got here," Henry said. "But Pwmpen has been showing me around..."

"Maybe you can talk him out of being a barber," the father said.

"Hair stylist!" Pwmpen shouted.

"It's not a *real* job!" his father replied.

"Pwmpen," his mother said quietly, "perhaps you could put the pet fish down and we could eat lunch?"

"Yes, Mother..."

Pwmpen gingerly placed Finneus and his bowl on a small table in the entryway and the four of them went into the dining room.

Jessica Doric spent the first night at the excavation site in one of the semi-permanent structures the Dahl had set up there. It was more of a tent than an actual building, Doric noted, made from blue canvas decorated with intricate, gold scrolling.

Elisan Mossdale brought her dinner to the tent and arranged the meal on a short table in the center. The two sat down with their legs crossed. A pot filled with stew, with flatbread on the side, was the primary course, with a bowl of fruit for dessert.

"Did you make this yourself?" Doric asked.

"Actually," he confessed, "I heated it up from the food they send us from the university."

She touched his arm, which made Mossdale blush.

"That's alright," she replied. "It smells delicious!"

Over dinner, they talked about the dig and Doric's fascination with all things Dahlvish.

"I'm a little surprised," Mossdale admitted. "Most humans aren't interested in such things."

"Most people are idiots," she said candidly. "But I feel fortunate to have this opportunity. And to meet a real Sylva in the flesh is exciting too."

"True, there aren't as many of us around as the Dahl."

"If I may ask," she went on, "do you feel any friction with them?"

"Why?"

"It's just," Doric said, "I know the Sarkans are at odds with them. I'm really not sure how the Sylva feel about the Dahl."

Mossdale tore off some bread and dunked it into his bowl of stew, considering his answer.

"We get along," he said and took a bite.

"I'm sorry," she said. "I hope I'm not being inappropriate."

"Not at all," Mossdale replied with a smile. "There was a time when we were all one people. The breakup of the Empire is what divided us, I suppose."

"Is that why you study history? To learn more about your people?"

"I guess so, although there's a lot of reasons..."

Doric waited for him to say more but Mossdale finished off his bread instead.

"You know," she began a new topic, "it's a warm night. We could go for a walk?"

The Sylva choked.

"No, we can't do that," he said after clearing his throat.

"Why not?"

"It's not safe to be out at night," he replied.

Doric laughed. "Are you joking?"

"No," he said earnestly. "You shouldn't be out after dark, especially outside the camp."

Doric gave him a quizzical look.

"There's creatures in the woods nearby," he added. "They're rather territorial, I'm afraid. They don't really like us being here."

"Actually," Doric said, "I flew over a strange forest on my way here."

"Yes," Mossdale replied. "It's called *Coedwig Lledrith*, or the Forest of Illusions."

"Why do they call it that?" she asked, her curiosity piqued.

"It has a bad reputation, so the authorities suggest people stay clear of it. Supposedly, if you go there, you'll see apparitions. Nobody really knows why."

"But these creatures live there?"

"Yes," Mossdale replied. "They call themselves the *Kuent'l Nanzi.*"

For Henry, most meals involved heating noodles in a cup, so having lunch with Pwmpen's family was much better than what he was accustomed to. Pwmpen's mother brought out a series of bowls containing fruit and vegetables, followed by a massive fish on a serving platter. A cascade of colors reflected off the scales of the fish, although its eye stared at Henry judgmentally.

"I'm so sorry for serving fish," the mother told him. "I hope it wasn't someone you knew."

"That's alright," Henry replied. "Finneus is the only one I know around here."

"You named him?" Pwmpen's father asked.

Under the father's withering stare, Henry stammered, "Yes?"

"Humans always name their pets," Pwmpen said helpfully. "It's *normal.*"

The mother, who had already cut the fish into segments, started dishing them out onto plates.

"I always thought the Dahl were vegetarians," Henry said, accepting his portion.

"Some are," the mother replied, "but not all of us."

"What determines which animals you eat and which ones you keep as pets?" the father wanted to know. "And do you eat your pets when you get sick of them?"

Henry wasn't entirely sure how to answer. "Maybe on a farm..."

"Stop badgering him," Pwmpen said. "Humans can eat whichever pets they want!"

"Actually," Henry said, "we don't normally eat pets, but I'm not sure how we decide which animals are food."

"This all seems a bit haphazard, if you ask me," the father remarked.

"Nobody's asking you, Dad," Pwmpen said.

"When my grandfather was a boy," the father said, "things were different."

Pwmpen was shaking his head violently.

"Of course, that was before the humans arrived..." the father kept going. "The Dahl were in charge and the universe was better off."

"We heard about this in class," Henry said. "Professor Grimfeather was talking about the Dahl Empire..."

"That's right," Pwmpen's father said, ignoring his son's silent pleading. "Elder Brenin ruled for light-years in every direction. There were none of these rebellions you see now. He kept everyone in line..."

"Dear," Pwmpen's mother said. "You promised not to talk politics at the table."

The father scoffed.

"It's history, not politics," he said. "It's not like I'm going on about the *Echuio*."

Pwmpen dropped his fork on the floor.

"Who's that?" Henry asked.

"It's not a *who*," the father replied. "It's a *what!*"

"Sounds Spanish," Henry said.

"Well, it's not whatever that is," the father replied. "It's a group that wants to bring back the Dahl Empire."

"Is that allowed?" Henry asked.

"No, which is why we're not *supposed* to be talking about it!" Pwmpen said.

The room became suddenly quiet. Henry searched the expressions of the others around the table, but even the father had stopped speaking.

"I've never heard of them," Henry admitted.

"The Dahl are a people of knowledge now," Pwmpen said. "The Empire was a dark time in our history. The idea that there's still some of us that want to return to those days is shameful."

"Are there a lot of Dahl like that?" Henry asked.

"Nobody knows," Pwmpen's mother replied. "The Echuio are very secretive. It's not even clear whether they really exist."

"Oh, they exist all right," the father said. "I know someone who knows someone who's pretty sure there's members in the government, perhaps even on the Elder Council."

Henry listened, but the smell coming from his plate drew his attention away. He put a forkful of fish into his mouth and savored the flavor.

Delicious, he thought, the dinner conversation drifting into the background. *I just hope Finneus doesn't see this...*

Besides offices and classrooms, the Archeology and History departments of Prenwyn University shared a small lounge where professors and their assistants could mingle and eat meals.

Professor Rhun took a break from studying the Singing Lantern and decided to find something for lunch. After passing down a hallway full of students, Rhun found the faculty lounge almost empty. Almost empty, except for an enormous owl creature hunched over one of the tables.

"Hello, Professor Grimfeather," Rhun said.

The Orubea's head turned around nearly 180 degrees until his large eyes fixed on the Dahlvish professor.

"Greetings," Grimfeather said without enthusiasm before his head rotated back again. In his talons, he was holding a plastic container. With a choking, gurgling sound, he regurgitated a dark ball of fur and bones into the container.

Professor Rhun's face turned a paler shade of white as Grimfeather inspected the furry pellet the size of a man's fist.

"I don't remember eating that," he remarked to himself.

Rhun went to the refrigerator but opened the door only to find he was no longer hungry. He closed the door again and discovered the other professor was staring at him.

"You're studying that artifact, aren't you?" Grimfeather asked.

"Yes," Rhun replied weakly.

"The one that the humans brought?"

"Yes..."

"I wish you could keep them on a leash," Grimfeather said. "I had one of them wander into my classroom."

"Henry, I assume?" Rhun replied.

"I'm beginning to wonder how the Imperium functions with such humans running it."

"I don't get the impression Henry has any administrative duties," Rhun said.

"And there's another one about?"

"Jessica Doric is her name."

"Haven't seen much of *her*, thankfully," Grimfeather said.

"She's perfectly competent," Rhun replied, "for a *human*."

"And that artifact they brought," Grimfeather went on. "That's from the Imperial period, yes?"

Professor Rhun straightened proudly. "It's a real find."

"If you say so."

"It's your area of expertise as well, isn't it?" Rhun asked.

"Academically," the Orubea replied, "but practically, I'd rather not get my paws dirty."

"Well, thankfully Miss Doric doesn't share your aversion."

"What does that mean?"

"I sent her out to see one of my graduate students at our excavation site," Rhun said.

Grimfeather's pupils enlarged like full, black moons.

"The one near *Coedwig Lledrith*?" he asked in alarm.

"The same."

"Is that entirely wise?"

"She's perfectly safe," Rhun replied.

"*Safe* is a relative word," Grimfeather said. "If anything were to happen to her, we'd never hear the end of it!"

"No need to ruffle your feathers," Rhun said, trying to make a joke. "My students are able to protect her, and themselves for that matter."

Grimfeather was not amused.

"It will all end in tears," he said, and produced a second, sealed container. He opened the lid, and a large rodent poked its head out and took in the room.

"What's that?" Rhun asked.

"My lunch," Grimfeather replied. "You may want to turn away..."

Professor Rhun took his advice and left, a noise he chose not to identify coming from behind him.

Doric and Mossdale talked into the night, but eventually the Sylva left, leaving Doric alone. Although the shelter was just a tent, it contained several pieces of furniture including a dresser and a bed. The latter had a soft mattress and an oak headboard carved with a pair of wings.

Doric slid under soft, cotton sheets and before long she had fallen fast asleep.

She then woke to a noise outside.

Only dimly aware she wasn't back home in her own bed, Doric struggled to pull herself out from under the covers. She took a few seconds, her feet dangling over the side, to remember she was on an alien planet and in a tent, no less.

She also remembered how much she hated camping.

The sounds outside grew louder, and it dawned on Doric that they were voices shouting. Jutting her feet into a pair of slippers the Dahl had provided, Doric dressed herself quickly and stepped outside. Just beyond the folds of the tent flaps, she saw Dahl running back and forth in the night. Without warning, a great stream of fire erupted less than a dozen yards away, lighting the dark in a long arc of bright orange. The fire came from one of the Dahl, his hands outstretched and facing toward the forest.

They're using psionics! Doric thought.

More Dahl began shooting flames, while others fired streams of ice shards, but everyone was aiming in the direction of the woods.

The flashes made seeing difficult, but Doric strained her eyes at whatever the Dahl were firing at. At the edges of the light, she could just make out forms in the distance. As far as she could tell, they were humanoids riding creatures with many legs. They held poles with long blades on the end, the shiny metal reflecting the bursts of fire.

Mossdale appeared at Doric's side. He held a blaster and waved it toward the tent.

"Get back inside!" he shouted.

"What's happening?" Doric asked, but Mossdale was already running toward the others.

"Get inside!" he shouted over his shoulder.

Doric ducked back into the tent and looked hurriedly for a weapon. She half wished Maycare was there but shook off the thought. She searched through the tent without finding even a butter knife.

Still unarmed, she took cover behind the oak bed, her eyes fixed on the entrance flap. Outside, the shouting only intensified.

"At least Henry isn't here," Doric said to herself.

An explosion erupted in front of her tent, knocking Doric on her back. Looking up at the tent roof, Doric saw a blade cut into the canvas above her, slicing down toward her head.

Doric rolled sideways and scrambled to her feet, only to fall again as she tried to run. Through the rip in the canvas, a thing slipped in, its eight long legs expanding once it was through. A torso with two arms and a head straightened itself from the spider-like body, the top of the head nearly reaching the roof. It held a pole blade in its hands.

Doric heard someone screaming before realizing it was her.

With the body of a giant spider and the torso of a humanoid, the Kuent'l Nanzi, as Mossdale had called it, lunged forward. Before Doric could move, a beam filled the tent with light, striking the creature in the chest. The Nanzi's legs staggered backward before crumbling beneath the body. The weapon dropped from its hands.

Doric turned to see Mossdale behind her, his blaster still aimed at the creature.

The braziers in the four corners of the stone room painted the rough walls in a blue, flickering light. At the center of the room, seven robed figures, each wearing a mask, formed a circle. The masks were silver except for one made of gold.

"Are we prepared?" the one behind the gold mask asked in a male voice.

"I remain opposed," someone said.

"Noted," the gold mask said. "Let's begin..."

With outstretched arms, they made swirling motions toward the middle of the circle while chanting in an archaic version of the Dahlvish language. At first, nothing seemed to happen until finally the dust on the flagstone floor began to stir, slowly moving in a clockwise direction. From this came larger pebbles and bits of dirt pulled from between the flagstones.

The chanting grew louder.

Low and close to the floor, this semi-translucent mass churned and grew denser until chunks of ice appeared intermixed with the dirt. For nearly a minute, the temperature in the chamber dropped noticeably until a ribbon of fire weaved into the icy whirlwind as it began to rise. Like a tornado, the twisting mass tightened into a spout nearly reaching the ceiling. Finally, the air in the room crackled as gnarled fingers of electricity flashed in and out of the cyclone.

Over the din, the chanting was only barely audible until the voices stopped all at once and only the man in the gold mask shouted, "I call forth Elder Brenin! Take shape and heed our call!"

When the whirlwind had grown dense with dirt, fire, ice, and lightning, the vague outline of a person took shape, still visible amongst the chaos.

"Come forth!" the gold mask repeated his demand. "Heed our call!"

The braziers in each corner went out, leaving the room in darkness except for the flashes of electricity. Backlit, the form at the center of the maelstrom became more defined until a pair of glowing white eyes opened and surveyed the robed figures surrounding him.

"Who calls me from the Otherworld?" the spirit of Elder Brenin asked, his voice deep and commanding.

The others, including the one in the gold mask, fell to their knees and bowed their heads.

"Your servants," the gold mask answered. "We require your guidance..."

The tone of the spirit's voice softened.

"Rise," he said. "None of you are my servants. You serve a higher purpose than *me*."

The robed figures got to their feet again, but instinctively kept their heads facing the ground.

"It's been a long time since I crossed over," Elder Brenin went on. "My children have strayed far from the lessons I've taught them."

"We're sorry for our transgressions," the gold mask said.

"Indeed," the spirit agreed, his face obscured by his blazing eyes. "You have become selfish and passive, only interested in your own enlightenment instead of the enlightenment of others."

"We've given counsel to the humans—" one of the others protested.

Brenin sneered.

"The invaders? The humans have corrupted you!" he shouted. "You've become complicit in the enslavement of others, relegating the other races to servitude."

The gold mask looked directly at the spirit.

"We have failed you for too long," the leader of the Echuio said. "But what should we do?"

Below the glowing eyes, a smile appeared.

"We were once an Empire!" Brenin replied. "Take back what you so easily discarded. Only then can you use that *strength* to help the weaker races. How can they become better if you don't lead them down the proper path? It is your destiny and *duty* to them and to yourselves!"

The robed figures once again went to their knees, all except the one in the golden mask.

"We will!" he said, shaking his fist. "Long live the Empire!"

"Long live the Empire..." the spirit replied and faded, along with the surrounding whirlwind. The braziers in each corner bloomed again in flame, filling the dark room with bluish light. Grit and bits of melting ice formed a pile in the center.

The robed figures stood and stared at each other in muted silence. Their leader in the gold mask took a step forward, the dirt and ice grinding under his shoe.

"Can someone get a broom?" he asked.

CHAPTER EIGHT

Ramus and Roxie Blues walked along a gravel path lined with trees full of pink blossoms.

Traditionally, the Dahl were cremated when they died, and their ashes mixed with the soil at the base of a tree. A small, brass placard engraved with the name of the deceased was then affixed to the trunk.

The cemetery was more like an orchard than a graveyard, Ramus thought.

Roxie stopped at one of the trees, staring at the two names written on the brass plate.

"Your parents?" Ramus asked.

"Yes," she replied pensively.

Only the two names were inscribed, without dates of birth or death. Ramus wondered if that was really enough to signify a person's life, but it was typical of the Dahl to leave out more than they revealed.

"I'm sorry," Ramus said, not knowing what else to say.

Roxie stood before the tree silently, her head bowed and her hands clasped together. The Dahl had no religion, but they still prayed to the departed, hopeful that their thoughts would somehow cross the barrier between this world and the next.

Of course, Ramus knew they could contact the dead, if need be, but this was strictly taboo for those directly related.

"I never got to say goodbye," Roxie said.

"But if they were still alive, they wouldn't have recognized you," Ramus replied.

"Yes," she said, "but at least they could've gotten to know me *now*, gotten to see what I've become..."

A bird with bright plumage landed in a nearby cherry tree and started singing something sweet and cheerful. Ramus wanted to wring its neck.

"The Dahl," he said as if talking about some other race, "are brutal. They act like they're wise and all-knowing, but they erased the parts they don't want to remember. They're cruel to the people they'd rather forget."

"Mmm," Roxie murmured.

"This is your family plot, right?" Ramus asked after another long pause.

"Yes."

"Will the authorities allow you to be buried here when you die?"

"I don't know," she replied.

The bird, which had continued to get on Ramus' nerves, flew off with a parting tweet to annoy him. Ramus watched it go until Roxie broke the silence.

"Your parents are still alive, aren't they?" she asked.

Ramus shrugged. "As far as I know..."

"I think you should go see them," she said.

"No thanks."

She touched his hand. His first instinct was to pull away, but he held his arm steady and felt her warmth.

"You have to tell them you exist!" she said in earnest.

"I'd rather they died in ignorance," he said.

Roxie's face flushed.

"Sorry," Ramus said. "That wasn't what I meant—"

"I know," she replied. "But you don't want to be like me. You should tell them."

"It won't do any good."

"You don't know that," Roxie said. "Give them a chance. Maybe they'll be glad to know they have a son."

"No."

He felt her hand tighten around his and her eyes staring hard at him.

"Please," she said.

After a long pause, Ramus broke her gaze and stared at the crushed gravel at his feet.

"Okay," he said.

Humans are nothing but trouble, Chancellor Telyn thought. He regretted agreeing to their presence on campus, and now Elder Blynora was in his office for the second time in less than a week.

"It was irresponsible," she was saying.

"As you may recall, Elder," Telyn replied, "I was not in favor of allowing Miss Doric to stay here in the first place."

"That's beside the point," the elder said. "The fact remains that one of your professors sent a human into a potentially dangerous situation and now we must deal with the consequences."

"What consequences?" Telyn asked.

In her silvery robe, Elder Blynora raised her arms in exasperation. "Who knows at this point?"

"As I see it," Telyn said, "that Sylvan graduate student, Mossdale, handled the situation adequately. No harm done..."

"But what if Miss Doric had been injured or, worse yet, killed?"

"More to my original point, Elder," Telyn replied. "The humans shouldn't be here in the first place!"

Blynora took a seat in one of the high-backed chairs stationed in front of the chancellor's desk. Telyn could not recall seeing the elder in any other way than standing before. Perhaps this was more serious than he thought.

"Are you alright?" he asked.

Blynora paused, staring at the Sprite robot floating quietly in the corner.

"Our history is a long one," she said finally. "Sometimes I think only the Pool of Memory truly remembers it all..."

Chancellor Telyn glanced briefly at the robot as one might acknowledge the presence of a toaster tucked away on a kitchen counter.

"That *is* its job, isn't it?" he remarked.

"Quite," she replied with a sigh. "The Kuent'l Nanzi have been a thorn in our sides for millennia. Some on the council, your wife being one of them, have suggested we should deal with them once and for all."

"I imagine others disagree?" Telyn asked.

"Of course," Blynora said. "The humans think we're all of *one* mind, but it couldn't be further from the truth..."

"And yet we must maintain a unified front, at least in *their* eyes."

"Obviously," the elder agreed. "Our wisdom must seem universally true, or the humans may question the advice we give them."

"Well, we wouldn't want *that*," the chancellor replied somewhat sarcastically. "It's best to keep up appearances."

Elder Blynora grumbled deep in her throat.

"Our greatest strength as a people," she said, "is our usefulness to the Imperium. Without that, we are no different than any of the other non-human races. That could lead to our own subjugation."

"They wouldn't dare!" Telyn exclaimed.

"What's to stop them?" she replied.

"We were once an empire of our own—" the chancellor said.

"That was a long time ago," Blynora interrupted. "Don't forget that."

"The Pool of Memory is not the only one who can remember," Telyn said.

Elder Blynora rose while shaking her head.

"Arrogance is what led to our downfall," she replied, turning to go. "Let us remember *that* as well..."

On Orkney Fugg's home planet, day drinking was the national pastime. The Gordians took drinking of all sorts seriously, but getting plastered during the day was important business. On board the *Wanderer*, Fugg finished his usual routine in the engine room, followed by an extended break in the galley where he cracked open one fungus beer after another.

"What about me?" Mel asked, seeing Fugg slowly getting wasted.

"What *about* you?" he replied.

"A good host would offer me a beer," she said.

"I'm not a good host," he admitted. "And I don't *like* you!"

"Afraid I'll drink you under the table?"

Fugg nearly spat out his mouthful, which on his planet was an unforgivable sin, and pointed to the fridge where the bottles were kept.

"Fine!" he said. "You can have *one!*"

One beer, as it happened, turned into several and, as time wore on, empty bottles accumulated on the table, the galley floor, and in a few of the cupboards. Gen the robot had done her best to collect the empties, but eventually gave up and escaped to her cabin to listen to music.

"When did Ramus leave with that singer?" Fugg asked, his speech slurred.

Mel stared at him bleary-eyed. "Over three hours ago!"

"Are we just going to just sit here and wait?"

"What do you suggest?" Mel asked.

"Let's go and get that thing ourselves..."

"What thing?"

"The thing!" Fugg shouted, gesturing vaguely in the air.

"Oh, *that* thing," she replied. "The *Lantern!*"

"Do you know where it is?"

"On campus somewhere, obviously."

"Well, let's go get it then!" Fugg said.

Mel gave the empty bottle in her hand a regretful look. "Are we out of beer?'

"Yesh."

"Okay then," she said. "Let's go..."

The two stumbled down the ramp onto the tarmac but, as responsible drunks, ordered a gravtaxi to take them to Prenwyn University. The driver, a Dahl wearing a white cap and a disapproving expression, dropped them off just outside the campus walls. Mel and Fugg then spent the next 30 minutes searching for a door to get inside. Once this was accomplished, they wandered clumsily along the sidewalks between buildings until reaching the Commons where they took a respite beside the fountain.

Mel rested her rubbery legs on the rim while dragging her hand through the water. The cool liquid felt relaxing.

"Such a beautiful place," she remarked.

"Meh," Fugg snorted. "Too bad it's full of Dahl!"

Some of the passing students, hearing this, exchanged scowls with the Gordian who gave them a rude salute with one of his fingers.

"Where is the Lantern anyway?" Fugg asked.

Mel scratched her pink hair, which was approaching Henry-levels of dishevelment.

"The archeology department maybe?" she said.

"Well, it would've been nice to know that before we left," Fugg replied, his buzz starting to wane.

"It's not like I have a map!" Mel protested. "All these buildings look alike."

Across the open square a familiar voice shouted, "Mel!"

Through a haze like cotton fibers, the Gnomi stared off toward the sound. Henry himself was waving at her while standing beside a rotund Dahl with an atrocious haircut. Henry smiled broadly and ran toward them, followed tentatively by the Dahl who carried a fishbowl.

"What are you doing here?" Henry asked Mel in surprise.

Mel stood, looking for words. "Visiting..."

"Have you been drinking?" Henry said. "In the middle of the day?"

"There's nothing wrong with that!" Fugg protested. "It's a proud tradition where I come from!"

"Have you two met, Henry?" Mel asked. "This is Orkney Fugg from the *Wanderer.*"

Henry hesitated. "Captain Ramus mentioned him a few times..."

"Who's the fat one?" Fugg asked, pointing a doughy finger at Pwmpen.

Mel gave the engineer a dirty look. "Look who's talking!"

"This is *all* muscle—" Fugg replied.

"Covered in fat!" Mel said.

Not sure the yelling was over, Henry waited and then said, "This is my roommate Pwmpen."

"I've never met a Gordian before," Pwmpen said timidly while holding Finneus Finnegan's bowl tightly against his chest.

"I've never met a chubby Dahl!" Fugg replied.

Several passing students stopped to see about the commotion but quickly set off again, wanting nothing to do with whatever *this* was. Henry tried changing the subject.

"We just came from lunch with Pwmpen's parents," he said.

"Oh?" Mel replied with genuine interest.

"Yes!" Henry went on. "It was nice to show Finneus around a bit."

"Who?" Mel asked.

"My goldfish."

"Of course," Mel replied.

"You're a Gnomi, aren't you?" Pwmpen asked.

Mel straightened, though she was still shorter than the Dahl. "Damn right!"

"Henry knows so many different people!" Pwmpen said, beaming at his roommate.

"Well, I try," Henry said and, as if trying to show off his knowledge, leaned in to convey something secret. "Mel, have you ever heard of the Echuio?"

"Shush!" Pwmpen whispered and waved his hands, nearly dropping the fishbowl. "Not in public."

"What's an Echuio?" Fugg asked loudly.

"It's an underground organization," Henry continued. "A bunch of Dahl wanting to overthrow the Imperium."

"Good for them!" Mel said.

Both Henry and Pwmpen stared at her.

"I mean," Mel added, "humans haven't exactly been good for the rest of us..."

"We're not so bad," Henry said.

"Bunch of racists, if you ask me," Fugg said.

Pwmpen stuck up for his human friend.

"Henry's been nothing but nice!" he said. "And he takes good care of Finneus!"

Fugg snorted. "How do we know the fish ain't racist too?"

"He's not, probably!" Pwmpen replied hotly as some of the water sloshed out of the bowl. The goldfish steadied himself as best he could.

Mel felt a migraine coming on.

"Anyway!" she shouted at them all before fixing her attention on Henry in particular. "Where's Jessica?"

"She's out visiting a dig site," Henry replied.

"Oh," Mel said, "Well, maybe *you* could help us then, Henry."

"Sure," he said.

"A little bird told me the Singing Lantern was on this planet," she said.

"Sure," Henry replied. "There's a Dahl professor looking at it."

"I'd love to see it again," Mel said.

"Well, I don't know," Henry wavered.

"I suppose you won't help us either," Fugg muttered. "Typical *human*."

"Wait," Henry said. "I could sneak you in..."

"No, Henry," Pwmpen said warily. "I don't think that's a good idea."

"Why not?" Henry asked. "What's the worst that could happen?"

Pwmpen took the goldfish back to the dorm, leaving Henry to bring Mel and Fugg to the archeology department on his own. In the hallway down from Professor Rhun's office, Mel and Fugg waited around the corner while they listened as Henry called for the professor just outside the door.

"Sorry, Professor," Henry said, his voice echoing down the corridor, "Chancellor Telyn wants to see you."

"He does?" Rhun replied. "Oh, it's probably about the attack."

"The *what?*" Henry asked.

Mel heard Rhun cough uncomfortably.

"It's nothing," the professor said. "Nothing at all, Henry."

After Rhun's footsteps receded down another hallway, Mel and Fugg joined Henry in front of the professor's office.

"Good work, Henry," Mel said. "Is the Lantern in there?"

"Yeah, come on," he replied and headed inside.

The office was not a tinker's workshop, but Mel still found the various artifacts and miscellaneous doodads on the tables strongly enticing. She had the urge to start stuffing her pockets with whatever she could get her hands on.

"There it is," Henry said, pointing to a desk where a crystal shape sat silently in the back.

Mel forgot about the rest and moved hurriedly to the Lantern. Meanwhile, Fugg remained beside the human.

"Why don't you do something useful and be a lookout in the hall," Fugg suggested.

"Oh, sure!" Henry replied and disappeared through the doorway.

When Fugg arrived at Mel's side, she was leaning over the device, studying the glass-like structure.

"Well, is that going to work?" Fugg asked.

"It should," she said. "Now we just need to cut off a piece."

"With what?"

"A plasma cutter would be ideal," she replied, her eyes giving the room a quick once-over.

"I don't see one," Fugg said.

She spotted something on the neighboring table. "This'll work."

Mel grabbed a hammer and chisel and sized up where she wanted to start.

"What kind of crystal is this?" Fugg asked skeptically, rubbing his chin.

"No idea," she said, "but it focuses psionic energy so it must be unique."

"And you're going to chip off a piece?"

Mel shrugged. "Sure, why not?"

She positioned the edge of the chisel against the Lantern and gave it a cursory tap with the hammer.

"Here," she said, "hold onto it for me."

Fugg came around Mel's other side and gripped the base of the Lantern.

"It's not going to blow up or anything, is it?" he asked.

"Probably not," Mel replied.

Fugg tensed and closed his eyes while Mel pulled back the hammer and gave the chisel a good whacking. When Fugg opened his eyes, Mel was staring disappointedly at the Lantern.

"Not a scratch..." she said.

"Well, hurry up!" Fugg said.

Mel tried again, putting as much force behind the strike as possible but the surface of the crystal remained stubbornly untouched.

"What the shit?" she swore.

Through the doorway, Henry appeared, closing the door behind him.

"What's going on in here?" he asked.

"Nothing, Henry," Mel replied innocently.

"Why are you holding a hammer?" Henry said.

Mel lowered the tools. "No reason."

"Maybe we should just grab the whole thing?" Fugg suggested.

"What?" Henry asked.

Mel dropped the hammer and chisel on the nearby table, and ushered Fugg toward the door.

"Thank you for bringing us, Henry," she said. "We've seen enough."

"But..." Henry sputtered, but Mel and Fugg were already past him.

"Talk to you later, Henry!" Mel shouted.

"Yeah, later, human!" Fugg snorted, and the two were gone.

Back in his dorm room, Henry sat in a chair with a sheet over his shoulders while Pwmpen gave him a trim. Pwmpen had promised him a proper haircut, but Henry's mind was elsewhere, thinking of Mel holding a hammer and chisel.

"Thank you for letting me try a few things," Pwmpen said.

"Huh?" Henry replied. "Oh, sure."

Someone knocked on the door.

"Come in!" Henry called.

The door opened, revealing Jessica Doric. She took a step forward, but stopped, seeing Henry facing her on the chair.

"Are those bangs?" she asked.

Pwmpen stopped cutting and both of the roommates stared blankly at the newcomer.

"It looks good," Doric said weakly.

"You're back from your trip already?" Henry asked.

Doric closed the door behind her. "Yes."

"This is my roommate, Pwmpen," Henry went on.

"Hello," the Dahl said and went back to trimming the back of Henry's head.

"Guess who I ran into—?" Henry began.

"Before you start," Doric cut in, "something happened..."

"What?" Henry asked.

"I was attacked," she replied.

Both roommates this time, "*What?*"

"Apparently there's a race on this planet called the Nanzi," she explained. "They attacked the camp and one of them broke into my tent."

"Did it hurt you?" Henry asked.

"No," she replied, "but it was horrible. They have the body of a giant spider and the torso of a person. I could've been killed."

"I'm sorry," Henry said.

"The trip was going really well up until then," Doric said. "I met a Sylvan student named Mossdale and he showed me around."

"Oh?" Henry replied.

"I've never seen a Sylva before and he was very handsome," she said.

"Oh?" Pwmpen asked.

"Yes," Doric said. "He was the one who killed the Nanzi who got into my tent. If he hadn't shown up, I just don't know..."

Henry felt his face growing hot.

"Are you feeling sick?" Doric asked. "You look flushed."

"I'm fine."

"I've heard of the Kuent'l Nanzi," Pwmpen said. "My mother told me they'd come and drag me away if I didn't eat my vegetables."

"I met his mother," Henry remarked. "We all had lunch together."

"Good," Doric said without much interest.

"Have you heard of the Dahl Empire?" Henry asked, trying to impress her.

"Of course," she replied, perking up.

"Well, what about the Echuio?" Henry asked.

"Henry!" Pwmpen scolded. "You don't have to tell *everybody*!"

"What's the Echuio?" Doric asked.

"Oh, just a secret society," Henry said with a sly grin.

Pwmpen stopped cutting and put away his scissors. "They want to revive the Empire."

"I wanted to tell her!" Henry shouted.

"They probably don't exist anyway," Pwmpen said. "It's just a bogeyman mothers use to scare their children."

"Well," Doric said, "I can tell you the Nanzi are real..."

"At least you have that Woodland Dahl to protect you," Henry told her, his eyes examining the hair clippings at his feet.

"Sylva," Doric corrected him.

"Whatever," he replied grumpily.

"Anyway," she said, "who did you say you met?"

Henry shrugged beneath the sheet. "Never mind. It doesn't matter."

Truth be told, Chancellor Telyn hated politics. He liked the power of his position, but not the petty squabbling and partisan backstabbing that infected all levels of academia. Of course, Telyn would not have reached his position without playing the game, even when that meant playing dumb from time to time.

The chancellor saw Prenwyn University as a place of learning, first and foremost. Over the many years as its leader, Telyn had forgotten more about teaching than most of these professors would ever know. Yet, academia was also a hotbed, a sanctuary for areas of thought that should be best left in the past. Not the least of which were certain schools of psionics, Dark Psi especially, that were simply too dangerous for common practice.

Shortly after Elder Blynora left Telyn's office, Professor Rhun stuck his head in the doorway with a quizzical expression.

"You wanted to see me, Chancellor?" he asked.

For the life of him, Telyn couldn't remember sending for Rhun, but maybe the professor had learned to read minds on the side.

"Yes, actually," the chancellor replied.

Rhun came in the rest of the way and sat in the chair in front of Telyn's desk. The chancellor always found professors from the archeology department rather unkempt, and Rhun was no exception. Telyn wondered if they only owned one outfit and wore it until the thing disintegrated into rags.

"Elder Blynora just came to see me," the chancellor began.

"Really?" Rhun replied. "How is she?"

"A bit rattled if you ask me—" Telyn started to say and then stopped himself. "Never mind! She came by to talk about the *humans*."

"Miss Doric and Henry?"

"Do you know of any other humans on this planet?" Telyn replied.

Rhun squinted his eyes at the ceiling and thought. "I don't *think* so..."

"Yes, *of course* I mean them!"

"Ah, very good," Rhun replied. "I thought I had forgotten someone."

"The Elder is very concerned about the recent attack on Miss Doric," the chancellor said.

Rhun nodded. "A disagreeable business."

"Exactly!" Telyn said. "And Elder Blynora somehow blames *me* for allowing it to happen!"

"I don't see why," Rhun replied. "You have no control over the Kuent'l Nanzi. No one does, it would seem..."

"Well, yes, that's true," Telyn said. "I didn't say the Elder was being *fair*. But, as the humans say, the dung rolls downhill, so now I'm talking to *you* about it."

"They *say* that?"

"Humans have many rustic expressions about excrement," the chancellor said, "but that's beside the point. You shouldn't have sent Miss Doric to the dig site in the first place."

"Oh?"

"It put her in danger, obviously."

Rhun considered this.

"I suppose you're right," he said finally. "How embarrassing..."

"Well, don't feel too bad about it," the chancellor went on, not wanting to upset the professor. Academics were often a sensitive lot.

"I trust your research on the artifact the humans brought is progressing?" he added.

"Indeed!" Rhun replied. "Most satisfactory!"

"Well, alright then," Telyn said, waving his hand in the direction of the door. "You should probably get back to it..."

Professor Rhun rose from his seat and made his way out. At the threshold, he passed another Dahl on the way in. The two couldn't have looked more different: Rhun's ordinary appearance contrasted sharply with the other Dahl's flaming red hair.

Rhun disappeared into the hallway while the newcomer strode into the office like he had been there a hundred times. Chancellor Telyn looked at him but could have sworn he had never seen him before.

Captain Ramus stopped in front of the chancellor's desk.

"Hello, *Father*," Ramus said.

CHAPTER NINE

The Magna raider arrived at the rendezvous point without fanfare, which was precisely how it was supposed to be for a secret meeting. Truth be known, Captain Ra-Gor would have liked a *little* fanfare, but that was generally frowned upon since this was an intelligence operation. The ship was on the wrong side of the Imperial border, so keeping a low profile was preferable.

Although both the Imperium and the Magna Supremacy kept a network of remote sensors along the demilitarized zone separating them, a small ship could slip past without drawing much attention. This allowed Ra-Gor to do his job, even if it meant having to deal with sub-species like the Sarkan, and one Sarkan in particular named *Enrion*. The fact that Enrion insisted that he was not actually inferior to Ra-Gor and the Magna was especially infuriating.

It got under the captain's green skin.

On the bridge of the raider, one of the crew turned to the captain: "No sign of the Sarkan's ship, sir."

Ra-Gor felt the heat rising on the back of his neck.

"Then we wait!" he growled.

From childhood, each Magna learned they were above all others. They were the master race, and unlike all the other races who thought *they* were the master race, the Magna really meant it this time. Their manifest destiny entailed the universe was theirs for the taking, but their supreme patience also meant they could wait until the universe inevitably fell into their grasp.

In the meantime, Captain Ra-Gor had to cool his heels until the lowly Red Dahl arrived in that pathetic ship of his.

"Captain," the Magna crew member said, "a vessel has just emerged from hyperspace."

About time, Ra-Gor thought.

"It's not the Sarkan ship!" the crew member added urgently.

"Put it on screen," Ra-Gor ordered.

The front of the bridge changed from a view of empty space to a close-up image of an impressive warship, a cruiser of Imperial design.

"They're hailing us..."

Ra-Gor's nostrils flared. "Let's hear it!"

"This is Captain Robert Maycare of the HIMS Baron Lancaster," a human voice said over the speakers. "Surrender and prepare to be boarded!"

While most people know space is big and empty, most people have no idea just *how* big and empty it really is. The odds of two ships happening to reach the same exact point in space at the exact same time is practically zero, which made this meeting with an Imperial vessel even more unlikely without a little *help*.

And Ra-Gor had a pretty good idea who had done the helping.

"Enrion!" the captain shouted, slamming his fist onto the arm of his command chair. Then, glaring at his helmsman, he said, "Evasive action!"

Like a forge set alight, the engines of the Magna raider flared. Meanwhile, the Baron Lancaster, a much larger ship studded with plasma cannons, wasted no time and began firing. Streams of blazing energy struck the raider's shields, illuminating the dark vacuum around it with orange fire.

The captain's chair rattled beneath Ra-Gor as he yelled more orders.

"Plot an emergency jump! More power to the shields!"

One of the consoles on the bridge exploded, peppering the officer at that station with shards of plastic and bits of metal. He slumped to the floor, trying to stem the black blood gushing from his face.

From his own tactical display, the captain watched the Imperial warship close in for the kill. With its added momentum from exiting hyperspace, the Baron Lancaster was approaching much faster than the Magna ship could accelerate from a near standstill.

Another salvo from the Lancaster erupted against the shields which flickered before dying out completely.

"Shields are down!" a bridge officer shouted.

It was hopeless, Ra-Gor knew, but he was not ready to give up just yet. While humans were nearly as merciless as the Magna — and that was reason enough for the captain to respect them — he would never suffer the humiliation of surrendering willingly.

"Return fire!" he shouted. "All power to the weapons!"

His only regret, Ra-Gor thought as the Lancaster loomed larger, was that he could not see that treacherous Sarkan one last time and snap his skinny neck. The sound of the cracking bone would have been most satisfactory.

While the wires in the ceiling fell around him like burning vines, Ra-Gor muttered, "Enrion..."

As a boy, Ramus was known as Rowan and, like all the other Dahlvish girls and boys, he learned about psionics at school. Of course, other topics were taught, like reading, writing, and arithmetic, but in these formative years, a young Dahl's powers began to manifest themselves and the focus turned to the type of psionics they did best.

Much to the consternation of his parents, however, Rowan was not particularly good at any of them. While his mother, Elder Arwyn, was understanding, his father the chancellor was not.

"He doesn't get this from *my* side of the family," Telyn said, his eyes glaring across the dinner table.

"Now, dear," Arwyn replied, "he's sitting right there."

Rowan looked at his lap and wondered if he should crawl under the table.

"What are we going to do?" his father asked.

Arwyn smiled reassuringly at her son. "We'll wait and see."

In fact, not every Dahl was blessed with strong psionic powers, although every Dahl had at least some ability. This was cold comfort to Chancellor Telyn who viewed his son's low acuity as a sign of weakness and a personal affront to his family's name.

For Rowan, his father's continued disappointment did not go unnoticed.

By the time the boy had grown older and had entered college, Rowan no longer felt he could achieve much of anything. Even his mother was no longer optimistic, which hurt Rowan most of all.

Then, quite by accident, he got lost one day in the library at Prenwyn University and found himself in an area of the stacks nearly buried in dust and cobwebs. It was in this long-forgotten corner that a leather-bound book jutted slightly out from the shelves as if calling to him. Curious, he removed the tome and blew dust off the binding. The lettering was old Dahlvish, but Rowan had learned enough to read the title, *The Art of Forbidden Magic.*

I should walk away, he thought, and so he did but only *after* tucking the book under his shirt.

In the following weeks, he secretly read the ancient text, careful not to let anyone see him doing so. The pages were brittle with age, but the words on them were still as clear as the day they were printed, likely dating back long before even the Dahl Empire had existed.

Late at night, when respectable students were tucked in their beds, Rowan sneaked out of the dormitory to an empty field behind the geology department and began practicing what he had learned.

Psionics came in as many shades as the colors of a rainbow. There was the orange of pyrokinesis and the blue of cryokinesis. Female Sylva even practiced a green type of psi connecting them with nature. If the psi Rowan had found had its own color, it would have been a deep purple, like the night just as the moon begins to rise.

Contrary to all the other psionics Rowan had tried, this purple psi was something quite different. For one thing, he was pretty good at it.

He started small, using the lessons of the ancient text to manipulate the cells of plants that grew in the field. Weeds were unheard of on Gwlad Ard'un, so Rowan began changing the colors of the flowers from pink to blue and back again. He then mutated the plants to grow additional buds where none had existed before.

Once he was confident with flora, he moved on to bugs that preyed on the plants. If he concentrated, Rowan could enlarge or shrink a beetle and even give it bioluminescence, its shell glowing with a cyan brilliance. He then started to branch out, so to speak, by giving the bug eight legs instead of six, and a few extra eyes for good measure.

The Art of Forbidden Magic taught Rowan everything about this new kind of psi and opened new ways of thinking he had never experienced during the traditional classes at school. He began wondered why no one, especially his parents, had ever mentioned it before.

Tired of plants and insects, he turned to warm-blooded animals.

Late at night, mouse-like rodents would roam the field looking for tasty beetles. This was made easier by the fact that many of the beetles were now glowing in the dark. Rowan caught one of the mice and explored what changes he could make to it. The fur, a little ratty in places, became soft like mink. The beady eyes turned turquoise with enhanced infrared abilities so the mice could hunt other creatures besides bugs. To help facilitate bigger prey, Rowan also made the rodents larger with sharper fangs and claws that could rend apart flesh. He watched with morbid curiosity as his creations tore non-modified mice into shredded pieces.

Coming across one of these unfortunate victims, Rowan shooed the attacking mutant away and examined the dead rodent. It was mostly intact with just a few bite marks around the neck.

Toward the end of the book, Rowan had read several passages about cellular rejuvenation, but he had been reluctant to try it until now. He was young but not entirely stupid, and knew reanimation was a step most Dahl would consider too far. However, it had also occurred to him that perhaps his parents, and other adults, *did* know about this school of psionics, but had been keeping it a secret. Why else would he not know about it?

The other Dahl had been keeping this power to themselves and that wasn't fair!

Carefully crouching over the dead mouse, Rowan focused his mind and formed his hands into a triangle. Within moments, energy grew like streamers of purple miasma, running between his hands and the corpse. The bands of violet bent and swirled, twisting through the inanimate cells, changing something within them that Rowan didn't fully understand. The ripped flesh around the rodent's neck knitted back together, healing before Rowan's eyes, and the blood below the skin started pumping again. Then, as if given an electric shock, the mouse jumped to its four little feet, its eyes open and looking around for whatever had just killed it. Perhaps realizing it had a second chance at life, the animal took one glance at Rowan looming over it and dashed for the cover of the surrounding plants.

Rowan watched his new, rekindled friend disappear into the night.

A week or two later, Elder Arwyn had just left a meeting of the Council when she received a message from her husband:

COME SEE ME IN MY OFFICE
LOVE, THE CHANCELLOR

Always the romantic, Arwyn thought.

When the elder reached the university, she found Telyn pacing in front of his desk.

"What's wrong?" Arwyn asked.

Telyn stopped and stared at her for a moment, wide-eyed.

"Calm down," his wife said.

The chancellor took a deep breath before exhaling loudly.

"The beetles are glowing," Telyn said flatly.

"What?"

"And the mice are enormous, with fangs like razor-sharp needles!" he went on.

"Have you been smoking something from the confiscation closet again?" Arwyn asked.

"No!" the chancellor barked.

"Perhaps if you started from the beginning, dear?"

"Very well," Telyn said and leaned against the heavy desk. "There were reports of something strange in the field behind the geology department."

"Well, they're always digging up something," the elder remarked.

"This is something else, Arwyn," the chancellor replied. "Strange plants and wildlife have started appearing there."

"Like glowing beetles?"

"Exactly, and rather ferocious rodents. Also, pink flowers that are now *blue* for some reason!"

Arwyn gathered her robes around her and sat in one of the chairs.

"Did you find out why?" she asked.

"I investigated," her husband said, "and it appears they were all manipulated at the cellular level."

"You're sure?"

"Do you think I'd call you if I wasn't?"

"This is serious," she said.

"You have no idea!" he replied, his voice shrill, which was not normal for him.

"What haven't you told me?" she asked.

"I waited hidden in the field last night," he said. "Sometime after midnight I saw a student arrive with an old book in his arms."

Arwyn heard a knock at the chancellor's door and nearly jumped out of the chair. She was relieved when her son Rowan let himself in.

"You wanted to see me?" the young Dahl said.

Arwyn's face turned ashen as she swung her head around to look at Rowan's father.

"What's going on?" Rowan asked and went to stand beside his mother.

"I know what you've been up to," Telyn said gravely.

Rowan shifted his feet, saying nothing.

"Where did you get the book?" Arwyn asked.

"What book?" Rowan replied.

"The one you use to cast Dark Psi!" his father shouted.

"I don't even know what that is!" Rowan yelled back, his face matching his reddish hair.

"It's the most dangerous psi ever invented," his mother explained. "The Elder Council outlawed it centuries ago..."

"Why?" Rowan asked. "It's powerful!"

"It's *too* powerful!" Arwyn replied.

Rowan put his hand on his mother's arm.

"But I'm good at it..." he said.

"You don't know what you've done," the chancellor said. "We have to tell the authorities."

"But Mother *is* the authorities!" Rowan said. "She could keep it a secret."

The elder stood, pulling her arm away from her son's touch.

"Your father's right," she said. "This is something bigger than me or this family. I *must* tell the Council..."

She stared into her son's eyes.

"I'm sorry," she said.

In the valley of red flowers called Dôlgoch, the Elder Council convened on their stone benches, sitting in judgment of a young Dahl. Standing before them, Rowan endured their steady gaze, flanked by his father on one side and his mother on the other. Off in the corner, shielded from psionics beneath a special glass box, *The Art of Forbidden Magic* lay on a marble pedestal.

Rowan had been in trouble before, but this seemed something different.

Elder Blynora rose from her seat and turned toward her fellow members.

"This is a sad day for all of us," she said. "The son of an elder and the chancellor of our greatest university stands accused of a heinous crime."

"He didn't know what he was doing," Telyn said. "He's never been very smart, but since when is ignorance against the law?"

Elder Blynora gave Rowan's father a hard look.

"He's ignorant no more," she said. "I dare say he knows more about Dark Psi now than anyone on the Council. That makes him *dangerous*..."

"Why?" Rowan asked, still incredulous that *any* knowledge would be forbidden. "What makes it so terrible?"

"You have gone against both nature and science," Blynora replied. "You have manipulated the very fabric of living tissue and brought back to life what was no longer living."

"But is it not true," Elder Arwyn protested, "that we've manipulated the trees to always show their blossoms? And have we not eradicated weeds so they no longer grow at all?"

A few of the council members grumbled, and one or two even approved of Arwyn's point. Seeing this, Blynora waved her hand to silence them.

"No!" she said flatly. "Those changes were done over centuries with great care and consideration by the Council itself. No single Dahl has been so bold as to mutate the very essence of our flora and fauna at the cellular level. And what's to stop a dark wielder from changing themselves, to make them into something unrecognizable as Dahl? No, it is too powerful for any single Dahl to possess."

"Then let us all have the power!" Rowan shouted despite his father having been clear about such outbursts. "If it's wrong for one person to have it, why not give it to *everybody*? Why keep it a secret?"

The other elders frowned, and some crossed their arms. Perhaps his father was right, Rowan realized.

"Do you see?" Blynora said to the others while pointing directly at the young Dahl. "He lacks the maturity to even understand the dangers he has unleashed! We have no choice..."

"What do you mean?" Rowan asked his parents, but neither met his gaze. "What is she talking about?"

"Banishment!" Blynora said. "He must be exiled before he teaches others what he knows."

"Leave Gwlad Ard'un?" Rowan said. "When will I see my parents again?"

"Never," Blynora replied, "but they won't miss you, child. They won't even *remember* you. You shall be erased from our memories and become one of the *Forgotten*."

"This is total bull—" Rowan started, but Telyn stopped him.

"The Council has decided," the chancellor said. "There's nothing more we can do."

The elders, for once, seemed to be in agreement. They nodded one by one until Elder Blynora had their unanimous consent. Rowan looked pleadingly at his mother, but she nodded as well, her face sunk in despair.

Guards, who had been waiting in the wings, appeared at Rowan's side as his parents moved aside.

"Take him away," Blynora ordered. "Once he's off-planet, the Council will reconvene at the Pool of Memory and perform the Ceremony of the Forgotten. No one except the boy will remember any of this from that point on."

"No!" Rowan shouted as the guards pulled him away, his heels dragging on the paving stones. "I'll *never* forgive you for this!" he yelled at his parents. "I'll *never* forget!"

In the present day, after Professor Rhun had disappeared into the hallway, Captain Ramus stopped in front of the chancellor's desk.

"Hello, Father," Ramus said with an expression of both dread and triumph.

Chancellor Telyn examined the mysterious Dahl before him, looking him up and down.

"I don't *have* a son," Telyn replied.

CHAPTER TEN

In her room aboard the *Wanderer*, Gen was taking the opportunity to watch videos of her favorite band. On the screen, K-bots were dancing and singing in perfect synchronization while Gen watched with rapt attention. Fugg and Mel had been gone for hours, and Roxie Blues had returned earlier, without Captain Ramus, and retreated to her own cabin without talking. Left to her own devices, Gen decided to practice some self-care by polishing her outer casing and listening to music.

Mel and Fugg disturbed this tranquility by suddenly barging into the room Mel and Gen shared.

"That was a huge waste of time!" Fugg complained. "And my buzz is *completely* gone!"

"Then get another beer!" Mel countered, sitting on the bed.

"You drank it all!" Fugg yelled.

Mel huffed at the injustice of his remark. "You *helped*!"

"What's happening?" Gen asked, pausing the video.

Mel and Fugg stared at the robot as if seeing her for the first time.

"We found the Singing Lantern," the Gnomi replied, "but we couldn't get a piece to take back to Uncle Artie."

"Oh, dear," Gen said. "What will you do?"

Fugg, who had remained standing, planted his hands on his hips. "Yeah, what *are* you doing to do?"

"Hell if I know!" Mel admitted.

"Maybe the captain can help?" Gen asked.

"Not likely," Fugg said with a snort. "He's too wrapped up with that lounge singer lady..."

Mel laid back, resting on her elbows. "Where are those two anyway?"

"Miss Blues is in her cabin," the robot replied, "but I don't know where the Captain went. I hope there wasn't an argument because Roxie seemed sad if you ask me."

"Nobody's asking," Fugg remarked.

"Well, it doesn't matter," Mel said. "We'll have to figure this out for ourselves."

"*You'll* have to figure this out," Fugg said. "I'm done helping."

"You were never any help to begin with, Fugg!" the Gnomi replied.

"I brought beer!" he retorted.

He turned his back on the bunk beds, fixing his attention on the robot and the monitor behind her.

"What the hell are you watching?" he asked.

Gen grinned excitedly and unpaused the video. The robots on the screen began dancing again, their arms and legs rotating in directions physically impossible for most organic creatures.

"It's a band called *Sparks!*" she said. "Aren't they great?"

"No!" he said. "Is that even singing?"

"Of course!" Gen replied without losing her enthusiasm. "They're programmed to perform all their greatest hits!"

"I'd like to hit them myself," Fugg muttered.

"Will you two keep it down?" Mel asked loudly from the bed. "I can't hear myself think."

"Your uncle's going to be pissed when you get back empty handed," Fugg replied as Gen paused the video again.

"He's not going to be mad," Mel said. "I'm like his daughter."

"And a terrible disappointment too, I bet," Fugg added.

"Shut up!" Mel replied. "I'm going to get that crystal one way or another..."

"And how do you plan on doing that?" he asked.

Mel swung her legs around until her feet touched the floor. Her lips had curled into a grin.

"I'm going to get it the only way a Gnomi knows how," she said.

"Yeah?" Fugg asked.

"I'm going to *steal* it!" Mel said proudly.

Ramus hadn't been in his father's office in years, but it was just as he remembered it. A creature of habit, Chancellor Telyn had kept every book and every memento in exactly the same place. Most of all, Ramus recognized the expression of his father's disapproval.

"What do you want?" Telyn asked bluntly.

"I'm your son," Ramus said.

"As I've said," the chancellor replied, "I don't have a son. It's quite impossible."

"You never wanted children?" Ramus asked.

The chancellor faltered. "No, but—"

Ramus saw a fleeting memory cross his father's stern face, but it disappeared immediately.

"I don't know who you really are," Telyn said, "but I think you should leave."

Instead, Ramus sat in one of the chairs and got comfortable.

"I came here with a friend of mine," he began. "She came to see her parents."

Telyn tapped his fingers on the desk impatiently. "Fascinating..."

"She knew they wouldn't remember her," Ramus went on, "but she came anyway."

"Some people are just forgettable I'm afraid."

Ramus scowled but continued. "Anyway, they weren't there. They had both died in an accident."

"Really, whatever your name is, I have better things to do—"

"She never got to say goodbye and now it's too late," Ramus said.

The chancellor exhaled in exasperation, but his tone softened.

"I admit that sounds tragic," he said, "but I fail to see what that has to do with me."

"She's one of the Forgotten," Ramus replied. "All memories of her were erased from her parents' minds and the minds of all other Dahl except herself."

Telyn's face drained of what little color it had to begin with.

"You've heard of the Forgotten?" Ramus asked.

The chancellor waved his hand philosophically. "In principle, yes."

"Oh, it's not hypothetical," Ramus said, his gaze riveted on his father. "Exile is a very real thing and I should know; I'm a *Forgotten* too."

"What is your name?" Telyn asked.

"You knew me as Rowan, but I took the last name *Ramus* when they kicked me off this damn planet."

Calmly, the chancellor gathered himself.

"Listen, Mr. Ramus," he said. "I'm sorry for whatever may have happened to you, but it is none of my concern."

"It's *Captain* Ramus, actually. I own my own ship, the *Wanderer*."

"Be that as it may," Telyn went on, "you are clearly not wanted here, one way or another. Also, if you were really exiled, by law you shouldn't be on *Gwlad Ard'un*."

"Are you going to call the police?"

The chancellor considered the question. "No, I suppose not, although I have every reason to."

"Well, that's something."

Telyn rose from behind the desk and offered his hand. "Safe travels to you."

Ramus got up as well and, with a moment's hesitation, shook his father's hand.

"Goodbye," Ramus said.

"Goodbye," Telyn replied.

The janitorbot rolled along his usual route through the history and archeology building, largely ignored by students and professors alike. A set of four small wheels supported the robot's body, a slender pillar of blue metal from which spindly arms protruded. A single eye on a telescoping neck pivoted from side to side, searching for loose garbage.

The robot entered each office and classroom without expecting a greeting, and he never received one. He found the trash can and quietly emptied it into a hopper he pulled behind him. It was a routine the janitorbot had done millions of times, but sometimes he would stop and examine the lessons on the board to break the monotony. He had learned a great deal about Dahlvish history this way, finding most of it even more tedious than his daily route.

"Fleshlings!" he grumbled disparagingly.

After finishing a full circuit around the building, the janitorbot returned to the custodial closet where he dumped the trash from the hopper into a central compactor. Closing the door behind him, the robot found the usual cleaning supplies but also something new: a person with pink hair.

"Who are you?" the janitorbot asked.

The fleshling, who was shorter than the average Dahl, stepped forward from the only window in the room. She flashed an ID card of rather questionable authenticity.

"I'm with technical support," she said, sliding the card back into her pocket before the robot could get a good look at it.

"Oh, really?" the robot replied doubtingly. "You don't normally meet me in the closet."

"Ah," she stammered. "Change in procedure."

The Dahl were often particular about following protocols, the robot thought, although this one appeared decidedly unlike most Dahl he had seen. On the other hand, fleshlings all looked pretty much the same.

"What do you want, then?" the janitorbot asked.

"I need to update your software," she replied.

The robot lifted his slender arms and shrugged. "Fine."

The technician attached a cord to the robot's port and transferred several new lines of code. When the tech was done and had withdrawn the cable, the janitorbot rebooted his system.

"How do you feel?" she asked when the robot came back online.

"The same as always," the janitorbot replied. "Can I go back to my work now?"

"Of course," she said.

The robot left the closet and continued on his well-worn route. Eventually, he came to the office of Professor Rhun. Inside, the robot found the room empty except for the Sprite floating in the corner. In general, the janitorbot found Sprites aloof and not much for conversation, so he ignored it and went directly to the garbage can near one of the work benches. Along the way, however, his single eye spotted something unusual.

Someone had left a piece of garbage just sitting there on a table.

"Good grief!" the robot said. "It's not like Professor Rhun to be so careless!"

With a mechanical sigh, the janitorbot reached up and, with considerable effort, pulled down the crystal piece of junk and dropped it with a *thud* into the hopper. He then emptied the regular trash can and went about his duties.

The support technician was waiting for him when the robot returned to the closet.

"How did that go?" she asked.

"Good, I guess," the robot replied.

The pink-haired person peeked into the hopper and made a noise, which may or may not have been a chortle since the robot had little experience with such things. The tech pulled the crystal junk from the bin, placing it in a leather satchel sitting on the floor.

"What do you want with that garbage?" the robot asked.

"Nothing important," she replied and slung the satchel over her shoulder. Without another word, she climbed through the window and disappeared.

The janitorbot's eye peered at the open window.

"Fleshlings!" the robot said.

Ramus returned to the *Wanderer* to find Roxie Blues waiting at the bottom of the ramp, a pile of cigarette butts stomped out at her feet.

"I didn't know you smoked," Ramus said.

Roxie, dressed in a billowing silk kaftan, gave a quick shrug.

"You were gone a long time," she said. "I got worried."

"Afraid the authorities grabbed me?"

"Something like that," Roxie replied.

Ramus motioned for them to head up the ramp. At the top, he punched the button that closed it.

"I saw my father," he confided.

Roxie's jaw dropped. "Really?"

"It went about as well as you might expect."

"What did he say?" she asked.

Ramus did his best Telyn impression: "*I don't have a son!*"

"Oh," Roxie said.

"It doesn't matter," Ramus went on. "I saw him; he saw me. We even said goodbye."

"Well, that's more than what I got," Roxie replied.

"I know."

The two ended up in the galley, deserted except for empty bottles of fungus beer scattered about.

"Where is everybody?" Ramus asked.

"Mel came back a while ago with a big satchel," Roxie said. "Don't know where she went after that."

Ramus pursed his lips. "They're up to something."

"Do you want to talk about your dad?"

"No," the captain replied. "Later, maybe. I want to see what the terrible two are doing first..."

"I'll be in my cabin," she said. "Come and see me when you're done."

Ramus found Mel and Fugg in the hold, standing inside the secret compartment with the lid off. At the bottom, a bag of tools lay beside the Singing Lantern.

"What the hell?" Ramus shouted.

Mel almost dropped the plasma torch in her hand.

"Oh, hey," she said innocently.

"Did you steal that?" Ramus asked, his eyes glaring.

"Maybe a little," Mel replied.

"I thought you were going to just cut a piece off or something," Ramus said.

Fugg pointed a fat thumb in Mel's direction. "Bonehead here forgot her tools."

"I have a good excuse," she protested. "I was drunk!"

"Anyway, we have it down here so hopefully nobody can spot it on scanners," Fugg said.

"*Smart*," Ramus said with wry sarcasm.

"Nobody saw me," Mel said. "I do this kind of thing all the time."

"Tell me about it," Fugg remarked.

"Shut up!" she yelled.

"You need to take it back," Ramus said. "As *soon* as possible."

Mel waved the lit plasma torch around. "First, I gotta figure out a way to get a sample."

Ramus crouched, peering into the compartment. "The torch doesn't work?"

"Nothing works!" Fugg replied.

Ramus scrutinized the Lantern.

"It's made from crystal," he said. "Maybe use a sonic lance after you synchronize the harmonics."

"That sounds like techno babble..." Fugg replied.

Mel rubbed her chin. "Actually, that *might* work."

Ramus slapped the top of Fugg's bald dome.

"Listen to *me*," the captain said.

Chancellor Telyn and Elder Arwyn ate dinner on their terrace that evening, fireflies filling the garden like blinking stars. Traditionally, the couple enjoyed their meals in silence, but Arwyn's husband surprised her this time by taking a stab at dinner conversation.

Setting his long, elegant fork down on the now empty plate, Telyn said, "A strange man came to see me today."

Arwyn was still chewing, but managed to mumble, "What?"

"A *who*, actually..." Telyn corrected her.

She swallowed. "*Who*, then?"

"That's the thing," Telyn went on. "He claimed to be my son."

Arwyn dabbed her mouth with a linen napkin, considering her reply.

"Are you admitting to an affair, dear?" she asked.

"No, of course not!" he protested. "He's not my son, obviously."

"What did he want?"

"He called himself *Ramus* and said he owned a freighter called the *Wanderer*."

"A Dahl owning a freighter?" Arwyn replied. "What will they think of next..."

"Regardless, the *takeaway* is that he insisted *I* was his father."

"Did he provide any evidence of that?" Arwyn asked.

"No," Telyn replied.

"Well, I wouldn't let it trouble you, dear," she said. "Perhaps he was mentally unbalanced..."

The chancellor's face turned thoughtful. "He told me a story."

"Yes?"

"He knew a Dahlvish woman who came to visit her parents," Telyn said, "but they had died in an accident."

"Tragic," Arwyn remarked.

"But apparently they wouldn't have remembered her anyway because she was one of the *Forgotten*."

Arwyn's eyes widened. "What did you say?"

"This freighter captain said he was one as well," Telyn replied.

The elder said nothing, waiting for her husband to continue.

"At any rate," Telyn said, "this Ramus person said his goodbyes and left. I must say it was all very strange."

"I can imagine."

The chancellor wiped his mouth, placing his napkin gently over his plate, and got up from the table. As he headed inside, he stopped.

"One other thing," Telyn added, "This Ramus fellow said we knew him as *Rowan*. Does that ring a bell with you?"

"No, dear," she replied. "I'm afraid it doesn't."

"Alright then," he said and left his wife alone on the terrace. Once she was sure he had gone upstairs, Arwyn called the Sprite they kept in the home. The domed sphere, its mechanical arms dangling below, floated effortlessly out to join her.

"Tell me," Arwyn said. "Do I have son?"

Inside the transparent ball, the liquid shimmered in shades of gold. After what seemed like ages, the Sprite replied, "Unable to respond."

Arwyn scowled at the hovering robot. "What do you mean?"

"The information is unavailable."

"You mean the answer is *No?*" she asked.

The Sprite didn't reply.

"Do you *have* the information?" she asked, growing more irritated.

"Yes."

"Then respond!"

"Unable to comply," the Sprite said.

"Why not?"

"The information is sealed by order of the Elder Council."

Arwyn drew a quick breath, nearly choking on it. After a minute, she leveled her gaze on the robot.

"By order of Elder Arwyn," she said, "unseal the information I requested."

The liquid inside the sphere sparkled and even a bubble or two meandered its way up from the bottom.

"Done," the robot said.

"Now tell me," Arwyn said eagerly, "*Do* I have a son?"

The Sprite was taking too long, Arwyn thought. So long, she was about to start pounding on the globe.

"Yes," it said finally.

Jessica Doric loved her rental house at the university. Designed for dignitaries, the furnishings were lavish and tapestries of the finest Dahlvish silk hung on the walls. It was certainly a step up from the sparse furniture of her tent at the dig site, but even so, Doric couldn't help but feel a fondness for that place as well. She wondered what the Sylvan grad student was doing right now...

Rousing Doric from thoughts, the doorbell rang, followed by a series of frantic knocks. Henry was banging on the door when Doric opened it.

"You're still here!" he said, out of breath.

"It's evening, Henry," she replied. "Where else would I be?"

"I thought they took you already!" he said between pants.

"Who?"

"The police!"

"Calm down and come inside," Doric said and closed the door behind him. "What are you talking about?"

"Somebody stole the Singing Lantern," Henry replied. "The police came to the dorm and wanted to arrest me. They think we stole it!"

"You and Pwmpen?"

"No, me and *you*!"

"That's absurd," Doric said. "There must be a misunderstanding..."

Henry shook his head. "No, the police were pretty sure we took it."

"How did you get away?" Doric asked.

"It was Pwmpen," Henry replied. "He went at the police with a pair of cutting shears. I've never seen anything like it!"

"Oh my god!"

"He told me to run."

"What did you do?"

"I ran!"

An authoritative knock at the door turned Doric's blood cold.

"We need to go!" Henry urged.

"But where?"

"The *Wanderer* is here on Gwlad Ard'un," he said. "I'm sure Captain Ramus would help us escape..."

"Ramus is here?" Doric asked. "How do you know?"

"I ran into Mel and Engineer Fugg on campus."

"Well, why didn't you tell me?"

Henry paused before answering. "I forgot."

The knock at the door became a steady pounding, but Doric still waited while considering what to do.

"We need to go!" Henry shouted.

"They'll be watching the starport," Doric said. "We'd never make it to the ship."

"Then what should we do?"

"I have an idea," she replied.

Taking the back door, Doric led Henry into the stand of trees behind the house and headed toward the university lot where vehicles were kept for staff use. Since it was after hours, the area was empty. When she came to one of the gravtrucks, Doric stopped.

"Do you know how to drive that thing?" Henry asked.

"Of course!" she said. "I watched the driver when we took the truck to the dig site. It can't be that hard."

"Okay..."

"Get in."

Inside the cab, the controls appeared more complicated than Doric remembered, but not much different from a regular gravcar. Henry fastened his seatbelt, which Doric found vaguely insulting, but after thinking about it, she did the same. Within minutes the craft was airborne and heading into the night.

"So, where are we going?" Henry wondered.

"I still think this is a mistake," she replied. "We just need somebody on our side."

"Like Professor Rhun?"

"Actually, I was thinking of someone else," she said. "*Elisan Mossdale.*"

"Oh," Henry muttered.

"I'm sure he can help us..."

The gravtruck continued into the darkness while Henry stared out the window at the lights of the university receding behind them. After an hour, he noticed a red light blinking on the dashboard.

"What's that?" he asked.

Doric stared at the indicator, but there was nothing that indicated what it actually meant.

"Probably nothing," she said reassuringly.

A few more minutes passed, and Doric realized their altitude was dropping. She quietly cursed under her breath.

"What?" Henry asked.

"Nothing."

The number on the altimeter continued to drop faster and faster.

Through the front window, the line between the stars of the sky and the blackness below the horizon began to rise noticeably.

"Is something wrong?" Henry asked, a hint of panic rising in his voice.

"Nope."

Another red light lit up beside the first one, along with a yellow one for good measure. Sweat started rolling down the back of Doric's neck.

This time Henry's voice was clearly concerned. "Are we going to crash?"

"No," Doric replied. "Probably not."

A sizable branch crashed against the window, causing both Doric and Henry to jump in their seatbelts.

"The trees are really tall here," Doric said.

The gravtruck hit the top of another tree, shaking the craft and cracking the windscreen.

"Okay," Doric said calmly, though her heart was pounding. "You may want to hold onto something..."

The last thing Doric heard before the crash was Henry screaming loudly into her ear. Then there was nothing but dark and silence

CHAPTER ELEVEN

Ta Demona descended on the Boneyards like a plague, her gravcar coming to rest just outside of Uncle Artie's burrow. The door to the vehicle swung open and the Psi Lord agent stepped out onto the muddy dirt, the sun glinting off the circuits running across her emerald skin. She swept into the inventor's den, much to the Gnomi's surprise.

"Why, *hello* there!" Uncle Artie said, looking up from his tea. Z-4T, who was in mid-pour, nearly dropped the kettle.

"I came to inspect your progress," Demona replied grimly.

"You've come in person, I see," Uncle Artie replied. "How wonderful!"

His voice suggested this was not wonderful, but Demona already knew that, having read his mind when she entered.

"Quite rude not to call first," Zat remarked.

"Now, now," Uncle Artie said, "it's always a pleasure to get visitors! Of course, your boss Solan normally projects himself here..."

"Since you haven't been updating him on your progress," Demona replied, "he felt a face-to-face meeting would be more *useful*."

"Is he coming?" the robot asked.

"No," the agent replied. "I'm his eyes and ears."

Demona's breathing was audible through her filter mask like a set of bagpipes without music.

"Wonderful!" Uncle Artie repeated.

"Show me what's done!" Demona demanded.

The Gnomi jumped to his feet, pausing to rub his back after moving too quickly, and tottered toward his work bench. Demona joined him there, casting a disapproving eye over the schematics laid out on the table.

"As you can see," Uncle Artie said nervously, "we've made quite a *lot* of progress..."

"I see plans, but no prototype," Demona replied.

"Well, these things take time," he said.

"You've had nothing *but* time," the agent hissed, "and you have nothing to show for it!"

"Now, see here!" Zat shouted and came forward.

Demona turned on the robot in a flash, extending her arm in his direction. A cloud of purplish fog poured from her outstretched hand, engulfing the robot. Insects burst from beneath Zat's feet, crawling up his metal legs and covering his body. The swarm enclosed his head in a solid mass of teeming bugs, stopping the robot in his tracks.

"I can't see!" Zat yelled, clawing his eyes.

"Oh, dear," Uncle Artie said.

"Now then," Demona continued, returning her attention to the inventor. "What do you have to say for yourself?"

"Well..." the Gnomi stammered, "as a matter of fact, I've put my daughter on the project."

"Indeed," the agent replied, knowing what he was about to say before he said it. "She's gone to retrieve the focusing stone."

"Why, yes," Uncle Artie said. "I haven't heard from her recently, but I'm sure she's making headway."

"Are you? Are you *sure*?"

Uncle Artie fiddled with his fingers. "Mostly sure..."

The Psi Lord agent leaned closer, her brilliant blue eyes radiant against the green of her face.

"Solan is dissatisfied with your progress," she growled. "You will supply him with the device soon or Solan will show you just how he deals with those who disappoint him."

"Yes, well," he replied, noting his robot still scraping the insects out of his eyes. "I wouldn't want that."

"Nor should you," she said, pivoting toward the door.

"The *Artie Augmenter* will be done in no time!" Uncle Artie declared while pointing a diminutive finger toward the ceiling.

Already walking away, the agent stopped.

"*Psi Wand* has a better ring to it," she said.

Behind her, she heard a grumble.

"Well, let's agree to disagree," Uncle Artie said.

Henry was having the most wonderful dream. He lay in a meadow of flowers while a fairy princess, with a voice much like Jessica Doric's, whispered in his ear. At first, he couldn't make out what she was saying, but as the voice became clearer, it sounded like:

WAKE UP!
WAKE UP, HENRY!

Henry opened his eyes.

"Wake up!" Doric was shouting, shaking Henry by the shoulders.

"What?" he mumbled.

Doric leaned back in her seat in the crashed gravtruck.

"You were unconscious," she said.

Henry rubbed his forehead and, finding it wet, drew away his fingers covered in blood.

"I'm bleeding?" he asked.

"The windshield shattered," Doric replied. "One of the shards cut you."

Henry absentmindedly wiped his hand on his shirt and looked around the cab. The dashboard was wrecked, loose wires arcing in the near darkness. A broken branch hung through the jagged gap in the window.

He also became dimly aware of a pain below his right knee. An emergency light gave just enough illumination beneath the dashboard.

"Is my foot supposed to be pointing that way?" Henry asked.

Doric covered her mouth, stifling a scream, which prompted Henry to take a closer look. Through the haze of his mind, he concluded that his right shoe was at a nearly ninety-degree angle, which was a bit more than usual as far as he could remember.

"I think it's broken," Doric said. "Does it hurt?"

"Kinda," he replied.

"You might have a concussion too," Doric added. "I'm going to find some sticks and make you a splint. I'll be back."

"Okay."

With considerable effort, Doric forced open her door and disappeared into the night. Meanwhile, Henry's leg started hurting more, much more in fact. He grimaced, grinding his teeth. He closed his eyes and, when he opened them, wasn't entirely sure whether he was unconscious again.

Someone was staring at him through the broken window. Someone with tiny, delicate wings like a dragonfly.

"Hello," Henry waved weakly.

The creature was a female humanoid, only a few inches tall, with green hair and wearing a red tunic like autumn leaves. Hovering, she studied him, her head cocked to one side.

Then she flew away.

"Bye," Henry said.

"Who are you talking to?" Doric asked, appearing on Henry's side of the gravtruck.

"A fairy princess," Henry replied.

Doric placed her hand on the truck door.

"You're hurt worse than I thought," she remarked and opened the door. Reaching in, she unfastened Henry's seatbelt and placed a pair of sticks at his feet.

"We can't stay here," Doric said. "They'll be looking for us."

"Where can we go?" Henry asked.

"I think the dig site is that way," she replied, pointing into the blackness. "I think..."

"Then I can meet your *boyfriend*," Henry whined.

"I don't have a boyfriend," Doric replied.

"That Sylva, Elisan Mossdale," he said.

"He's *not* my boyfriend, Henry," she replied. "We only met once."

Henry waved his hands in the air. "And had a wonderful dinner together..."

Doric ignored him and tore strips of cloth from her pant leg.

"And he *saved* your life!" he said, pointing an accusing finger.

"Shut up, Henry," Doric said. "Now, brace yourself. This is going to hurt."

"I already—" he started, but his screaming cut the sentence short.

Doric discovered a utility knife in a storage compartment and fashioned a crutch out of a large tree limb. She also cut up some of the cushion material from the seats to wedge beneath Henry's arm, hoping it would make things more comfortable for him.

"How's that?" she asked.

Henry leaned against the stick, taking as much weight off the splint and his broken ankle as possible.

"Good," he said, but Doric saw drops of sweat appearing on his forehead.

"It hurts?"

He ventured a pained grin. "Maybe..."

"I'm sorry, Henry," Doric said. "We really need to get away from the crash site before the authorities arrive."

Henry nodded without answering, taking a few tentative steps, which were more like hops than walking. The base of the crutch sank slightly into the soft ground, but Henry managed to take a few more hops in the general direction of the dig site. Doric passed him, taking the lead.

Using a flashlight also from the cab, she scanned the forest in front of them. The harsh light reflected off the bare, white bark of the trees, their trunks like gnarled skeletons. This was the same forest Mossdale had warned her about, but there was no helping that now.

"This way," Doric said.

After several minutes, Henry spoke behind her.

"You're sure this is the right direction?" he asked.

"Absolutely," Doric replied, beaming the light ahead.

"You're *sure* you're sure?"

"Henry!"

"Sorry," Henry mumbled.

They hiked through the night and into the early morning, the stars just visible among the upper branches. Without a thick canopy, the forest undergrowth had grown dense in places, slowing Doric and Henry's progress even more. A thorn slashed Doric's face, cutting her cheek.

"Ouch!" she yelped.

"Are you alright?" Henry asked.

"It's nothing."

"Can we take a rest?"

"Yes," she said and, sweeping the area with the flashlight, found a log where they could sit.

Henry gingerly set himself down, stretching his leg and propping the crutch to one side. Doric took a place on the log beside him.

"Do you want me to take another look at your ankle?" she asked.

"No thanks," he said.

"Why?"

"It's embarrassing."

"Don't be silly, Henry."

"It's just," he went on, "I'm slowing you down."

"It's not your fault," she replied. "I'm the one who crashed."

"I know, but..."

"What?"

"I'm always screwing up," he said.

Doric smiled and patted him on the shoulder. "Oh, Henry."

She switched off the light to conserve the battery, dropping them into near total darkness. Henry laughed nervously.

"How's your head?" Doric asked, but Henry was silent. "Henry?"

"Do you see that?" he said.

"See what?"

Henry's black outline pointed into the woods. "There..."

Between the trees, perhaps fifty feet away, something white was moving around the thorn bushes.

"Is it a ghost?" Henry whispered.

"Don't be silly," she replied, her voice lacking conviction.

Smaller than a human, but definitely humanoid, the pale specter floated, passing easily through the undergrowth and then directly through a tree.

"I think my concussion is getting worse," Henry said.

"I see it too," Doric replied.

The spirit approached until it was a mere twenty feet away. Doric realized she was holding her breath and forced herself to breathe. By then whatever it was had come within ten feet and Doric could see its face. Although she didn't recognize it, Doric noticed the pointed ears of a Dahl.

"There's more!" Henry shouted.

Additional specters appeared, moving about the forest in seemingly random directions. Each was unique, dressed in clothing reminiscent of the kinds Doric had seen the Dahl wearing around campus. They floated aimlessly at times or stopped to mime actions like eating or working on a computer.

"Do some of these ghosts look familiar?" Henry asked.

"Who?" Doric replied.

"That one over there," he said, gesturing with his crutch. "That one looks like Pwmpen, doesn't it?"

Doric recognized a certain plumpness about the ghost.

"I think he's cutting someone's hair," Henry added.

Doric squinted and could make out a pair of scissors, just as eerily transparent as the rest.

She and Henry watched the image of Pwmpen, as well as the others, for much longer than Doric would have liked. By the time Doric realized it, the first rays of dawn were cutting through the dead branches. As the beams fell on the ghosts, the apparitions slowly faded away.

In the morning, Ramus woke up alone in Roxie Blue's bed. Her room was technically Fugg's cabin, but the chief engineer had relinquished it after much arguing and storming off to sleep in the engine room.

Roxie had done her best to give the cabin her own flair, including some sandalwood incense. Even so, the room still reeked of its former Gordian occupant. Also, there was a not-so-tasteful picture of Fugg's mother or possibly father — Ramus wasn't sure — hanging on the wall.

Ramus pulled himself out of bed and got dressed before heading to the galley where the delicious aroma of pancakes greeted him. Roxie, wearing a rose-colored robe, was pouring more batter into a pan.

"I didn't know you could cook," Ramus admitted.

Roxie looked up. "I'm full of surprises."

On the radio, music was playing from a local station. Ramus recognized the melody from his childhood, a classic Dahlvish song featuring a lute and harps.

"I haven't heard a lute in a while..." Ramus remarked sarcastically.

"You don't like it?" Roxie asked.

"Classical music was never my thing."

"Well, if you want cyber death metal," she said, "you may have to ask Gen."

Ramus pulled out a chair and took a seat in front of a plate already stacked with pancakes.

"Where is everybody?" he asked.

"In the cargo hold presumably..." she said, flipping the cakes on the stove.

The music stopped abruptly, replaced by the voice of a Dahl announcer.

"Attention!" the man said. "Be advised that a pair of humans are currently on the loose, accused of stealing a priceless artifact from Prenwyn University. If you see a male and female human, do not attempt to apprehend them yourself. Call the authorities immediately!"

The announcer repeated the message twice before the radio went back to music.

"Well, shit," Ramus said.

"Humans?" Roxie said. "There can't be many of *those* on the planet."

Ramus tapped his fingers on the table.

"It's got to be Jessica Doric and her assistant," he replied. "Mel said they ran into Henry."

"At least they don't suspect *us* of taking the Lantern," Roxie said.

"Yeah, but that doesn't mean they won't figure it out. Anyway, we can't let Jessica take the fall for something our knuckleheads did."

"You're such a good guy," Roxie said with a smile.

Ramus rolled his eyes.

"Not even close," he said.

Gen appeared at the galley doorway but stopped after seeing Roxie in her robe.

"Oh," the robot said.

"It's alright," Ramus said. "What is it?"

"There's a person at the ramp who wants to see you, Captain," Gen replied.

"What kind of person?" he asked.

"A very nicely dressed lady," the robot said.

"Fine," Ramus replied, sliding out of the chair. "I'll take a look, but I should probably add a doorbell at this rate..."

Reaching the top of the ramp, Ramus saw the robes of an elder at the bottom. Even though it had been years, he recognized her immediately.

"Mom?" he blurted out.

Much to Ramus' surprise, Elder Arwyn made no effort to deny it.

"Hello, son," she said.

Henry had grown accustomed to the perpetual bloom of the trees on Gwlad Ard'un, so the twisted, bare branches of this forest were disconcerting. Also, when the sun rose in the morning sky, Henry began sweating profusely. His broken ankle was hurting as well and, although Doric had done an admirable job carving the crutch, the stick was slightly shorter than needed and now Henry's back was beginning to spasm.

On top of that, he had seen a bunch of ghosts.

"Are we sure they were real?" Henry asked Doric a few steps ahead.

"I told you *yes*," she replied, her tone rising at the end.

"But what if it was my concussion?"

"I saw them too," she said.

"But what if you have a concussion too?" Henry asked.

Doric stopped.

"Then we wouldn't have the *same* hallucination," she said.

"Right," he replied.

They started again, but after a few minutes, Henry slowed. Sensing this, Doric stopped.

"Are you okay?" she asked.

"I'm thirsty," he said.

Doric's shoulders dropped as her lungs heaved a sigh.

"Sorry, Henry," she said. "I'm sure the dig site will have some water."

"Hmm," Henry replied.

He pictured the vague image of a Sylva holding a frosty glass of water and Mossdale and Doric laughing over how sweet it tasted. Henry's version of Mossdale, whom he had never met or seen before, bore little resemblance to the real Sylva, especially the devil horns.

Do Woodland Dahl have horns? he thought. *No, that's fauns. What's that noise anyway?*

"Do you hear that?" Henry asked aloud.

"Hear what?" Doric replied.

"A high-pitched noise," he said.

Doric paused, casting her head from side to side.

"It's like a voice," she said finally. "But from somebody who's been inhaling helium..."

She took a few steps to the right.

"It's coming from over there..." she added.

Doric kept moving in that direction and disappeared into the underbrush. Henry did his best to follow, but the end of his crutch kept sinking into the ground. By the time he had caught up with Doric, Henry was nearly doubled over in pain from his leg and his back. When he straightened up again, he saw Doric standing before an enormous spider web stretching across two dead trees.

Henry came closer and found a tiny person with wings stuck to the web, the same fairy princess he had seen the night before.

"Are you going to help me?" the fairy asked. "Or just stand there like a couple of idiots?"

"It's *you!*" Henry said in astonishment. "You're the one I hallucinated!"

The fairy glanced at Doric.

"He's not very bright, is he?" the fairy asked.

Taking a moment to process what she was seeing, Doric said finally, "Who are you?"

"I'm Mistral," she replied, pulling on the web, "but can we talk later? They'll be coming soon..."

"Who?" Henry asked.

From deeper in the woods, twigs snapped as if something large was coming closer.

"Hurry!" Mistral cried.

Doric quickly pulled her free from the webbing. Her wings still covered in sticky fibers, Mistral couldn't fly so Doric cradled the fairy against her body.

The noises were growing louder as the shadows of what appeared to be many legs approached. The hairs on the back of Doric's neck stood stiff.

"Kuent'l Nanzi," she whispered.

"What?" Henry asked.

"Shut up and run!" Doric shouted.

Doric, with Mistral pressed against her, charged into the trees with Henry doing his best to keep up on his broken ankle. They had not gone far, however, before he fell face-first with a groan. Doric gave him a boost up, but Henry winced in obvious pain.

"I don't think I can make it," he groaned.

"Yes, you can!" Doric replied sternly.

"No, he's right," the fairy said.

"Well, I'm not leaving him!" Doric shouted, which surprised Henry but gave him a warm feeling.

The Nanzi chasing them were getting closer, the daylight glinting off the blades of their polearms.

"Gross!" Henry yelled. "They're *spiders* with *spears*!"

"Just hold me out," Mistral said, and Doric obeyed, stretching out her arm.

The tiny fairy made a whirling motion with her hands and a circle of golden sparkles appeared in the air. Like glimmering dust, the sparkles floated from Mistral and landed over Henry's aching leg. He felt a tingle run up his body, which was both disconcerting and comforting at the same time.

Nearby, harsh voices echoed through the trees.

"Put weight on your foot," Mistral told Henry.

Not entirely trusting her, Henry still used the crutch to steady himself, but realized there was no pain coming from his leg anymore.

"It's healed!" he shouted.

Doric shushed him before hissing, "Come on then!"

Henry discarded the crutch and the three rushed along the forest floor with the Nanzi in hot pursuit.

"They're gaining on us," Doric panted.

"Don't worry," Mistral replied.

The fairy spread her arms to either side, leaving a twin trail of magical dust behind them. From this dust, mirror images of the two humans materialized, perfect doppelgangers of the originals. The set of twins split off to the left and right, running in opposite directions. At the same time and while in full stride, Mistral cast more sparkles over Doric, Henry, and herself.

Henry nearly ran into a tree as his legs slowly disappeared. He saw Doric and the fairy fade away as well, the three of them becoming invisible.

Quietly, Mistral told them to stop.

"Don't make a sound," she said.

Behind them, the crashing of the pursuers stopped momentarily and the Nanzi erupted into angry and confused voices. After a brief argument, they broke into two groups and chased the diverging copies as they disappeared deeper into the forest to the North and South.

When the Nanzi had receded to a safe distance away, Mistral made the three of them reappear.

"I've never been invisible before," Henry remarked, staring at his hands.

"With a face like yours," Mistral giggled, "maybe you should try it more often."

"Alright," Doric said. "Can you help us find our way out of this forest?"

Freed from her constraints, Mistral buzzed into the air, making a few loops before coming to a steady hover near Doric's face.

"Where are you headed?" the fairy asked in her high-pitched voice.

"We were going to the Dahl dig site," Doric said, "but I have no idea which direction that is anymore. Can you take us?"

"Well, first we need to return to my village," Mistral said. "Everybody will be worried about me."

"They must not know you very well," Henry muttered.

Mistral dove at Henry's head, forcing him to duck and cover.

CHAPTER TWELVE

Now that Henry's leg was healed by Mistral's psionics, Henry, Doric, and Mistral made good time through the forest. After an hour, they came to a patch of woods where the trees seemed a little less bare, leaves filled the canopy, and the underbrush was not as thick.

Mistral left the two humans for a moment and soared up into the branches where she was met by other fairies, their tiny wings glittering. They danced high above Doric's head as she strained her neck to watch. After a while, Mistral returned, her wings fluttering excitedly.

"It's good to be back home!" she said.

"How many of you are there?" Doric asked.

"Hundreds," the fairy replied with a frown. "But there used to be thousands until the Kuent'l Nanzi arrived."

"What are your people called?" Doric asked.

"We are the *Sylph*," Mistral said. "We've lived in these woods for as long as anyone can remember."

"The Dahl never mentioned you," Henry said, crossing his arms.

"Why would they?" Mistral replied angrily. "This forest was beautiful before the Dahl began experimenting. Now, we're just reminders of their biggest failure!"

"What kind of experiments?" Doric asked.

"Dark Psi," Mistral replied. "They mutated the woodland creatures and created the Nanzi."

"The Dahl created the Nanzi?" Doric asked.

"Yes, and *we've* been stuck with them ever since!"

"Then why don't you find someplace else to live?" Henry asked.

"Leave our home?" Mistral replied. "This is our land!"

Doric shook her head. "I can't believe the Dahl are responsible."

Mistral laughed scornfully.

"They're not as perfect as they lead everyone to believe," she said. "They hide their dirty laundry behind a pretty curtain."

"I've done that," Henry admitted.

"Anyway," Doric said, ignoring him, "I'm sorry they did this to you."

"You'll be a lot more sorry if the Dahl ever find out you know about us," Mistral replied.

"What do you mean?" she asked.

"Weren't you listening?" Mistral said. "The Dahl aren't going to let you leave the planet knowing about their shame!"

"They wouldn't hurt us," Doric asserted.

"Maybe," Mistral replied, "but they might erase your memory. They've done it to their own people. Why not you?"

"I choose to believe those things are in the Dahlvish past," Doric said. "They're different now. I'm sure of it!"

"What about the Echuio?" Henry asked.

"It's a minority," Doric replied. "They don't speak for the rest of the Dahl."

"Whatever you say," Mistral said, "but don't say I didn't warn you."

"Will you still take us to the dig site?" Doric asked.

"If that's what you want," Mistral replied.

"Yes," Doric said.

"Well, it's getting late," Mistral went on, "so we'll leave in the morning."

Mistral showed Doric and Henry a soft area of moss below one of the trees that the rest of the Sylph called home. Up along the trunk, the fairies had carved terraces out of the shelf fungus and built little houses. A few came down to examine the strangers, but most kept their distance.

Mistral brought the humans some fresh water and berries for a late dinner.

"Don't mind my brothers and sisters," she said. "We don't get visitors often, or *ever* for that matter..."

"The Dahl never come here?" Doric asked.

"Not if they can help it," Mistral replied, her wings buzzing in the night air.

"They're probably afraid of the ghosts," Henry remarked.

"What ghosts?" the Sylph asked.

"You know," Henry went on, "the spirits walking around. I'm surprised we haven't seen them tonight..."

Mistral's face brightened.

"Oh, you'll see them," she said, "but they're not ghosts."

"What are they?" Doric asked.

"They're a kind of psychic projection," Mistral explained. "Like a reflection of what the Dahl are thinking and doing."

Doric took a sip of water from a leaf that had been woven into a cup. "Do they know they're being projected?"

Sylph shrugged.

"It's all a result of their experiments," she replied, "and that was centuries ago. Hard to say if anyone cares what's happening here anymore..."

"Have you ever asked for help against the Nanzi?" Henry wondered with a mouth full of berries.

Mistral made a disgusted face, though it was unclear if she was reacting to the Nanzi or seeing Henry talk with his mouth full.

"The Dahl have abandoned us," she said. "We're on our own."

"I'm sorry," Doric said.

Mistral waved her tiny hand.

"It's not your fault," she said. "Now, get some sleep. I'll lead you out of the forest in the morning."

She did a mock curtsy in the air and darted away into the tree above. In the darkness, save for the light of the moon, Doric and Henry laid down on the moss. Henry was fast asleep immediately, but Doric lay awake, her mind swimming with all that she had learned about the Dahl. Almost none of it matched with what she thought she knew.

Sitting up, the soft moss beneath her, Doric began seeing ghostly projections appear among the trees just like the night before. Feeling restless, she stood up and walked into the woods. She was careful not to go too far, afraid of any Nanzi that might be about.

Doric took some pleasure in watching all the different Dahl, but felt guilty that she was spying on them. Most were simply living their lives, carrying out the normal activities of their regular evenings.

As hauntings go, it was quite boring, Doric thought.

Passing an old, dead trunk, Doric came to something different. Two figures wearing robes and masks stood close together, sharing an intimate moment. One removed her silver mask and revealed the face of a female Dahl. Doric didn't recognize her, but when the other figure removed his golden mask, she knew him right away.

"What is going on?" Doric asked aloud.

Her face grew even more puzzled when the two figures shared a passionate, translucent kiss.

They came just before dawn when the forest was at its darkest. Doric had just settled down to sleep again. Henry lay nearby on the moss, gently snoring.

Doric heard the noises first: hairy, scurrying legs rustling through the undergrowth. Then, fire. Orange flares of torchlight erupted at the base of the trees, illuminating the dark and throwing shadows of long, angular limbs and bladed weapons.

They found us! Doric's mind shouted while adrenaline tore away whatever sleep might have been lingering. She bolted up before crouching again when she realized they would see her. Doric kicked Henry in the back.

"Get up!" she shouted as quietly as possible.

"Mmph..." he murmured, but didn't open his eyes.

Doric kicked him again. "Get up!"

The Nanzi were everywhere, setting the surrounding trees on fire. Flames leaped up the dry wood and into the Sylph village above. For their part, the Sylph descended and showered the attackers with fairy fire of their own.

"Is it morning yet?" Henry's voice said faintly. "Why's it so bright?"

"We're under attack!" Doric shouted.

"What?" he replied, rubbing his eyes. Doric kicked him some more, partly to make herself feel better. "Ow!"

From the corner of her eye, Doric saw Mistral streak past along with some of her people. A Nanzi opened his mouth and a wet lump of webbing shot out, hitting one of the Sylph who became glued to the side of a tree. A second Nanzi stabbed the silk bundle with the tip of his blade.

"Monsters!" Mistral screamed in her shrill voice. She circled around and blasted the second Nanzi with a stream of flame. The fine hairs of the creature's body were set alight and the creature dropped his weapon, running back into the woods on fire.

Henry was finally upright and on his feet. "What do we do?"

Doric's mind reeled. Between the Nanzi and the fires, she and Henry were completely surrounded.

"I don't know," she said.

Doric felt Henry grab her by the arm and she closed her fingers around his wrist in return. Holding onto each other, they watched the melee all around them.

The trees glowed red hot and orange, the heat on Doric's skin unbearable. She wondered if this was how she was going to die, in the arms of her former graduate assistant.

As if in response, a particularly large Nanzi emerged from the fight after spotting the two humans. His curved, metal blade was painted brightly by the fire. He brandished it at Doric and Henry, but it was Doric who pushed Henry aside so she could stand between him and the Nanzi.

The creature glared at her with shining, purple eyes. He smiled, revealing pointed teeth, before opening his mouth further and spitting a clump of webbing. The sticky, silk filaments wrapped around Doric's legs and encased her feet. She tried to move, but fell as another salvo pinned her hands together.

Henry knelt by Doric's side, but he, too, became victim to the webbing and dropped next to her.

While the battle raged, the Nanzi strung the two humans by a thick thread and pulled them away into the forest.

Ramus arrived at his parents' house in the late morning for brunch. After his talk with Telyn, Ramus hadn't really expected to see Elder Arwyn, but her arrival at the loading ramp of the *Wanderer* somehow didn't surprise him. His mother had always been the smart one.

"You know who I am?" Ramus had asked her.

Standing in her elder garb at the foot of the ramp, Arwyn looked contrite.

"I didn't believe it at first," she had admitted, "but I found out the truth."

"Too bad you had to forget the truth in the first place," Ramus replied bitterly. "But you had a lot to do with that, didn't you?"

His mother cast her eyes down at the tarmac. "I imagine so."

"What do you want from me now?" he asked.

"I'd like you to come to the house," she said. "I know I can't expect your forgiveness, but I want to catch up on what we could've had... and what we've lost..."

Now, the house where Ramus grew up stood before him like it always had, just the way he remembered. Like his father's office, not much had changed. The Dahl were fond of the status quo.

He rang the bell and Chancellor Telyn opened the door. He wore one of his many tunics, only slightly less official than the ones he wore on campus.

"Greetings, Captain Ramus," his father said with all the warmth of an iceberg.

"No need for formalities," Ramus replied mischievously. "You can just call me *your dear boy.*"

Telyn coughed. "Perhaps later..."

Inside, Arwyn was waiting at a table in the drawing room where a small spread of fruit and pastries was laid out, along with glasses and a bottle of wine.

"A little early for wine," Ramus remarked.

"Not at all," his mother said. "This is a special occasion!"

Unlike Ramus' father, Arwyn was more informal, wearing a flowing silk dress with a cherry blossom design. She pulled out a chair and offered it to her son.

"Thank you," he said, taking a seat. Arwyn and Telyn also sat down, though the latter looked ill at ease.

"I'm surprised to be seeing you again," Ramus told his father.

"I couldn't agree more," Telyn replied.

Arwyn scowled at her husband.

"Don't mind him," she told Ramus. "He's worried you'll get us into trouble."

"Aren't you worried too?" Ramus asked.

"Perhaps," Arwyn said, "but we'll cross that bridge when we come to it. Isn't that something the humans say?"

Ramus nodded.

"It must be so fascinating," Arwyn added. "Being surrounded by them all the time."

"Actually," Ramus replied, "I try to avoid them, and they're happy to keep non-humans like me at arm's length."

"Even the Dahl?" Telyn asked, despite himself. "After all we've done for them?"

Ramus raised his shoulders in a shrug. "They're not a grateful bunch..."

This led to his father grumbling under his breath.

"I suppose I should pour us some wine?" Arwyn offered. "This is a local vintage from one of Telyn's professors. I believe she has a winery somewhere in the hills."

She reached to pour Ramus' glass but missed, spilling the wine on his shirt.

"Careful!" Telyn yelled.

"Oh, calm yourself," Arwyn replied coolly before taking a towel and dabbing it on the crimson stain.

"It's fine," Ramus said.

"Telyn has enough tunics to outfit an army," his mother replied. "Why don't you come up and we'll pick one out for you?"

"One of *my* tunics?" Telyn asked.

Arwyn gave her husband another look, which quieted him immediately.

"It's no trouble," she said. "Your father is just being territorial."

With some hesitation, Ramus agreed and followed Arwyn upstairs.

Telyn's walk-in closet was lined with tunics and pants, almost none of them casual in any way. Ramus pulled a tunic at random from the rack, the fabric interlaced with silver and green thread, but his mother had selected a different one with a gold motif.

"Seems fancy," Ramus remarked of Arwyn's pick.

"They're *all* fancy, Rowan," she replied with a smile, and it was just like Ramus was a boy again, his mother calling him by his name.

Ramus relented, removing his stained shirt. The archaic tattoos running up his arms caught the attention of his mother, but she refrained from commenting on them. The gold stitching ran throughout the garment and there was a small pocket on the front, just big enough for something like a watch. Trying on the tunic, Ramus found it stiff, but he expected nothing less from his father.

They went back downstairs and rejoined Telyn at the table. Seeing his son wearing his outfit, the chancellor nearly hurt himself rolling his eyes.

"I still don't understand why you invited me here," Ramus remarked after taking his seat.

"My sentiments exactly," Telyn muttered.

Arwyn was careful in her reply.

"I'm a mother," she said, "who didn't know she had a son until not that long ago."

"So, maternal instinct?" Ramus replied skeptically. "Not something our people are known for..."

"Perhaps," she said, "but I can try, can't I?"

"If our minds were wiped and Captain Ramus was exiled," Telyn said, "there was likely a *good* reason for it."

"The Sprite told me all about it," Arwyn admitted, "but that doesn't matter."

"Of course it does!" Telyn said. "What was it?"

"I learned Dark Psi," Ramus replied for himself.

"What?" his father asked.

"As I said," Arwyn replied, "it *doesn't* matter. We have our son back and that's what's important."

"Actually, it was *you* who reported me to the authorities, mother," Ramus said.

"I was wrong," she said flatly.

"On the contrary," Ramus' father replied. "That seemed quite appropriate. Dark Psi is too powerful to fall into the wrong hands."

"What are the right hands?" Ramus asked.

"Not a *boy's*," Telyn replied. "Do you still practice it?"

"Sometimes."

Telyn scoffed and pointed his fork at the exile.

"Then you were right to be banished," the chancellor said. "And should have *remained* so!"

"Calm down! I doubt Rowan plans to stay," Arwyn said, turning to her son. "Why are you here, if you don't mind me asking?"

"As I told father," Ramus replied, "I brought a fellow exile who wanted to see her parents, but they had died. I decided I didn't want the same thing happening to me."

Arwyn smiled. "I'm glad you did."

"Yeah," Ramus replied and found himself grinning too.

Telyn scowled, first at his wife and then his son.

"This will all end in tears," the chancellor said.

Dragged through the forest, his hands and feet tightly webbed together, Henry tried to protect his face but still managed to hit his head on a rock and fall unconscious. When he woke again, the world was dimly lit and upside-down. It took an embarrassingly long time for him to realize *he* was the one who was upside-down, wrapped tightly in a cocoon from the neck down (or *up*, in this case).

"What's happening?" Henry asked. "Is it night already?"

"We're underground," Doric's voice said.

Henry tried to turn toward her but couldn't move. "Are you topsy-turvy too?"

"Yes," she replied. "All the blood has rushed to my head."

"Oh," Henry said. "That's why I have a headache. Also, I might have another concussion..."

"Again?" Doric replied. "We should get you to a doctor."

"Do you think they have a doctor here?" he asked.

"I don't think so..."

Henry surveyed his surroundings and had to agree. They appeared to be hanging in a cavern with torches providing the barest of light. Roots dangled in places from the ceiling, along with webs suspended like lace tapestries.

From an adjacent chamber, a large Nanzi appeared with a torch in one hand. She was bare-chested, but Henry tried not to blush.

"You're awake," she said.

"Who are you?" Doric asked.

"I am the Queen of this nest," she replied while her sparkling, violet eyes examined them. "You are a strange kind of food."

"We're not food!" Henry yelled, which only made his head hurt more.

"Then why are you hanging in my larder?" the Queen asked sensibly.

"We're humans," Doric said. "You should let us go before they come looking for us."

The Queen's expression turned thoughtful. "I've heard of humans..."

"We're very important!" Henry shouted again and then made a mental note to stop doing that.

On her spider legs, the Queen scurried up to him, her face looking down on his.

"Funny," she said, "you don't *seem* very important to me."

"If you hurt us," Doric said, "our kind will lay waste to this entire forest."

The Queen laughed.

"Such empty threats," she mused. "My kind have been here for millennia! Where have the humans been hiding?"

"We've been busy," Henry said, quietly this time.

The Queen lifted Henry's face closer to hers, using the torch to illuminate his features.

"Are you a boy or a man?" she asked.

"A boy— a man!" he sputtered. "I have my own apartment!"

"I don't know what that is," she replied, shaking her head. "But you seem young and supple, and I will suck your juices until you're dry."

Henry again tried not to blush, although all the blood pooling in his face made this difficult.

A loud noise jolted the underground cavern, dirt spilling down from the ceiling. The Queen released Henry who swung back and forth by his feet.

"I told you," Doric said.

The Queen hissed at her and hurried away, her torch disappearing around the corner.

"You were very brave, Henry," Doric said.

After the shaking stopped and the dust began to settle, Henry spotted a new light on the wall where the Queen had disappeared. He gasped when he imagined the Queen returning, but it wasn't a torch producing the light. Mistral flew into the room, her tiny wings glowing.

"You're alive!" she shouted in her high-pitched voice.

"Thanks to you, I think," Doric replied.

"Oh, it wasn't just me," Mistral said. "After the Nanzi attacked, I knew we couldn't rescue you on our own, so I went to get help..."

Holding a flashlight in one hand and a blaster in the other, Elisan Mossdale came around the corner. His beam landed on Henry and Doric.

"I heard you could use some assistance," Mossdale said.

Ramus went back to the *Wanderer*, still wearing his father's tunic. He carried his wine-stained shirt in a little woven basket his mother had given him. He felt silly striding up the ramp into the ship, but the warmth from seeing his family again still lingered.

"Look at you!" Fugg remarked with a snort at the entrance. "Did somebody go shopping?"

"It's my father's," Ramus replied. "And you can shut the hell up!"

Fugg lifted his hands in surrender. "So sensitive!"

In the galley, Ramus found Gen.

"Captain!" the robot said. "Please tell me all about this thing they call *brunch*!"

"It went fine," Ramus replied sheepishly.

"And they gave you clothes?"

"Enough about my wardrobe," he grumbled. "What's going on around here? Did Mel return the Lantern?"

"Not to my knowledge," Gen said. "But I believe she's built her prototype."

So, my idea worked, Ramus thought.

"I'll check in on her later," he said. "Where's Roxie?"

"In her cabin," Gen replied, covering a wide smile with her mechanical hands.

"What?" Ramus asked.

"I was curious why the two of you were sharing a cabin," Gen went on, "so Chief Fugg explained it to me."

"Fugg doesn't know what he's talking about," Ramus replied. "And anyway, it's none of his business..."

"Yes, Captain!" Gen said and went back to what she was doing.

Inside Roxie's room, the lounge singer was straightening the sheets on the bed. She laughed when she saw what Ramus was wearing.

"And they say *I'm* overdressed!" she said.

Ramus grunted as the door slid closed behind him.

"Everybody's got an opinion about me today," he said.

Roxie rearranged the thick material around Ramus' shoulders, staring into his eyes.

"Well, it's a bit much..." she said.

"My mother gave it to me."

"Oh," Roxie said softly. "It went well then?"

"She wants a fresh start, apparently," Ramus replied. "I'm not sure my father agrees, though."

Roxie sat on the side of the bed. "Either way, I'm glad you're getting the chance."

Ramus removed the tunic and laid it beside her on the bed.

"I'm sorry about how things turned out for you," he said.

"Don't be," she replied. "Like I said, I'm happy for you."

"Maybe I should bring you next time?"

"You want me to meet your parents?" she said with a smirk. "Moving kinda fast, Captain Ramus..."

"Stop it."

Roxie touched the tunic beside her, running her hand down the fabric. "This is nice."

"Only the best for my father," Ramus said wryly. "He's the Chancellor, you know."

"So I've heard..."

Her hand reached the small pocket at the front. Poking her fingers inside, she pulled out something on a golden chain. Examining it, she held it out for Ramus to inspect.

"What's this?" she asked.

Ramus bent closer and saw a round amulet in the palm of Roxie's hand. His heart skipped a beat when he recognized the sunburst design of the Dahl Empire.

CHAPTER THIRTEEN

A fast courier ship arrived above Gwlad Ard'un with a message from Lady Veber, the Imperial Regent, requesting an audience with Elder Blynora. The elder had not met with the regent since the crowning of the new emperor and she was not particularly eager to do so now. Still, she wondered what Lady Veber wanted and there was only one way to find out.

Standing alone in Dôlgoch, where the Elder Council assembled, Blynora closed her eyes and concentrated, channeling her psionic powers. She became ethereal and traveled across space far faster than any ship, projecting her image directly into the chambers of Lady Veber as the message had required. When she opened her eyes, Blynora saw the regent sitting behind a heavy desk while a young man, still in his teens, stood beside her. He wore the green of the Groen family and a golden circlet on his head.

Elder Blynora bowed, her body like a bluish, translucent ghost.

"Your Imperial Majesty," she said to Emperor Jack, "and the Lady Regent..."

"Elder Blynora," Lady Veber replied. "It's good to see you finally, if not in person."

"My apologies," Blynora said. "The affairs of the Dahlvish home world have kept me quite busy."

"Too busy to pay your respects to the Emperor?" Lady Veber asked.

"I promise I will attend when the young man comes of age and takes full control of the throne."

Lady Veber had a wide, welcoming face, but her eyes were hard like she had lost something and was not inclined to lose anything more. The emperor was less formal.

"It's okay!" Jack replied. "It's no big deal!"

Elder Blynora smiled, but Lady Veber did not.

"Jack is kind as always," the regent said, "but he can afford to be... for now."

"Indeed," Blynora replied. "Nevertheless, I'm curious why you've called this meeting. Your message was vague, to say the least..."

Lady Veber kept her eyes fixed on the elder.

"Some information has come to our attention," Lady Veber said sternly, "about a secret organization on Gwlad Ard'un."

"Oh?" Blynora replied. "What kind of organization?"

"A group called the *Echuio*," Lady Veber went on. "Our informant said they intend to rise up against the Imperial government."

"That's nonsense!" the elder said with a laugh. "I would know if such a group existed."

"Perhaps you *do*," Lady Veber replied.

The elder turned serious. "I'm sure I do not."

"Then let me enlighten you," the regent said. "They are members of your upper elite who pine for the days of the Dahl Empire."

Blynora waved her hand dismissively.

"The old empire was relegated to history long ago," she said. "If the Echuio exist, they are nothing more than a fringe gathering of sentimentalists nostalgic for what once was..."

"Or they are a danger to the newly crowned emperor," Lady Veber said, casting a quick look at Jack beside her. "Either way, it is something we cannot ignore."

"What do you mean?" the elder asked.

"Gwlad Ard'un has remained largely independent since the founding of the Imperium," Lady Veber said. "Perhaps this was a mistake."

"On the contrary, Lady Regent," Blynora replied. "The Dahl have remained ever loyal, providing our wisdom to your leadership since the beginning."

"But who benefits most from this so-called wisdom?" Lady Veber asked. "Your special status has always elevated the Dahl above other races in the galaxy. It would not surprise me if the Dahl have grown too accustomed to the privilege, perhaps even wished for the total control they once had."

Elder Blynora shook her head.

"We live to serve—" she started but the regent cut her off.

"Words are meaningless without action," Lady Veber said. "After consulting with the Emperor, we believe assigning a military governor to Gwlad Ard'un would be prudent. Someone to keep a closer watch on your home world."

"Absolutely not!" Blynora protested. "That's unacceptable!"

Lady Veber sprung to her feet, leaning forward with her fists on the desk.

"No?" she shouted back. "How *dare* you!"

"Wait," Jack said. "Let's not get excited. Maybe Elder Blynora can do something..."

Lady Veber returned to her seat. "What do you have in mind?"

"Well," Jack explained, "if the Elder could investigate these Echuio guys, maybe she could take care of them herself. Could you do that, Elder Blynora?"

Her transparent image flickered as Blynora gathered herself.

"Yes, of course," she said. "It would be my pleasure."

"Very well," Lady Veber said, sighing. "But you have seventy-two hours and no more. Then, I will dispatch a warship with a military governor to your planet, Elder."

"Understood," Blynora bowed again.

The elder felt the floor fall away and soon her consciousness was back on the soft ground of Dôlgoch. A trickle of sweat wound its way down her cheek.

"Humans," she said aloud and then remembered a human strategy called *good cop/bad cop*, wondering if she had just experienced it personally.

In the cargo hold of the *Wanderer*, Mel had fashioned a work bench where she had assembled the psi wand based on Uncle Artie's original design. Mel had also added three metal prongs on the end which were now holding a small, rounded piece of crystal.

Fugg was not impressed.

"How does it work?" he asked doubtfully.

"I *told* you already!" Mel replied.

"Yeah, but I still don't get it."

Mel rolled her eyes in disgust. "You're a mental midget!"

"Who are *you* calling short?" Fugg protested.

"You're both idiots," Ramus said, entering the hold with Roxie Blues alongside him.

"No we're not!" Mel and Fugg replied in unison.

Ramus and Roxie stopped beside the work bench.

"Gen told us you've got that thing finished?" the captain said.

Mel's mood turned from anger to pride. "Damn straight!"

"So she says," Fugg added, "but she hasn't tested it yet."

"Where's the Lantern?" Ramus asked.

Mel pointed to the metal flooring that covered the secret compartment. "It's in there."

"Can a scan pick up that piece in the wand?" Ramus asked.

"This little thing?" Mel replied. "It's too small for a scan to see."

"Either way," Ramus went on, "you need to take back what's left of the Lantern."

Mel blew a raspberry.

"It's fine!" she said. "I took a little chip off the bottom. Hardly noticeable..."

"Good," Ramus said.

"So, how *does* it work?" Roxie asked, gesturing at the wand.

Mel waved the device in the air.

"It acts as a conduit for psionics," she said. "The wand focuses your psi energy, making it more powerful. Fugg's right, though, I haven't tested it yet."

Everyone stared at Ramus.

"Not a chance," he said, raising his hands. "I'm no guinea pig."

"I'll do it," Roxie offered.

"You?" Fugg replied. "Since when do *you* know psi?"

Roxie blushed. "Well, I'm not very good at it..."

"I don't care," Mel said, handing her the wand. "Give it a shot."

Roxie examined the instrument in her hand while the others instinctively took a few steps back.

"It's not going to explode, is it?" she asked.

Mel shrugged. "Probably not."

Ramus and Fugg took an additional step back.

"You don't have to do this," Ramus said.

Roxie collected herself and held the wand out straight. "No, I want to."

They watched while the singer hummed deep in her throat, her eyes tightly closed. Ramus eyed Mel as if to suggest he would kill her if anything went wrong. For her part, Mel scowled in return, confident in her workmanship.

As Roxie concentrated, the wand began to hum and the crystal suspended between the metal prongs slowly started to glow, first in a pale yellow, then turning an intense gold. The dimly lit cargo hold grew brighter and Roxie's hand holding the wand started to shake.

"Roxie..." Ramus began, but the singer's eyes remained shut while the crystal radiated more energy. With a sharp crack in the air, a sound wave erupted from the wand, traveling across the room and hitting a crate on the other side. The box shattered into tiny pieces, showering the hold with bits of plastic.

Everyone jumped, including Roxie.

"What the hell was that?" Ramus asked.

"That's a result!" Mel shouted in reply.

Roxie took a deep breath.

"I use ultrasonic psi while I sing sometimes," she said. "You know, to make my voice stronger. But it's never been like that! This is amazing!"

Ramus slowly took the wand out of Roxie's hand.

"Maybe don't use this while you're singing to an audience," he suggested. "You'd take their heads off..."

A slow smile crossed Roxie's face. "Okay..."

Ramus slipped the wand into his coat pocket and started to leave.

"Where are you going?" Fugg asked.

"I need to meet somebody," the captain replied.

"Why are you taking my invention with you, then?" Mel wanted to know.

"Safekeeping," Ramus replied. "I don't trust you maniacs with it."

"Even me?" Roxie asked.

"I'll see ya," he said and left.

Mel crossed her arms and watched the door slide shut.

"He better not break it!" she grumbled.

The Horticulture Department at Prenwyn University maintained a rose garden on campus. It was a circular ring of flowers with a fountain in the center made from a bronze bowl over seven feet wide. When the column of water splashed on the inside of the bowl, it made a soft, ringing noise that most Dahl found soothing. Ramus, who was about as zen as a house on fire, did not.

Wearing her gown, Arwyn lingered at the fountain, watching the water splatter the bronze. Ramus was glad they appeared to have the garden to themselves.

She looked up as Ramus arrived.

"Hello, dear," Arwyn said. "Did you bring the tunic?"

"I left it on the *Wanderer*," Ramus replied, stopping beside her.

"Actually, your father will probably want it back..."

"What about this?" Ramus asked, holding out the amulet with the sunburst insignia.

Arwyn studied the medallion in Ramus' palm but didn't reach to take it.

"Where did you get that?" she asked.

"I think you know," he replied, closing his hand into a fist.

Arwyn gazed into the fountain without speaking.

"You spilled that wine on me," Ramus continued, "and then you practically forced me to wear Father's tunic with this in the pocket. Why?"

His mother hesitated and then asked, "Have you heard of the Echuio?"

"I've heard rumors," Ramus replied. "My crew said the humans were talking about them..."

Arwyn looked at her son. "It's more than rumors. They're real."

"What's that got to do with my father?" Ramus asked.

She walked to the roses surrounding the fountain and took a flower, cradling it in her hand.

"I've had suspicions about Telyn lately," she said. "But I didn't want to believe them..."

Ramus simmered with frustration. "Just tell me!"

"I think your father is leading the Echuio," she said.

"You can't be serious," Ramus replied.

His mother snapped the stem and let the rose fall to the ground.

"I *am* serious," she said earnestly.

"Do you have any evidence?"

"I didn't at first," his mother explained, "but then I found a gold mask hidden in Telyn's belongings."

"Yeah?"

"Tribunals in the old Empire would wear masks like that," Arwyn said. "They're incredibly rare now, found only in ancient dig sites."

"So, how did he get one then?"

"Exactly my point," she replied. "And there's been other things: he's been acting more distant of late, and secretive. I didn't know what to do..."

"You're a member of the Elder Council," Ramus said. "Why couldn't you go to them?"

"And implicate my own husband?"

"You turned in your own son," Ramus said bitterly.

"I know!" she replied, covering her eyes. "I've made terrible mistakes. I didn't want to make another one..."

Ramus' heart softened. He rolled the amulet over a few times in his hand.

"I'll do it," he said.

Arwyn uncovered her face to get a better look at her son. "Do what?"

"I'll turn him in."

"But they'll know you're an exile," she said. "They'll send you away again. Maybe even erase our memories like they did the first time."

"Maybe," Ramus replied, "but I never planned on staying and maybe it's better if you forgot about me."

"But I *want* to remember..."

"We don't always get what we want," Ramus said.

His mother stepped closer and gave her son a hug, squeezing Ramus as tightly as she could.

"You're a good son," she said.

"*No*, I'm *not*," Ramus replied.

Henry felt a grudging relief while traveling in the gravcar on the way to the dig site. Sitting in the back, watching the heads of Elisan Mossdale and Jessica Doric in the front, he was thankful for the rescue by the Woodland Dahl, but not without a little resentment. Henry was so focused on his own feelings he didn't notice that Doric was quiet. Mistral, who had demanded to come along, was quiet too, but mostly because she was excited to stare out the window at the passing treetops.

The gravcar landed among the camp shelters where Mossdale lead the way to his own tent. Inside was a bed and dresser of Dahlvish design, but Mossdale had added a few Sylvan touches of his own, including a mirror decorated with a carved acorn motif. On a table, a few relics from the dig were lined up in an orderly fashion, although Henry couldn't tell what they were. Most were covered in rust and in the process of being cleaned. Mossdale had a few glass cloches on the table as well, the dome protecting the precious items beneath.

"I'm so glad you're safe," Mossdale said. "If your friend hadn't found me at the camp, I'm not sure what would have happened!"

Mistral fluttered her wings, practically bouncing in the air.

"You would've been Nanzi food!" she said.

"I could've gotten us out," Henry replied so unconvincingly that the hovering Sylph just laughed. Henry winced. "I was waiting for my moment," he added.

Mistral was about to say something snide when Doric interrupted.

"Are you going to arrest us?" she asked Mossdale.

"Why?" he replied.

"Because of the Singing Lantern," she said.

"Well, did you steal it?" Mossdale asked.

"No!" Doric said.

"I thought as much," Mossdale replied. "And since you didn't have it with you, either you lost it in the woods or you're innocent."

Doric relaxed her shoulders as if a weight had been lifted. Meanwhile, Mistral buzzed around the tent, stopping above the table of artifacts.

"What are all these?" she asked.

"We dug them out of the ground," Mossdale replied, approaching the table and eager to talk about his work.

Henry drew Doric aside.

"I guess your friend isn't so bad," he told her.

"Of course," Doric said. "Did you think he was?"

Henry stammered. "I mean, I didn't know for *sure...*"

"Really, Henry," she replied, shaking her head disapprovingly.

" ...and this one was apparently a silver hairbrush," Mossdale was saying.

"I brush my hair with a *stick*," Mistral confessed.

"Elisan," Doric said, "there's something else I need to talk to you about."

The Sylva raised his head. "Yes?"

"I saw something while I was in the forest," she replied.

"I'm not surprised," Mossdale said. "It's the Forest of Illusions, after all."

"But they're *not* illusions," Doric replied. "That's just it. They're psychic reflections of real-life Dahl."

Mossdale turned serious. "Oh?"

"Yeah, we see what you Dahl are doing all the time," Mistral said. "There's no secrets in the forest..."

"Oh?" Mossdale said again.

"I saw the Echuio," Doric continued in earnest. "I saw their *leader!*"

Mossdale took a moment to absorb what Doric had said before turning back toward the table.

"Elisan?" Doric said.

Taking one of the empty cloches, Mossdale swung it over Mistral, trapping her between the glass dome and the wooden base. He slammed both hard on the table while the fairy pounded against the glass.

"Hey, let me out!" she shouted and made a puff of fire which filled the tight space with flame. She dropped to the bottom of the cloche, her wings slightly singed.

" Elisan?" Doric asked again weakly as the Sylva ran to the tent entrance.

"Guards!" he shouted. In mere moments, a pair of security officers came rushing inside.

Henry pointed at Mossdale and laughed.

"I knew it!" he blurted out.

"What's going on?" Doric asked.

"I'm sorry," the Sylva said. "I'm afraid you're under arrest after all."

"But—" Doric started as the two officers grabbed her and Henry by the arms, clamping handcuffs across their wrists.

"Take them away," Mossdale said.

Telyn did not appear pleased to see his son when Ramus entered the chancellor's office with a bundle of cloth under his arm. He seemed even less so when Ramus dropped the bundle on the desk, causing a few of the items on top to scatter or tip over.

"I must say," Telyn muttered, "I wasn't expecting to see you again so soon, Captain Ramus."

Ramus sat in the chair in front of the desk.

"Me either," he said, "but I wanted to return your tunic."

"I'm sure you could have sent it by messenger," the chancellor said.

"Maybe," Ramus replied, "but I wanted to give you this personally..."

From his jacket, Ramus retrieved the medallion which dangled between his fingers.

"What's that?" his father asked.

"You don't recognize it?"

Telyn leaned closer in his seat.

"Ah yes," he said, squinting. "That's a necklace from the Dahl Empire. Where did you get it?"

"From your tunic," Ramus replied.

"My tunic? That seems unlikely..."

"Are you familiar with the Echuio?" Ramus asked.

"Of course, but I don't see—"

Ramus threw the amulet onto the desk. "Mother thinks you're their leader."

"Nonsense!" Telyn said with a sneer. "She wouldn't—"

"She does, or says she does anyway."

Telyn stared at the starburst lying among his things. He shook his head in disbelief.

"Arwyn is far too intelligent to accuse me of such treachery!"

"Well," Ramus said, "technically she wanted *me* to do it..."

"And I suppose you believe it's true?"

"No," Ramus replied. "Not at all."

Telyn's mouth hung slightly ajar, which was not a dignified expression for a chancellor.

"Your office has not changed since I was a boy," Ramus went on. "You're the poster child for the status quo, so there's no way you could be involved with anything as revolutionary as the Echuio."

Telyn straightened up in his chair.

"Thank you," he said.

"I mean, if they made a statue of you, I doubt anyone could tell the difference from the real thing."

"Alright..." Telyn said.

"Do the cleaningbots dust you at night?" Ramus asked.

"That's quite enough, Rowan!"

"You didn't call me *Captain Ramus*."

Telyn's eyes narrowed. "What do you want?"

"Funny you should ask," Ramus said, "but we'll get to that in a moment." From his other pocket, he pulled out the psi wand.

"Is that a weapon?" Telyn asked.

"Kind of," Ramus said. "You know the artifact that was stolen?"

"Yes."

"Well, I stole it," Ramus added. "I mean, technically someone from my ship took it, but this is the reason why."

"I should have guessed," Telyn said. "I'll tell the authorities to call off their search for the humans..."

"You may want to wait on that," Ramus suggested.

"Why?"

"Once Mother discovers I haven't turned you in," Ramus said, "she's probably going to send the police herself... for *both* of us."

The pair of security officers led Henry and Doric away from Mossdale's tent toward a waiting gravcar. Mossdale followed and stood silently while the two humans were loaded into the backseat of the vehicle.

"What are you going to do with Mistral?" Henry asked through the open door.

"Once you're gone," Mossdale replied, "I'll release her into the forest. No harm will come to her."

The door swung shut and the two officers got into the front. As the gravcar lifted off, Henry watched as Mossdale and the rest of the dig site grew smaller. Doric refused to look, staring out the other window.

"I was stupid," she muttered to herself. "I should've known."

"How could you?" Henry asked.

Doric didn't answer, her eyes fixed in the other direction.

The car flew just above the treetops, no one saying a word. Although the handcuffs hurt Henry's wrists, he drifted off to sleep for a while until Doric's voice woke him. She was talking to the guards.

"Where are we going?" she asked.

"Remain silent," one of the officers said from the front.

Henry scrutinized the woods passing below, but they just looked like trees, much fuller than the dead trunks of the Forest of Illusions. It only dimly occurred to him that the sun was in the wrong place.

"This isn't the way back to Prenwyn University," Doric remarked.

"We're not going there," the officer said. "Now be quiet."

Doric shot Henry a worried glance, but his mind was on other things.

"Do you think Mossdale was telling the truth about Mistral?" he asked. "Do you think they'll hurt her?"

"No," Doric said. "It's not her they're after."

Henry felt strangely relieved and went back to staring out the window. After what seemed like a long time, the car slowed to a hover and began descending into a clearing. Henry couldn't see any buildings at first, but as the vehicle lowered, he saw a ruin of some sort, half buried in the field below.

"Where are we?" he asked.

"I've no idea," Doric confessed.

The gravcar came to rest and the two officers opened the rear doors to let the humans out. The clearing was small, with no other structures besides the ruin. Vines covered the stone walls and vegetation grew around the broken blocks that were strewn about. From the air, a car could easily pass overhead without noticing anything out of the ordinary.

"This way," one of the officers said, directing them toward an ancient archway.

"What is this place?" Henry asked but got a shove in the back for his trouble.

"Quiet!" the officer said.

The two humans, with the Dahl behind them, walked into a partially collapsed chamber, the sky visible through the crumbling ceiling. The room was empty except for stairs leading down. With nowhere else to go, Doric and Henry took the steps until they reached a heavy wooden door flanked by torches. The flames flickered with an eerie, bluish light.

An officer pushed the doors open to reveal another chamber, this one bright with four burning braziers, one in each corner. In the center, seven robed and hooded figures with masks were aligned in a semi-circle. They each wore a gold medallion with a starburst around their necks. Once Doric and Henry had entered, the officers removed the handcuffs and left, closing the heavy doors behind them.

"Who are these guys?" Henry asked Doric.

"The Echuio," she replied.

The masks for all but one of the robed Dahl were silver. The other, standing in the middle, wore one made of gold. He stepped forward.

"Greetings," he said.

"I know who you are!" Doric shouted suddenly, making Henry jump.

The one with the gold mask laughed. "Well, I thought you'd recognize my voice..."

He pulled off the mask.

"Professor Rhun!" Henry said. "Are you a prisoner too?"

Everyone, including Doric, stared at him.

"Oh, right," Henry said and felt his skin turning hot.

"I saw you in the Forest of Illusions," Doric went on. "You were kissing a woman."

Rhun grinned sheepishly. "Oh, you mean her?"

One of the other robed figures removed her mask. Pulling back her hood, she revealed her auburn hair, braided into loops.

"Allow me to introduce myself," she said. "My name is Elder Arwyn."

CHAPTER FOURTEEN

As someone who studied the Dahl, Jessica Doric knew a lot about the Elder Council. She had even heard of Elder Arwyn, but she never dreamed one of their leadership could be a member of the Echuio. It made sense, in a way, but only in hindsight.

"How could you betray your people like this?" Doric asked the elder.

"Betray?" Arwyn replied. "On the contrary..."

"But you're on the Council," Doric said. "You're supposed to do what's *right*!"

"Do what's right for my people?" she scoffed. "Or do what's right for the *Imperium*? The imperial government is controlled by humans and it's the humans who benefit the most from it. The Dahl people are little more than servants to your emperor. Considering our proud history, our current state is a disgrace!"

Professor Rhun took Arwyn's hand. "Now, now, my love..."

Doric turned her eyes to the professor.

"After I saw you in the forest," she admitted, "I should've known Elisan was also part of the Echuio."

"Well, yeah," Henry remarked. "It's pretty obvious if you think about it..."

"Shut up, Henry," Doric replied under her breath.

"Yes, Mossdale has been a tremendous asset," Rhun said. "His knowledge and access to our ancient artifacts have been invaluable." He motioned at his medallion. "His dig sites have given us the treasures we're wearing today."

"Are you going to *sacrifice* us?" Henry cried.

Rhun laughed. "Of course not! We're Dahl, not savages!"

"Then what *do* you want with us?" Doric asked.

"As a matter of fact," the professor explained, "the two of you have joined us at an auspicious moment. We are about to launch the reawakening of the Dahl Empire, reborn after centuries of neglect."

"Why now?" Doric asked.

"Well, I must say the stars have aligned, it seems," Rhun replied. "With the young emperor on the throne, your Imperium has never been weaker. If there was ever a time to strike, it's now."

"The Imperium will destroy you!" Doric said emphatically. "Just like everybody else that tried to rebel."

Professor Rhun eyed Elder Arwyn.

"We think not," Rhun said. "In fact, you've brought us the very instrument that will help us defeat you."

"The Lantern?" Doric asked.

"Indeed."

"But it's lost... or stolen," Doric said.

"Oh, it was definitely stolen," Rhun added, "but we have a pretty good idea who stole it. I believe you're familiar with Captain Ramus and his crew?"

"Yes," Doric replied.

"It so happens that Ramus is Elder Arwyn's son," Rhun said.

"*Son?*" Henry asked.

"Even before I learned the truth," Arwyn said, "we had my son's ship under surveillance. We witnessed one of his crew steal the artifact and take it aboard the *Wanderer*."

Her face showed a hint of sadness.

"Frankly," she said, "I had hoped Rowan would join us, but eventually I decided it might be better if he implicated my husband instead, and perhaps got himself arrested in the process."

"Who's your husband?" Doric asked.

"Chancellor Telyn," the elder replied matter-of-factly.

"Oh, good lord!" Henry said, having trouble keeping up.

"As we speak," Rhun said, "security officers, loyal to our cause, are descending on Ramus' ship to recapture the artifact."

"But I still don't understand why," Doric said.

"To use the device as it was intended," Rhun replied emphatically. "We will communicate with our supporters simultaneously, across all of the Imperium. The Dahl are in high places of government after all, counseling our human masters, but we will rise up in unison and kill those we previously advised."

"It will be a sudden slaughter," Arwyn said, "but it will begin a new order, a new Dahl Empire!"

"Now I get it," Henry remarked. "Pretty obvious if you think about it."

"Shut up, Henry," Doric sighed.

In the chancellor's office, the father-son bonding session between Telyn and Ramus quickly descended into wondering what to do next. Telyn had several questions.

"I don't understand why Arwyn would want me arrested, or you for that matter," he said.

"Isn't it obvious?" Ramus replied. "She wants to divert attention away from the real leader of the Echuio."

"Why?"

"Because she's *one* of them," Ramus said.

"Don't be absurd!" Telyn exclaimed.

"Well, you can ask her all about it when you see her next," Ramus said, standing up. "But one thing's for sure, we can't stay here. The only question is where do we go?"

"That's a good question," Telyn said, rubbing his chin. "If an elder on the Council is one of the Echuio, there's no telling who else could be involved."

"Is there anyone who is definitely *not* a member?"

"Besides you and me," the chancellor started, "it's hard to say. However, since this is a Dahlvish conspiracy, we could assume it's someone who isn't Dahl."

"Such as?" Ramus asked.

"Follow me," his father said.

Whisking past his secretary without a word, Telyn led his son down some stairs and into the courtyard outside the building. Students and faculty alike filled the common space, any of whom could have been the eyes and ears of the Echuio. Ramus gripped the psi wand in his pocket, stifling the urge to start shooting, but his father swept through the crowd like a plow over a field.

They continued across campus until they reached the archeology building.

"Here?" Ramus asked.

The chancellor didn't answer. He entered the building and ascending more stairs. In the back of Ramus' mind, he wondered why his people were averse to elevators.

On the third floor, Telyn stopped to get his bearings before pushing ahead down a corridor and barging into one of the offices. Behind the desk, a creature looking like a cross between a bear and an owl glared at them with his large, round eyes.

"Chancellor Telyn," Grimfeather said tepidly, "I suppose knocking was out of the question..."

"There's no time for that," Telyn replied. "Oh, this is my son, Rowan."

The Orubea's feathers ruffled. "Son?"

"I'm just visiting," Ramus deadpanned.

The chancellor leaned on the professor's desk. "Grimfeather, I need to know if you're part of the Echuio."

"Well," the professor replied, "I'd hardly tell you if I was, would I?"

"Perhaps," Telyn continued in earnest, "but it appears my wife *is* one of them."

"Dear me," Grimfeather replied. "That's terrible."

"And she's trying to get me and my father arrested," Ramus added.

"That stands to reason," the Orubea said. "I've long suspected something was brewing at the university. These places are often a hotbed for malcontents. I'm sure they want the chancellor out of the way so the Echuio can work unimpeded."

"You think some of the students are involved?" Telyn asked.

"Most likely," Grimfeather replied, "and a good many of the professors too, I assume."

"This is madness!" the chancellor shouted. "Don't they know the Imperium will crush us?"

Grimfeather chuckled from his wide, feathered chest.

"The more extreme the view," he said, "the more insulated from reality it becomes. Especially if they've recruited from an impressionable student body. The students' own zeal then encourages the leadership and vice versa. It's a snake feeding on itself..."

"So, what do we do about it?" Ramus asked.

"We need to alert the Council," Telyn said.

"But Mom is *on* the Council!" Ramus replied. "They might *all* be conspirators."

His father nodded.

"Perhaps," he said, "but I'm willing to bet one of them is *not...*"

Light bending was another discipline of psionics taught at Prenwyn University, and the senior security officer was one of their finest pupils. When she gained command of her unit, she taught them everything she knew, making them virtually invisible to the unaided eye. This explained why Roxie had no idea she was surrounded until a group of six security officers appeared around her as if from thin air.

Standing beside a fresh pile of cigarette butts at the foot of the *Wanderer*'s ramp, Roxie uttered a little scream.

"What do you want?" she asked, visibly shaken.

The senior officer, her uniform so crisp and clean that it was a shame to be invisible much of the time, stepped forward.

"You are the exile known as Roxie Blues," she said. "You're under arrest for illegally returning to the home world!"

"I just wanted to see—" Roxie began.

"Silence!" the senior officer shouted and placed handcuffs around Roxie's wrists.

With the singer in tow, the officer and her team climbed the ramp where they encountered Fugg running toward them with a blaster. The senior officer, who had also minored in telekinesis, flicked her hand, sending Fugg flying backwards into the bulkhead.

The chief engineer dropped the blaster and rubbed his head.

"Pointy-eared witch!" he yelled.

The security detail spent the next few minutes rounding up both Mel and Gen the robot, gathering them in the galley.

"What's this all about?" Mel asked, her hands bound behind her back.

The senior officer's dark hair was in sharp contrast to her crystal blue eyes as she stared down the Gnomi.

"You're all under arrest," she said coldly.

"For what?" Mel demanded.

"For the theft of the ancient Dahlvish artifact you call the *Singing Lantern*," the senior officer replied.

Gen, who was not handcuffed for some reason, covered her mouth. "Oh, dear!"

"Now, where is it?" the senior officer asked.

"No idea what you're talking about, *pig*!" Mel spat.

"What?" Fugg protested out of habit.

"No, not you, idiot!" Mel yelled.

"Never mind," the senior officer said and grabbed Roxie by the arm. "She can help us find it."

Roxie shook her head vigorously. "I refuse!"

"That's alright, exile," the senior officer said. "You just need to sing."

"Sing?" Roxie asked.

"Yes."

Mel's eyes grew big. "It's a trick!"

"Of course it's a trick!" the senior officer told Roxie. "But if you don't do it, we'll harm the others."

Roxie looked unsure what to do, but after hesitating, she sang a few notes.

"No," the senior officer said, giving Roxie's arm a sharp tug. "Not out loud. Sing in your head!"

If Roxie's expression was baffled before, it became even more so now. However, she did what she was told. After a few moments, a muffled sound came from somewhere down the adjoining corridor.

"Keep going," the senior officer commanded and pulled Roxie down the hallway.

The sound grew louder until the senior officer recognized it as an old Dahlvish ballad about lost love.

"Don't stop," she said.

Following the music, the senior officer tracked it to the cargo hold, to a spot in the floor near the middle of the box-filled room.

"Oh," Roxie said, finally understanding what had been happening.

"Why did you think it was called the Singing Lantern?" the senior officer asked, somewhat disappointed in her fellow Dahl.

"Well, now I feel foolish," Roxie admitted.

"You should," the senior officer replied, releasing Roxie's arm.

Raising both hands, the senior officer focused her mind until the heavy floor panel lifted in the air and flew off to the side. The officer stepped forward and peered into the secret compartment. The crystal Lantern lay at the bottom, still glowing as Roxie's song slowly faded.

In the valley of Dôlgoch, Blynora once again convened the Elder Council, but this time Elder Arwyn was late. With the other members seated on the stone benches in a semi-circle, Blynora waited impatiently for Arwyn to arrive until a gravcar landed in the neighboring field. However, it was Chancellor Telyn and another Dahl who got out and approached the hill where the elders were assembled.

"What is this?" Blynora asked. "Where is Arwyn?"

"I've no idea," Telyn replied, slightly winded from the climb.

"Then you and your companion must leave," Blynora said. "This meeting is for elders only."

"There's something important the Council must know," the chancellor said, "and it involves my wife."

"Is she alright?" Blynora asked.

"I assume so, although I doubt she'd wish the same for me," Telyn said.

Blynora's face turned sour. "Whatever does *that* mean?"

"We think she's part of the Echuio," Ramus said, speaking for the first time.

"Who's this?" Blynora asked the chancellor.

Telyn wavered, his reply caught in his throat.

"My son," he said finally.

"I wasn't aware you *had* a son!" Blynora said.

"Nor was I, until recently," the chancellor replied. "It appears our minds were erased."

"So, he's an exile?" Blynora shouted. "Are you mad, bringing one of the Forgotten to a Council meeting? You could be exiled yourself for such treachery!"

"Listen," Ramus said with a low growl. "My mother is a conspirator and she's trying to frame my father for it. Who knows what else the Echuio are planning?"

From the sky, another vehicle approached and landed in the field beside the first one. This time, Elder Arwyn emerged and joined the rest of the council on the hill.

"I see the rebels have arrived before me," she said, giving her husband and son a stiff smile.

"Drop it, Mother," Ramus said. "Nobody's going to believe Telyn is a revolutionary!"

Arwyn cast her eyes down. "It's true I was fooled at first, but I must inform the Council that my husband is, in fact, the leader of the Echuio."

"That's completely absurd!" Telyn protested.

Blynora considered for a moment and then asked Telyn, "Who do you expect us to believe? You may be the university chancellor, but Elder Arwyn is part of the leadership council."

Arwyn nodded at Blynora in appreciation. "Thank you, Elder. I've also taken the liberty of having my son's crew arrested as well. It appears they were the ones who stole the artifact from the university."

Ramus' face turned nearly as red as his hair.

"You people are idiots!" Ramus shouted and pulled the wand from his pocket.

"You brought a weapon here?" Blynora asked incredulously.

"You're goddamn right!" Ramus replied. "Come on, Father. Let's get out of here!"

Reluctantly, Telyn followed Ramus back to the gravcar as his son kept the wand trained on the council elders. Once the vehicle was gone, Blynora addressed the others.

"They won't get far, I promise you," she said. "I've already sent a telepathic message to the authorities."

"Thank you again," Arwyn said. "When I learned I had a son and Telyn had brought him back to Gwlad Ard'un, I was understandably shocked. I should have come to the council immediately, but as a mother, I was torn. I didn't know what to do."

"Yes, you *should* have come to us," Blynora replied. "But I understand."

"May I ask why you've assembled the council?" Arwyn asked. "Did you already know about my husband's treason?"

"No, but it appears related," Blynora replied. "I've been notified by the Emperor's Regent that she plans to send a military governor here to oversee the planet."

"Why?" Arwyn asked.

"Somehow they've learned of the Echuio," Blynora said, "and if we don't quell them immediately, the Imperial military will do so for us!"

Doric and Henry were back in Professor Rhun's office. The robotic Sprite floated in the corner as usual and the worktables had not changed at all since the last time the two humans had been there. Even the Singing Lantern was back on its perch on one of the tables, except now something ominous hung over the artifact.

Also, Rhun was smiling like a madman.

"What's so funny?" Henry asked.

The professor rubbed the crystal lantern like a genie's lamp.

"Oh, it's not so much funny as it's the culmination of so much hard work," he said, his eyes sparkling. "You really have no idea how long I've waited for this. How could you? The humans see us as faithful lieutenants. You would never sense the deep resentment we harbor for your people."

"You could have mentioned it..." Henry muttered.

"Not at all!" Rhun replied. "Then we'd fare no better than all the other races you've subjugated. You see, I understand *why* we've remained subservient for so long, but soon that time will end. Soon, we will rise again..."

Elder Arwyn entered with a pair of security officers. Her face was grim.

"What is it?" Rhun asked.

"There's trouble," she replied. "My husband and son were both at the Elder Council when I arrived. They were trying to convince Blynora that I was part of the uprising."

"Did they succeed?" the professor asked.

"No," Arwyn said, "but they escaped and there's no telling where they are now."

Rhun laughed.

"There's no trouble then," he said. "What can they really do against us?"

"There's more," she went on. "Blynora said the Emperor will assign a military governor to the planet within days. We hadn't planned on acting so quickly."

Rhun's eyes turned thoughtful before he began smiling again. He touched the Lantern as if for good luck.

"Then we'll simply move up the timetable," he said. "Alert the others that we'll be using the artifact later today."

While Rhun and Arwyn were talking, Doric felt like she was in a daze, far off and isolated from what was happening around. Now, a jolt went through her, shaking Doric from her stupor.

"Today?" she asked, fully awake.

"Why not?" Rhun replied. "We have the artifact. We have the other pieces in place. There's nothing to stop us..."

"But humans and Dahl have worked together for so long," Doric said.

Henry shook his head sadly. "And they say *I* don't pay attention..."

"I know this must come as a shock, Miss Doric," the professor said, almost tenderly. "I'm well aware of the high regard you've placed in my people. However, as I said before, you should feel fortunate. You're witnessing the dawning of a new Dahl Empire. Of course, it's also the fall of your own..."

Arwyn sneered at the human woman.

"Perhaps we'll use one of you as *our* adviser?" the elder suggested. "Or perhaps just a pet..."

"Enough," Rhun said. "Go tell the others while I prepare the artifact. Leave the guards here though, in case Chancellor Telyn and your son arrive to make trouble..."

She nodded at the officers as she turned back toward the door.

"Feel free to kill them if they show up," she said. "Don't spare my husband and son on my account."

As Arwyn disappeared through the doorway, Professor Rhun watched her go.

"She's a remarkable woman," he said to no one in particular. "Telyn was a fool to lose her, but then, he failed to satisfy her..."

"Ewww," Henry remarked.

Crime was a rarity among the Dahl, but they still maintained a few cells on Gwlad Ard'un for off-worlders who got themselves into trouble. In a security building not far from Prenwyn University, Fugg, Mel, and Gen the robot were incarcerated in a small room with a force field on one side. Bunk beds, a sink, and a toilet filled the rest of the cell.

"This is a fine mess you've gotten us into," Fugg grumbled at Mel, while Gen looked longingly out the narrow window opposite the force field.

"Me?" Mel protested. "What did I do?"

"You stole the Lantern!" Fugg shouted. "Gnomi are constantly stealing stuff!"

"I only stole it *once*," Mel replied. "So, not *constantly*."

"That was enough," Fugg said and gestured at the tiny cell. "Who knows when I'll get more fungus beer? That means it'll be toilet wine from now on!"

"Gross," Mel said. "Fungus beer..."

"You're going to miss it too!" Fugg replied.

Mel sat on the bunk dejectedly. "I know..."

"Where do you suppose they took Miss Blues?" Gen asked, turning away from the window.

"She's Dahl," Mel said, "so they aren't going to treat her like the rest of us."

"I heard some of the guards talking about Miss Doric and Henry," Gen said. "Apparently, they've been captured too, although I don't understand why. We're the ones who stole the Lantern..."

"Mel stole it," Fugg corrected the robot. "We're just *accessories.*"

"Oh!" Gen replied. "I've never been an accessory before."

"Gen makes a good point," Mel said. "Why would they arrest two innocent humans?"

"Who cares?" Fugg said. "They'll get what they deserve."

"What do you mean?" the robot asked.

"Executed, probably," Fugg replied.

"Fugg!" Mel shouted.

"Oh, wake up," Fugg said. "There's something in the air and it stinks..."

"That's your body odor," Mel replied.

"But why would they kill Jessica and Henry?" Gen asked. "They seem so nice."

Fugg rolled his eyes.

"Because they're *humans*," he said with a snort. "The humans have called the shots for too long and now it's time for their heads to roll."

"Don't frighten the robot," Mel said.

"Oh, *she'll* be fine," Fugg replied. "They may reprogram her, wipe her memory and whatnot, but there's always a use for robots."

"But I don't want my mind wiped," Gen murmured.

"It doesn't matter what you want," Fugg said. "And you can forget about your new civil rights. There ain't no way our new overlords — the Dahl — are going to keep *those* on the books anymore."

Gen's shoulders drooped and she stared at the ground.

From elsewhere in the building, the sound of shouting reached the cell. Then, something like heavy furniture crashed and sent a shudder through the floor beneath the prisoners' feet.

"What the hell is that?" Fugg asked.

The three of them went to the force field, the pale blue light reflecting in their eyes. The angle was too acute to see anything, but the din of more fighting came down the corridor. When the noise stopped, nothing happened for a few minutes until a dark shape appeared and came walking slowly their way.

Fugg was not surprised by who it was.

"Did they arrest you too?" Fugg asked the red-haired Dahl outside the cell.

"No, dummy," Ramus said and passed an ID card over the door controls. The force field vanished, leaving the way clear. "I'm here to get you out..."

CHAPTER FIFTEEN

Elder Arwyn gathered the other high-ranking members of the Echuio in Professor Rhun's office, their robed figures circling the crystal lantern on a table like they were attending a black mass. Although their hoods were pulled over their heads, they were not wearing their masks this time, the need for secrecy now over.

Jessica Doric and Henry were witnesses to the ritual about to take place, shooed into the corner and standing beside the hovering Sprite.

Rhun raised his hands above the relic.

"For centuries," he said, "our proud people have served the invaders, but this ends today! A birthright denied is a destiny lost, and the Dahl will no longer allow others to lead. We will take our rightful place as the rulers of the galaxy!"

Whispers of agreement came from beneath the hoods of the others. Only Arwyn's voice stood out with a resounding, "Yes!"

Henry pushed the Sprite out of the way so he could see better.

"What's happening?" he asked.

"They're going to broadcast to the Echuio agents all over the Imperium," Doric replied, barely above a whisper. "Then the agents are going to kill our leaders simultaneously."

Henry grabbed one of the metal appendages hanging beneath the Sprite and pulled the robot closer, ducking behind it.

"They're not going to kill *you*, Henry," Doric said, "...at least not yet."

Henry edged farther behind the robot.

"Concentrate," Rhun was saying, "and focus your thoughts on the message. Like a wave in all directions, our words will wash over the human empire, bringing our oppressors to their knees!"

The hooded figures bowed their heads toward the relic. Slowly, the Singing Lantern began to dimly glow. The light within the crystal structure grew brighter, but still remained murky.

"Something's wrong," Arwyn said.

Rhun waved his hand for the others to stop. He visually examined the Lantern before picking it up.

"Someone's damaged it!" he shouted. "There's a piece missing underneath..."

Arwyn stepped forward.

"Rowan's crew were the only ones to possess it," she said and then her eyes blazed. "My son had a device! It was a cylinder like a wand... and there was a small crystal on the end!"

Rhun grabbed Arwyn by the arm.

"We need that device!" he told her.

Arwyn pulled her arm away. "How?"

The professor thought for a moment.

"Where is that other Dahl in your son's crew?" he asked. "The singer?"

"Mossdale has her under guard," Arwyn replied.

"Then we'll use her to get the wand from your son," Rhun said. "Threaten to kill her if you must, but get that crystal!"

Arwyn nodded but before she could leave, a rock came crashing through one of the windows, scattering broken glass into the room. Doric took cover behind Henry who was shielded by the hovering Sprite.

Rhun went to the window and looked out. Down in the courtyard below, a hulking figure with a beak and feathers stood among a throng of students and staff.

"We know you're in there!" Grimfeather shouted up to the second floor. "Surrender or we're storming the building!"

Rhun turned to Arwyn.

"While you're at it," he told her, "mobilize our students and get them here as soon as possible!"

As a Dahl, Roxie Blues enjoyed certain rights that most of her shipmates did not. Instead of rotting in a jail cell, she was under house arrest at the lovely home of Chancellor Telyn and Elder Arwyn. If she didn't look outside where the guards were stationed, Roxie could even imagine the home was hers, something impossible on a lounge singer's wages. With that in mind, Mossdale, who was bringing her a cup of tea in the living room, could have been her husband.

"Why are you looking at me like that?" he asked, handing her the cup on the sofa.

"Oh, nothing," she replied wistfully.

Mossdale sat in the chair beside her and took a sip of his own tea.

"You're a student, aren't you?" Roxie asked, coming back to reality.

"*Graduate* student," he corrected her.

"When you told me your teacher, Professor Rhun, was the leader of the Echuio," Roxie went on, "I must admit I was a little surprised."

"There's no reason to keep it a secret anymore," Mossdale said.

"No, I mean I was surprised their leader is a professor."

"Why not?" he replied. "Many academics are revolutionaries."

"Maybe from economics or political science," she said, "not *archeology*."

Mossdale scowled, causing Roxie to question whether their imaginary marriage would last...

"Until now," the Sylva said, "the greatest days of the Dahl were in the past. Who else could appreciate that more than an archaeologist?"

"I guess," Roxie replied doubtfully.

"Anyway," Mossdale added, "starting today, the future will be even brighter."

"For the Dahl," she said, "but you're not really one of *us*, are you?"

"You're not one of them either," he replied, glaring at her. "You're an exile who was erased from their memories..."

Roxie stared into her cup. "I suppose so."

"It doesn't matter anyway," Mossdale said. "From now on, none of the Dahl and their sub-races will be shackled by the humans..."

Roxie heard voices at the front door. It swung open and Elder Arwyn swept inside wearing a hooded robe. Mossdale jumped to his feet.

"What's going on?" he asked.

"There's a complication," Arwyn replied while noticing Roxie sitting on the sofa. "Making yourself at home?" she asked her.

Roxie rubbed the upholstery. "It's a lovely place you have here."

"Well, don't get comfortable," Arwyn replied. "You need to come with me."

"Why?" Roxie asked.

"I think you already know," the elder said and turned to Mossdale.

"They damaged the artifact to make some sort of device," she told him. "The relic won't work properly without the piece of crystal they removed."

"Where is the device?" Mossdale asked.

"My son has it," she said.

"Good luck getting it back," Roxie remarked.

"Perhaps," Arwyn replied. "But it's fortunate that we have you as a bargaining chip..."

"What's that supposed to mean?" Roxie asked.

"I know my son," the elder said. "And I think he'd be more than willing to give up the wand if he knew we'd hurt his girlfriend."

"You know about us?" the singer asked.

"It's disgustingly obvious," Arwyn replied.

"Well, I wouldn't call it disgusting..." Roxie said.

"Where are we taking her?" Mossdale asked.

"To Rhun's office," Arwyn said. "Be careful. Professor Grimfeather has assembled opposing forces in front of the archeology building."

"How did they know?" Mossdale asked.

"I assume my husband told them," Arwyn replied. "But no matter. Gather our forces in the student body and meet me there. Once we're safely inside, I'll contact my son."

Pwmpen hadn't seen Henry since the night the security officers tried to arrest him. Pwmpen was no longer the outcast, hiding from the world in his dorm room. He was someone new and courageous. Someone he might never have become without meeting the human.

Unsupportive of the young Dahl's awakening, the security officers arrested Pwmpen anyway for aiding and abetting a fugitive.

When his parents came to bail him out, his father was not pleased.

"What has gotten into you?" he demanded to know. "That human is a *bad* influence on you!"

Pwmpen stayed silent during his parents' berating, but he knew he could never go back to being the old Pwmpen.

So, in the present, when Pwmpen heard a commotion in the dormitory hallway, he stepped out to see what was happening instead of locking the door.

"What's going on?" he asked a passing student.

The student stopped in surprise, unaware anyone actually lived in that particular room.

"Professor Grimfeather says there's rebels occupying the archeology building," he panted.

"What kind of rebels?"

"The Echuio!" the student said and hurried on his way.

Pwmpen joined the gathering throng as they congregated in the large, open area in front of the archeology building. He had no difficulty locating Professor Grimfeather who stood at least two feet taller than the students and faculty around him.

"Mr. Pwmpen," Grimfeather growled. "Nice of you to join us."

"Is it true?" Pwmpen asked and pointed at the second floor. "Are the Echuio up there?"

"Apparently," Grimfeather said, "but let's find out, shall we?"

At that, the professor took a paving stone in his paw and heaved it through the upper-story window.

"We know you're in there!" Grimfeather shouted. "Surrender or we're storming the building!"

"We will?" Pwmpen asked despite his newfound self-confidence.

The hulking professor leaned down.

"Always show strength when facing adversity," Grimfeather advised. "Sometimes your enemy will surrender to avoid a fight."

Pwmpen looked up at the broken window and saw Professor Rhun staring down at him.

"Is Professor Rhun one of the Echuio?" Pwmpen asked.

With his big, round eyes, Grimfeather looked for himself. "It would appear so."

"I would've expected someone from economics," Pwmpen remarked.

For his part, Rhun cupped his hand and shouted, "Go home, all of you! Return to your dorms immediately!"

Hearing this, a worried buzz went through the crowd and a few students turned to leave.

"Stay where you are!" Grimfeather commanded them.

Rhun cleared away some of the shards of glass still hanging in the window.

"Today is a great day!" he yelled. "Trust your elders to know what's right!"

Well, that's encouraging, Pwmpen thought.

"Don't listen to him," Grimfeather told the crowd. "Your elders are no better at making decisions that you are!"

"Are you going to listen to that foreigner?" Rhun asked the crowd. "He doesn't look like us! He's no more Dahl than the humans who oppress us!"

Some more of the students, and a few of the teachers, nodded in agreement and gave Grimfeather suspicious glances. Seeing this, Pwmpen remembered Henry sitting in their dorm room while Pwmpen cut his hair. Nobody else would sit for him, but Henry didn't hesitate.

He felt his heart pounding.

"It doesn't matter who he is!" Pwmpen shouted. "It doesn't matter how scary Professor Grimfeather looks! He tells the *truth*, so listen to him!"

Grimfeather blinked his eyes at the heavy-set Dahl.

"I don't mean to be scary..." he muttered.

"If we leave now," Pwmpen found himself saying, "we'll be letting this — whatever *this* is — happen without a say in it! We can't just hide away and watch! We have to do something!"

Someone in the crowd raised a fist and shouted a resounding "Yeah!", which probably surprised themselves as much as those around them. Some of the students who had started to leave, stopped and came back.

"We stand together, or we fall apart!" Pwmpen added loudly. "Who's with us?"

Now, a great many of the crowd cheered. Grimfeather once again leaned down, this time so Pwmpen could hear over the noise.

"Nicely done, Mr. Pwmpen," the professor said, and Pwmpen smiled broadly.

Henry would be proud.

As quickly as possible, Mossdale amassed the students recruited by the Echuio and arrived at the archeology department where he found Grimfeather's group attacking a psychic barrier surrounding the building. The barrier, presumably raised by Professor Rhun himself, was fading fast against the psionics being used by the loyalist students and faculty.

"We don't have much time," Mossdale said and directed his forces to attack the crowd.

From the elementalism department, a dozen rebel students unleashed a salvo of fire, bathing the front of the loyalists' group in a river of flames. The burning students pulled back immediately, stopping their own attack against the barrier.

Mossdale smiled in satisfaction.

"Get between them and the entrance!" he ordered. "Don't let them get past us!"

Mossdale scanned the opposing crowd and spotted Professor Grimfeather's eyes glinting in the fires of the students still ablaze. With his great, feathered arms, Grimfeather batted at the fires, quickly putting them out. He appeared to give orders of his own and, moments later, giant, humanoid shapes rose from the ground. Three in all, these golems made from dirt lumbered toward the rebel line.

Apparently, they have some elementalists of their own, Mossdale thought.

With his back literally against the building's front door, Mossdale shouted more commands. "Water psi, attack!"

Like fire hoses, powerful streams of water gushed from the hands of several rebel students. The streams struck the golems in the chest, blasting away mud and bits of stone. The loyalists scattered out of the way, shielding their faces from the debris.

"Hold!" Grimfeather's voice came thundering across the courtyard, but Mossdale saw several of the loyalists running away.

"Now, turn on the cold!" Mossdale yelled.

The spouts of water changed to shards of ice, tearing apart what remained of the dirt golems and cutting into the loyalist ranks. Several students fell wounded until others raised a psychic barrier of their own against the onslaught.

The battle outside the archeology department continued to rage. Shouts and screams reached the broken windows on the second floor when Elder Arwyn arrived with Roxie Blues. The latter was deathly pale, shocked by what she had seen outside as they had entered the building. The rest of them were as before, with Doric and Henry in the corner and Professor Rhun beside the Singing Lantern. The large room was crowded, and all eyes were on Ramus when he finally walked alone through the doorway. He was dressed in his usual attire, including a leather jacket with the wand stashed in the pocket.

"I got your message, Mother," Ramus said.

"I hope you came unarmed," Arwyn replied.

"Of course."

"Not that I don't trust you," she said, "but take off your jacket."

With a shrug, Ramus casually pulled off the coat and dropped it at his feet. Beneath, he wore his usual red t-shirt showed off the archaic tattoos running down his arms. As before, when he was trying on his father's tunic, Ramus noticed his mother eying the intricate ink. This time, however, she was making no effort to hide her dislike.

"You don't approve?" he asked her.

"To mutilate your body like that," she said disapprovingly, "it's just so... *un-Dahl.*"

"You have no idea," he replied wryly. "Actually, these were payment for working for the Psi Lords."

"I should have known," Arwyn said. "Their use of psionics to peddle information is an abomination. It's *beneath* you."

"Knowledge is power," Ramus said. "And it paid the bills after you abandoned me."

Professor Rhun interrupted.

"Be that as it may," he said, exchanging glances with Elder Arwyn, "what's important is whether you've brought the device."

"The wand is in my jacket," Ramus replied, "although I'm curious what you're going to use it for..."

"With the addition of the fragment in your wand," he said, "it's my hope the relic will once again work properly and let us signal our operatives around the Imperium."

"First let her go," Ramus said, pointing at Roxie. "Then you can have the wand."

"Very well," Rhun replied and waved toward the singer. Elder Arwyn gave Roxie a shove and she crossed the room to where Ramus was standing. Satisfied, Ramus bent down and removed the psi wand from his jacket. He tossed it carelessly to the professor who caught the device out of the air. Rhun laughed once it was in his hands.

"Perhaps now we can finally begin," he said, grinning.

"Knock yourself out," Ramus said.

Rhun took the wand and brought it toward the Lantern. As the professor did so, both the Lantern and the focusing crystal started glowing. The light grew brighter until Rhun held the wand next to the Lantern.

"Amazing," he whispered. "It's working..."

Meanwhile, Ramus gently nudged Roxie behind him while he fixed his eyes on Arwyn.

"Mother," he said.

"Yes, my dear?" the elder replied.

"When I said I was unarmed," he said, "I wasn't *exactly* telling the truth."

The tattoos on Ramus' arms began to glow like hot metal. With a blue radiance, they burned brighter than the wand or Lantern. At the same time, Ramus himself began to change.

"What are you doing?" his mother asked in horror. "What dark magic is this?"

"Dark psi," his son replied, his voice taking on a deep, growling quality.

Thick hair sprouted from Ramus' skin and his fingernails grew long and sharp. His mouth filled with monstrous teeth. Roxie, who was watching with as much horror as Ramus' mother, took several steps back.

Two security officers made the wrong choice and rushed toward Ramus.

Outside, the students and faculty were much too busy fighting to notice the windows of the archeology department. If they had, they might have been surprised to see a sizable spray of blood bathing the glass. After that, the reddened windows lit in bright flashes as a second battle broke out on the second floor.

When the battle in the courtyard began, the loyalists outnumbered the rebels, but as the clashes continued, many loyalists fled. Of those who stayed, nearly half ended up wounded or worse.

For his part, Pwmpen kept close to Professor Grimfeather, the Orubea's size giving the plump Dahl a sense of security. He was beginning to feel quite good about his chances when a bolt of lightning arced across the battlefield, striking both of them.

Sprawled on the ground, Pwmpen felt every nerve in his body twitching uncontrollably.

"Professor..." he managed to say but couldn't hear a reply over the buzzing in his ears.

Opening his eyes, Pwmpen saw Grimfeather lying motionlessly beside him and Mossdale standing over them.

"It's over," the Sylva said. "Just stay down."

"No," Pwmpen moaned, but he couldn't move.

"You're lucky," Mossdale said. "The professor took the brunt of that lightning attack. Otherwise, you would've been dead."

Mossdale showed Pwmpen the blaster he was holding.

"Maybe I should end it for you too," he said.

From the direction of the archeology building, a shrieking wave of sound split the clouds of smoke hovering over the scorched battleground. It struck Mossdale in the back, sending him flying over Pwmpen.

Pwmpen lifted his head toward the building and saw an attractive Dahl woman holding something in her hands.

Beside her were two humans.

"Henry!" Pwmpen shouted and one of the humans came running.

"Are you okay?" Henry asked, kneeling beside him.

"Not really..." Pwmpen replied weakly. "Who is that lady?"

"Roxie?" Henry replied. "Oh, she's a friend."

Holding something like a wand, Roxie pointed it at pockets of the remaining rebels, dropping them to the ground with sonic bursts.

"She's a singer," Henry added.

Pwmpen groaned. "She seems talented."

Just as quickly as it started, the battle was over. The remaining rebels were incapacitated and Doric and Roxie, along with the loyalists who were still standing, went about helping the wounded.

"How's Professor Grimfeather?" Pwmpen asked Doric when she came back.

She only shook her head grimly and said, "I'm sorry."

Pwmpen wiped his face, suddenly moist with tears. Dirt smeared down his cheek and Henry tried cleaning him up with a piece of his shirt.

"Grimfeather terrified me," Henry said, dabbing at Pwmpen's face, "but I'm sorry too..."

Doric left them and stopped next to Mossdale. Blood dripping from his ears, he stared at her defiantly.

"Professor Rhun and Elder Arwyn ran away," Doric told him. "The others are dead or under arrest."

Henry came and joined her.

"What did you do with Mistral?" he asked Mossdale.

"She's safe," Mossdale replied and coughed. "She's back in the forest where she belongs."

"She better be..." Henry muttered.

Doric looked around at the surrounding carnage.

"Was all this really worth it?" she asked.

Barely able to move, Mossdale rolled his head to one side so he could see the scene around him.

"Yes," he said.

The room was the same. In each corner, the braziers illuminated the stone walls in flickering, blue shadows, but only two robed figures were present now, Professor Rhun and Elder Arwyn. The professor's robes were tattered as if slashed by the claws of a beast, the material dark with dried blood. Rhun's left arm hung uselessly at his side while his right arm was raised toward the center of the chamber where a whirlwind of fire, earth, and air churned.

Elder Arwyn watched apprehensively.

"Come forth!" Rhun shouted. "Come forth!"

From the middle of the cyclone, a shape materialized among flakes of snow and jetting bursts of flame. The black form's white eyes opened and surveyed the two in the room. The whites narrowed to slits as the braziers went out.

"You have failed," Elder Brenin's spirit said.

Rhun lowered his hand and bowed his head. "Yes."

"Where are the others?" the psi ghost asked.

The professor was silent.

"Speak!" Brenin yelled.

"Dead or arrested," the professor replied quickly.

"And yet you still live..." the ghost growled.

"We escaped," Arwyn said, "but we were probably tracked here. The authorities will be coming soon."

"You were the leaders of the revolution," Brenin seethed. "What happened?"

"We were betrayed by my son," Arwyn replied. "He failed to see our vision — *your* vision."

Brenin chuckled bitterly.

"Your only vision was the return of our empire," he said. "A return of our people's place above all others in the galaxy."

"Yes," both Rhun and Arwyn said.

"Fools!" Brenin shouted. "Do you think that was the goal? The Dahl empire is but a means to an end, to bring enlightenment to the ignorant! What is the purpose of the Dahl? We teach others so that they may *see*! You see nothing... you are truly *blind*!"

Rhun and Arwyn fell to their knees before the whirlwind. The eyes glared at them.

"I have waited endlessly," Brenin said, "only to see my people fail once again. You squandered your chance, and who knows when there'll be another?"

"Forgive us, Elder!" Rhun said, his words vanishing into the blackness.

The spirit's eyes turned blood red. "No."

With a sudden flash, lightning erupted from the spirit, casting long shadows on the walls behind Rhun and Arwyn's bodies. Blue-white fingers of electricity twisted through the air, enveloping the robed figures. Their hands reached out toward the ghost before them, but the crimson eyes stared back without mercy.

Then, the light and the ghost were gone. Only bits of melting ice and clumps of dirt remained beside the smoldering robes, and those who wore them, lying on the floor.

The fire in the braziers reignited as a group of Dahl entered through the doorway. Elder Blynora and a few members of the Council were among them.

From behind the group, Chancellor Telyn stepped out when he saw his wife and ran to her side.

"Arwyn," he said gently.

She opened her eyes. "Telyn…"

"Why?" was the only question Telyn could think to ask.

The elder struggled to speak, but said, "There has to be something more… something more than *this.*"

"It was enough," Telyn said.

"Not for me," she replied with her dying breath.

CHAPTER SIXTEEN

The flowers of Dôlgoch were in perpetual bloom and a warm breeze gently blew across the valley. The Elder Council, minus Arwyn, had taken their places on the hilltop benches along with Chancellor Telyn, Captain Ramus, and Roxie Blues.

Elder Blynora stood beside the Singing Lantern resting on a small, silver table while Ramus had the psi wand tucked away in his pocket for safekeeping.

"This has been a difficult time," Blynora was saying in her most official tone, "but we are here today to thank those who helped us through it."

The elders clapped and even smiled slightly toward their guests, although with an awkwardness that Ramus could keenly feel.

"Chancellor Telyn," Blynora went on, "if you would join me?"

Telyn rose and took his place beside the senior elder. Much to Ramus' surprise, his father appeared uncomfortable, even nervous.

"As you know," Blynora said, "the Elder Council is lacking a member after the unfortunate demise of Elder Arwyn. Although we are saddened by Arwyn's betrayal, we cannot forget the many years she served the council and our people."

At least they can remember some things, Ramus thought.

"To replace our missing member, and to reward Chancellor Telyn for his lifelong service to Prenwyn University," Blynora continued, "we are happy to appoint him to this council as *Elder* Telyn."

Although Elder Blynora had already told him of the appointment, Telyn still smiled and, as far as Ramus could tell, seemed almost pleased.

"Thank you," Telyn replied graciously. "It is a great honor to join the rest of you on the council."

The elders, along with Ramus and Roxie, clapped politely.

"However," Blynora said, interrupting, "there is another issue that remains..."

Ramus and Roxie exchanged glances while Blynora nodded to Telyn and took a seat on one of the marble benches.

"For centuries," Elder Telyn began, "our people have exiled those who did not fit the standard of what we considered proper Dahlvish behavior—" Telyn glanced at Ramus, "—my son being one of them. However, it was my son and Miss Blues who were instrumental in defeating the Echuio and saving our way of life."

Telyn glanced at the other elders.

"Not much changes on Gwlad Ard'un," he said, "but the rise of the Echuio was a lesson for us all that some change must be allowed, or it may happen anyway against our wishes. As a teacher, I cannot ignore a good lesson..."

Ramus did his best not to cringe as his father waited for laughter that never came.

"Anyway," Telyn went on, "I have spoken with Elder Blynora and the council and, after much thought, they have agreed to make one of the greatest changes possible."

Ramus heard Roxie take a deep breath.

"With the aid of the artifact," Elder Telyn said, "and my son's device, we will remove the memory wipe that has erased the existence of countless exiles. Beginning today, the Forgotten will be remembered once again!"

Roxie exhaled and laughed, grabbing Ramus and giving him a hug. Feeling her arms around him, Ramus recalled the moment a few days before when his father had asked him what he was getting out of all this.

"I want you to end the exile," Ramus had said at the time. "The Forgotten don't have a home to come back to, or family to love them back. I want you to fix that."

"How?" his father had said.

"I know your psi power," Ramus said. "You can spread learning telepathically, can't you? Then do that across the Imperium using the Singing Lantern."

Telyn had shaken his head. "I still don't see how..."

"With the Sprites and the Pool of Memory," Ramus replied. "Mother unlocked memories of me, so I know the memories of the others can be unlocked too. Just make it happen... that's why I'm helping, so people like Roxie will never have to lose their parents again. And people like her parents never die without knowing they had a daughter."

Ramus, if he was being honest, didn't truly believe his father would be permitted to do so, since the chancellor was not a member of the council. However, that took care of itself better than Ramus could have dreamed. As Elder Telyn, his father had full access to the Pool of Memory and the memories of those who had been forgotten.

"As you know," Telyn was saying now beside the Lantern, "the crystal of the artifact was damaged, from one of my son's crew I believe..."

Ramus looked away.

"So, if you could bring that wand of yours up here," Telyn said, "we can start."

"You want to do this right now?" Ramus replied.

"It's been long enough," his father said.

Roxie let Ramus go and he went to join his father while taking the wand out of his pocket. The father and son stood next to the table, Ramus holding the focusing crystal at the tip of the wand as close to the Lantern as possible.

"Let's begin..." Telyn said.

When Lady Veber heard of what had transpired on the Dahl home world, she demanded that the Singing Lantern be returned to human hands. Since Lord Maycare was the owner of the artifact, he insisted that the Lantern be returned to *him* specifically. The Elder Council protested, but to no avail, and it was packed up for travel with Jessica Doric overseeing the work. Elder Blynora offered the use of a Dahlvish ship, but Doric, cognizant of her recent treatment, chose to travel on the *Wanderer* instead.

At the ship's loading ramp, she watched as the special crate containing the Lantern was carried onto the freighter by workers. Meanwhile, some distance away, Henry and Pwmpen were watching as well, although Pwmpen seemed preoccupied.

"What are you thinking about?" Henry asked.

The Dahl scrunched up his round face and looked at his human friend questioningly.

"Have you ever remembered something you didn't even know you had forgotten?" Pwmpen replied.

"No..."

"Since yesterday," Pwmpen said, "I keep remembering things."

"Like what?"

"I have an uncle — my father's brother — I never knew I had."

"Well, that's nice," Henry remarked.

"Apparently my father had him exiled before I was born."

"Oh, that's not so nice," Henry replied. "Why did your father do that?"

"My uncle liked to play the accordion..."

"Ah," Henry said. "Well, that's going to make for an awkward conversation."

"I suppose so," Pwmpen said with a laugh. He smiled at Henry. "I'm going to miss you."

"Me?" Henry asked.

"Of course!" Pwmpen replied. "It won't be the same without you. You've really brought me out of my shell."

"Sorry," Henry said.

The Dahl chuckled. "Don't be sorry! It's been great, no matter what my parents say..."

With the Lantern safely aboard the *Wanderer*, Doric joined Henry and Pwmpen on the tarmac.

"That's done at least," she said. "I'll be glad when we're home again."

"Aren't you going to miss Gwlad Ard'un and the university?" Henry asked.

Doric took a moment to think about it. "Not really."

"But—" Henry started.

"I know!" Doric replied defensively. "Let's just say this has been an eye-opening experience. The Dahl aren't exactly who I thought they were." She glanced at Pwmpen. "No offense."

"No, I suppose we're not," the Dahl replied. "Even to ourselves."

They stared at the ship for a while in silence until Henry finally spoke.

"Does Lord Maycare know his lantern was damaged?" he asked.

"Good heavens, no!" Doric replied.

"Really?" Henry said.

"Are *you* going to tell him?" she asked.

Henry's eyes widened as he shook his head. "No..."

"I'm the one who convinced him to let me bring it here," Doric added. "I'd rather not tell him there's a chip missing."

"Speaking of which," Pwmpen said, "what about the wand?"

"Captain Ramus said he's keeping it," Doric replied. "And anyway, it's a lot safer for everybody if the Lantern can't be used without the focusing crystal in the wand."

Everyone nodded in agreement.

"Do you think Lord Maycare missed us?" Henry asked hopefully.

Doric sighed.

"If he remembers we were gone," she said.

After inciting the Echuio to rebel against the Imperium and then sending an anonymous message alerting the Imperium of the very same Dahlvish group, Enrion had faded into the background in hopes his schemes would do as much damage as possible. When a full revolution did not materialize, however, the Red Dahl fled to the planet Fortunas IV.

Fortunas IV had been a sleepy planet until the trade routes from the Imperium arrived. The bazaars and eclectic nightlife that sprung up afterwards had become famous and a perfect place to lose oneself if the circumstances demanded it. Enrion needed to get lost and the miles of shops and trade stalls on Fortunas IV were just the thing. Even so, the vermilion skin of a Sarkan was hard to miss, so Enrion pulled his hood tighter as he skulked down the narrow streets.

He was sure someone was following him.

Enrion ducked into a storefront and found himself in a fabric shop, bolts of cloth propped up against the walls and samples stretched out on tables. The proprietor greeted him warmly.

"How may I help you?" the shop owner asked.

"Just browsing," the Sarkan replied. "Do you have a back door?"

"A back door? No, my friend. Just the entrance there..."

Enrion frowned and turned to head back out, only to find a large Magna blocking his way.

"Ra-Gor!" Enrion said.

The Magna captain seemed surprisingly happy to see the Red Dahl, although Ra-Gor's face showed scarring from burns that hadn't been there the last time Enrion saw him. One of his ram-like horns was also missing, blackened at the stump, which gave his head a lopsided appearance.

"You told the Imperial Navy the coordinates of my ship, didn't you?" Ra-Gor asked.

Enrion's red skin darkened. "I don't know what you mean..."

"You sold the information to the Psi Lords," the Magna went on, "and they sold it to the Navy."

"See?" Enrion replied. "The *Psi Lords* sold you out, not me!"

Ra-Gor took another step into the shop, which the shopkeeper took as a sign to leave the store entirely. He slipped past the Magna and exited the premises.

Now alone with someone at least two feet taller and quite angry, Enrion retreated slowly, coming to a halt against one of the display tables.

"I needed a way to contact the Dahlvish underground," Enrion explained. "I didn't have any money, so I gave the Psi Lords what they asked for. What they did with the information is hardly *my* fault. How did you find me anyway?"

"I asked the Psi Lords, naturally," Ra-Gor replied.

The Sarkan clenched his fist.

"You didn't just sell me out," Ra-Gor said. "You also left an anonymous tip about the Echuio as well!"

Ra-Gor moved closer while his head brushed the brass lanterns hanging from the ceiling.

"You wanted conflict!" Enrion shouted. "The Emperor needed to know the Dahl couldn't be trusted. I was sowing distrust! I was doing what you *asked!*"

Ra-Gor pulled a blaster from the holster on his hip.

"Never trust a Sarkan..." he said.

Enrion scowled.

"Not if you're smart!" he yelled. "You green-skinned fool!"

Just as Ra-Gor's fingers tightened around the trigger, a small sphere of energy materialized in Enrion's palm. He threw the ball of light, striking the Magna in the forearm and knocking the blaster away as it fired. The hot, orange plasma hit a bolt of cloth, setting it ablaze.

Disarmed, the big Magna leaped forward as another of Enrion's energy spheres exploded at the center of Ra-Gor's chest. The Magna landed on the Red Dahl, pinning Enrion on top of the display table.

"Get off me!" Enrion gurgled, feeling the Magna's hands closing around his throat.

The shop quickly filled with thick smoke, the flames spreading through the merchandise. Having a single exit and no smoke alarms would probably have been a safety violation on most planets, but regulations were infamously lax on Fortunas IV.

Beneath the Magna, Enrion cast more energy spheres into Ra-Gor's body, but with no effect. Choking from soot and the hands around his throat, Enrion couldn't be sure if Ra-Gor was even still alive, but the Magna's weight was too great to lift off him.

The shop became darker as Enrion slowly lost consciousness.

Outside, a crowd had gathered to watch the fire along with the shopkeeper. The proprietor wondered if his insurance had been paid in full that month as his store collapsed in the inferno.

Lady Veber recognized the dingy alley, having been there before. The life of an Imperial Regent wasn't always glamorous, but this was worse than usual. Nevertheless, she would do *anything* if it meant protecting her charge, the young emperor, and the Imperium itself.

Dressed inconspicuously, she stepped over a puddle of questionable liquid and passed through a secret door. She walked down a gently sloping passageway into a chamber heavy with the smell of incense.

Kanet Solan welcomed her.

"Lady Veber," he said. "What a surprise!"

"That's Lady *Regent* to you," she replied coldly.

"But of course!" Solan corrected himself. "I didn't expect to see you here again."

"I'm trying not to make a habit of it," Lady Veber said.

"We're always happy to help..."

"The Psi Lords are lucky I allow them to exist at all."

"And yet here we are," he said, unbothered by the veiled threat. "What can we do for you *this time?*"

Lady Veber came closer, as if concerned someone might hear her. She realized this was absurd since the room was undoubtedly bugged, even if Solan's green-skinned priestess wasn't there to read her mind.

"I need information, obviously," Lady Veber said.

"From the lowly Psi Lords?" Solan replied. "What could the *Regent* need from us? Don't you have the entire Imperial Intelligence Agency at your disposal?"

Lady Veber glared at him.

"Quite," she said, "but the Agency appears to be compromised, it seems. Frankly, I'm not sure who I can trust at the moment, which explains my visit."

"So, you trust *us* more than your own government?"

"Not at all," Lady Veber replied, "but I do trust your greed. I have little doubt the Psi Lords would sell their own mothers for the right price."

A tight smile crossed Solan's face. "Our mothers would understand..."

"As it happens," the regent went on, "it's come to our attention that there are certain elements close to our leadership that might have mixed loyalties."

"You're referring to your Dahlvish advisers, I presume?"

"You know about that?" she muttered.

Solan shrugged. "We're a data cartel, after all..."

"With that in mind," Lady Veber said, "I need you to root out the advisers who were sympathetic to the recent uprising on the Dahl home planet. They're still a danger until they're removed."

"Removed?" Solan asked.

"Arrested if possible. Killed if necessary."

"Well, collecting the information might take some time," Solan said. "We humans have grown particularly dependent on the Dahl over the years. There are advisers scattered throughout the Imperium."

"I don't care how much it costs," Lady Veber said. "I just need it done as soon as possible."

"I assume the boy Emperor has approved of this action?" Solan asked. "After all, your methods might be considered... *unconventional*."

"He trusts that I'll do whatever is necessary."

"Ah, that word again: *trust*," Solan said. "Perhaps we all take it a bit for granted."

"Can you do what I ask?" Lady Veber replied.

Solan laughed casually.

"Of course," he said. "As it happens, my best agent is attending to another matter, but once she returns, I will assign her to your request."

"Good," Lady Veber said, turning.

"Oh, Lady *Regent*," Solan called after her.

"What?"

"Please give my regards to the Emperor, would you?" he asked.

"Not on your life," Lady Veber replied, and headed back up the corridor and into the dirty alley beyond.

After the *Wanderer* landed at the Regalis starport on Aldorus, Mel and Ramus rented a gravcar and flew to Uncle Artie's burrow among the waste heaps. To the casual observer, the Boneyards were a never-changing wasteland, but for Mel, she knew that the daily arrival of more garbage from the rest of Regalis meant the mounds of debris were constantly refreshed with new junk. It was a tinker's paradise, which Mel was only beginning to realize.

Z-4T the robot met them outside as the unwelcoming committee.

"It's about time you got back!" Zat said, his mismatched hands on his waist.

"Did you worry about me?" Mel asked slyly.

"What?" Zat replied. "No! Of course not!"

"Where's Uncle Artie?" she asked.

"Inside," the robot said, "but be prepared..."

"Prepared for what?" Ramus asked.

Zat didn't answer, leading them inside where Mel and Ramus found the old Gnomi on crutches.

"What happened?" Mel asked in shock.

"Nothing to worry about!" Uncle Artie replied, trying to hobble over to them. "Just fell down is all..."

"Nonsense!" the robot said and pushed him as gently as possible into a chair. "That horrible woman from the Psi Lords did this."

"*Demona*," Ramus growled under his breath.

"Whatever her name is," Zat replied, "but she'll be back soon."

Mel produced the wand from a satchel over her shoulder and showed it to Uncle Artie.

"See?" she said. "I told you I'd make it work."

"Oh, it works alright..." Ramus added.

Uncle Artie took the device and rolled it around in his hand. "Nice craftsmanship."

"Thanks!" Mel replied, faintly blushing.

"The Psi Lords will pay handsomely," he went on.

"About that—" Ramus started, but in the doorway, Ta Demona suddenly appeared in her black priestess robes like a dark cloud.

"About *what?*" she asked, a purple aura manifesting in Demona's outstretched hand.

Ramus' eyes flared as he spun around. Zat ducked for cover behind the chair where Uncle Artie was laid up.

"Stop!" Uncle Artie shouted. "No fighting!"

Ramus relaxed ever so slightly and the glow in Demona's hand lost some of its color. A long time ago, the two of them had been lovers while they both worked for the Psi Lords. Even now, something still lingered between them.

"We have the device as promised," Uncle Artie told the Psi Lord agent. "Just take it and go!"

"No," Ramus said.

Uncle Artie glanced up in surprise. "What? Why not?"

"It's too dangerous for the Psi Lords to have," he answered.

"Of course it's dangerous," Demona said. "That's why we *want* it!"

"Well, I won't let you have it," Ramus replied defiantly.

The purple energy coming from Demona regained strength, now radiating from all over her body. From beneath Ramus' jacket, a blue light shone brightly from the tattoos on his arms. His fingernails turned into sharp claws, although his face remained largely unchanged.

"If you want the wand," Ramus said, "you'll have to go through *me!*"

This time, Mel was the one to speak.

"Stop!" she shouted. "Just stop!"

Neither Demona nor Ramus changed their demeanor, but neither began an attack.

"Ramus is right," Mel said. "I made the thing and it's wicked powerful for sure." She turned to Uncle Artie. "I'm sorry, but we can't give it to the Psi Lords."

"I see," Uncle Artie said. "That's a shame. I could've used the money..."

"I know," Mel replied. "I'll make it up to you somehow."

Zat, poking his head around the chair, was skeptical. "That'll be the day!"

"I will!" Mel yelled. "I promise!"

Demona, whose eyes had been steadily fixed on Ramus, shook her head while the purple aura disappeared around her.

"Solan won't like this," she said.

"Tell Solan he can go to hell," Ramus replied, his fingers returning to normal. "And you can also tell him that this family is under my protection. If anything happens to Uncle Artie or Mel, you'll have me to contend with."

"What about *me?*" Zat asked.

Ramus eyed him over his shoulder. "Sure, the robot too..."

Demona crossed her slender arms.

"At some point, Ramus, you'll fall through that thin ice you've been skating on," she said. "When you do, I'll be *waiting.*"

"Looking forward to it," he replied and watched as she left the way she came.

Ramus put his hand out in front of Uncle Artie. "I'm going to need that, if you don't mind."

The old Gnomi considered the device for a moment but gave it over to the ship captain. Ramus slipped the wand into his jacket while looking at Mel.

"You owe me, too," he said.

"Me?" Mel asked. "For what?"

Ramus scowled. "For your passage to Gwlad Ard'un and back!"

"Oh, right," Mel said. "How the hell am I supposed to pay for that *now?*"

"I'll think of something," Ramus replied.

After she had workers return the Singing Lantern to the display case in the mansion hallway, Jessica Doric found Benson, Lord Maycare's butlerbot, in the kitchen. He was preparing a tray of tea.

"Hello, Benson," Doric said.

"Good afternoon," the robot replied, not looking up.

"Glad to be back," she remarked. "Is that tea for Lord Maycare?"

Benson finally gave her a passing glance. "Well, it's not for *me*, I assure you..."

"Right."

"Is Henry with you?" the robot asked.

"No," Doric replied. "He's home with his goldfish, recuperating."

"Well, if you'd like to follow me," the robot said, "I'm sure Lord Maycare will be pleased to see you."

"Really?"

"Yes, there's been some excitement since you've been gone."

To Doric's surprise, the butlerbot did not lead her down to the basement forge, but rather into the study. Maycare lay in a ridiculously plush chair with his leg propped up on an ottoman and one arm in a sling. He was otherwise immaculate, his hair and pressed shirt perfect as always. Maycare smiled at her with pearly teeth.

"Jess!" he shouted. "You're back!"

Benson set the tray on a table and poured some tea into a china cup.

"Actually, I've been here since this morning," Doric said, "making sure the Singing Lantern was situated."

Maycare accepted the cup from Benson, took a sip, and handed it back immediately.

"Could use some more sugar..." Maycare said.

The robot rolled his eyes and dropped a pair of sugar cubes into the tea, stirring vigorously with a silver spoon. He gave the cup to Maycare who took another taste.

"That's better," he said.

"It was quite an adventure—" Doric said.

"It *certainly* was!" Maycare interrupted.

"You're not talking about my trip, are you?" she replied dryly.

"What? No!" Maycare said, chuckling. "I'm talking about my episode of *Break My Blade!*"

Doric dropped into the chair beside him in resignation. "What happened?"

"He nearly burned the place down," Benson replied for him.

Maycare shushed the robot.

"Let me tell it," he said. "I was making a blade with a 1000-layer Damascus pattern, but my billet was so big that when I took it out of the forge, the heat set the Benbot—"

"That's one of the judges," Benson explained.

"—on *fire!*" Maycare finished. "To be fair, if Benbot hadn't run around the studio yelling 'I'm on fire! I'm on fire!', I doubt it would've spread everywhere. It's really not my fault..."

"Of course," Doric said.

"Anyway, the insurance will take care of everything," Maycare said. "And they can always build another Benbot."

Benson scowled.

"Will that be all, sir?" he asked.

"Sure," Maycare replied absentmindedly.

Doric watched the robot go and then said, "I had an adventure too..."

"You were on Gwlad Ard'un, weren't you?" Maycare asked.

"Well, yes!" she said. "We were almost arrested and then we got attacked..."

"You didn't scratch my relic, did you?"

Doric stammered. "No, *I* didn't."

"Well, no harm done then..." he said.

"You know about the revolution, don't you?" she asked.

"I don't watch the news, Jess," Maycare said, sipping his tea.

Doric sighed. "Are you at least happy to have me back?"

Maycare slammed the cup back on the tray beside him.

"Of course!" he exclaimed. "I missed you and that other one tremendously!"

"Well, that's good, I guess..."

"Do you have any idea how boring it was with just Benson around?" he added.

"Well, it's good to be back anyway," she said.

"Since you *are*," Maycare said, "I heard about an artifact I'd like us to find. It was last seen on a planet where the rain melts human flesh..."

Doric rose from her chair and headed for the door.

"I'll get right on it," she said.

"And tell Benson to come back in here, won't you?" he said after her. "This tea is too sweet!"

"I will," she said over her shoulder. She was smiling but she didn't want Maycare to see.

It is good to be back, she thought.

The dive bar Le Sous-Sol was more crowded than usual, with at least a dozen people sitting around the little stage in the back.

Ramus was one of them.

Roxie Blues was finishing up her set of torch songs, her voice like an angel engulfed in cigarette smoke. When she was done, Roxie thanked the crowd for the smattering of applause and went to sit with Ramus.

"That was almost gratifying," she mused, pulling out a chair for herself.

Ramus set down his drink and smiled. "Did the bandbot get tuned up tonight?"

"Sam is always in tune," Roxie replied.

The two Dahl stared at each other across the table while Roxie drank from a champagne flute Red the bartender had brought her. Ramus needed a refill, but Red had ignored him.

"I wanted to thank you for everything you've done," Roxie said finally.

"You already did," Ramus replied, which brought a faint redness to Roxie's cheeks.

"Still," she said, "it's good to be remembered for a change."

"I won't forget."

She shook her head ruefully. "You know what I mean."

Ramus stared at his empty glass.

"Yeah," he said, "the Elder Council won't be able to exile people anymore..."

"I'm not sure of that," Roxie replied. "But at least people will still remember those who are sent away."

"Right."

"I suppose you'll be leaving?" she asked.

Ramus winced. "Yeah."

"I guess freighter captains don't stick around very long..." she said.

"No."

"It was nice of you to let Mel come with you," she said, smiling.

"Well, I'm not sure *she* thinks so," Ramus replied. "She needs to pay off her debt somehow, so working on the *Wanderer* was a good way to do it. Plus, she'll drive Fugg crazy, so that's a bonus."

Another awkward silence. Another sip of champagne.

"We shouldn't be sad," Roxie said. "We had a lot of fun!"

"We did?" Ramus asked. "I remember a lot of blood..."

Roxie glanced away before her eyes returned to him.

"If I hadn't gone," she said, "I never would've known what happened to my parents."

"I'm sorry they died before remembering you."

"I still remember *them*," she said.

"There's that."

"I'm sorry about your mother," Roxie added.

Ramus really wished his glass wasn't empty.

"She probably got what she deserved," he said, "but it doesn't make it feel any better."

"We make choices," Roxie said, her voice tinged with regret. "Then we have to live with them."

"Are you sorry about us?" Ramus asked.

Roxie reached across the table and touched his hand. "Not at all."

"I don't know when I'll be back here again," Ramus admitted. "It's a big universe..."

"I know."

It was almost time for Roxie's next set. Ramus got up from the table, came around to her side, and leaned in. She lifted her eyes, meeting his, and kissed him.

"I'll see you around," she said and watched him go, and then she went back on stage. Sam the bandbot started playing the next song and Roxie sang the blues.

For the continuing saga of the Imperium Chronicles, watch for the next volume in the series.

CHARACTER LIST

Abbot, The: The Dahlvish leader of the Dharmesh Monastery.

Arwyn, Elder: A member of the Elder Council. Wife of Chancellor Telyn.

Benson: Butlerbot of Lord Devlin Maycare. Replaced the previous robot, Bentley, after he was destroyed.

Blues, Roxie: Dahl lounge singer at the Sous-Sol.

Blynora, Elder: Leader of the Elder Council

Brenin the Great, Elder: Long-lived ruler of the Dahl Empire. Killed by a Magna assassin.

Demona, Ta: A ruthless agent for the Psi Lords who uses her abilities to collect information.

Doric, Professor Jessica: Head of research for the Maycare Institute of Xeno Studies.

Enrion: Sarkan agent for the Magna.

Finnegan, Finneus: Henry Riff's goldfish.

Freck, Arthur ("Uncle Artie"): Mel Freck's uncle.

Freck, Melinda ("Mel"): A tinker from the Gnomi race.

Fugg, Orkney: A Gordian and the chief engineer of the Wanderer.

Gen: A general purpose robot who works for Capt. Ramus.

Grimfeather, Professor: An Orubea and professor at Prenwyn University.

Groen, Emperor Jack: Emperor of the Imperium.

Maycare, Lord Devlin: Famous sportsman and playboy. Founder of the Maycare Institute of Xeno Studies.

Maycare, Lord Captain Robert: Captain of the HIMS Baron Lancaster. Nephew of Lord Devlin Maycare.

Mistral: A Sylph encountered in the forest.

Mossdale, Elisan: A male Sylva in the Department of Archeology at Prenwyn University. Like all male Sylva, he lacks psionic powers.

Naiad: The interface used to access the Pool of Memory.

Pwmpen: Henry's dorm roommate.

Ra-Gor: Magna officer/handler for Enrion

Ramus, Captain Rowan: Captain of the freighter the *Wanderer*. A Dahl outcast knowledgeable in the forbidden art of Dark Psi.

Red: Gordian bartender at the Sous-Sol.

Riff, Henry: Overly excitable assistant to Prof. Doric.

Rhun, Professor: Professor of Archeology.

Solan, Kanet: High-ranking member of the Psi Lords.

Telyn, Chancellor: The head of Prenwyn University.

Veber, Lady Rebecca: Matriarch and leader of the Veber family. Imperial Regent to Emperor Jack Groen.

Z-4T (aka Zat): Robot assistant of Uncle Artie.

GLOSSARY

Aldorus: The planet on which the Imperial government is located.

Ashetown: A district of Regalis where the poorest of the city live.

Augmentors: A monastic sisterhood who worship technology. Found on the planet Technas Delphi.

Baron Lancaster, HIMS: A heavy cruiser of the Imperial Navy. Commanded by Lord Captain Robert Maycare.

Blaenwaun Bay: A Dahl starship that carried Jessica Doric and Henry Riff to the Dahl home world.

Boneyards: An area of Ashetown where discarded machines and robots are dumped.

Break My Blade!: A popular TV competition that involves forging knives, which are then judged.

Coedwig Lledrith ("Forest of Illusions"): A dark wood which is, according to legend, haunted by tortured spirits.

Cyber Collective: An independent, interstellar nation founded by robots.

Dahl: An ancient race dedicated to the accumulation of knowledge. Physically slight, they coincidentally resemble elves of human folklore. Several sub-species of Dahl exist in Andromeda.

Dahl Empire: A vast empire run by the Dahl, spanning thousands of light years, and which existed long before humans arrived in the Andromeda Galaxy. Symbolized by a sun with lines radiating out.

Dark Psi: A school of psionics, outlawed by the Dahl, that can transform flesh and reanimate dead tissue.

Dharmesh Monastery: The home of a group of Dahlvish monks in the Palatine Mountains on the planet Aldorus.

Dôlgoch: Name of valley where the Elder Council meets.

Echuio ("Awakening"): A secret, outlawed organization bent on returning the Dahl Empire.

Elder Council: Executive government of the Dahl.

Erudites: A blue-skinned race with high intelligence.

Eudora Prime: A planet on the border between the Imperium and the Cyber Collective.

Five Families: The most powerful houses of the Imperial nobility. Direct descendants of the captains from the surviving sleeper ships that came from Earth.

Forgotten, The: Dahlvish term for any Dahl that's been exiled from their society. The memory of their existence is psionically erased from all non-exiled Dahl.

Fortunas IV: A distant planet of the Imperium known for its expansive bazaars and nightlife.

Gnomi: A diminutive race, no more than two to three feet tall. Derisively called *tinks*, the Gnomi are highly proficient with machines and electronics.

Gordian: A race of stubborn, boar-like humanoids with pig noses and tusks. Physically stocky, but shorter than the average human.

Groen: One of the Five Families.

Gwlad Ard'un: The Dahl home world

Imperial Conclave: A special meeting used to decide who becomes the Imperial Emperor.

Imperium: An empire largely controlled by humans. Founded 700 years ago, after humans arrived in sleeper ships from Earth after an 800-year journey.

Kuent'l Nanzi: Part-spider, part-humanoid race native to the forests of Gwlad Ard'un.

Magna: A race of green-skinned humanoids with devil- or ram-like horns. Larger and more physically imposing than an average human.

Magna Supremacy: A major interstellar power at odds with the Imperium.

Maycare Institute of Xeno Studies: An organization founded by Lord Devlin Maycare and run by Professor Jessica Doric. The purpose of the institute is to find and take possession of xeno technology before it falls into the hands of disreputable parties such as Warlock Industries.

Middleton: A district of Regalis filled with large businesses and middle-class neighborhoods.

Narwa: Name of Enrion's ship.

Nobles ("Aristocracy"): Families of the Imperium who are directly descended from the crews of the sleeper ships. The most powerful of these are called the Five Families.

Nodesphere: A network of interconnected computers (i.e.: an Internet).

Orubea: Race of large creatures that looks like a mix between a bear and an owl.

Pool of Memory: A liquid computer in which the collected knowledge of the Dahl is stored.

Prenwyn University: Largest, most prestigious university on the planet Gwlad Ard'un.

Psi Lords: A secretive data cartel that uses dark psi and espionage to gather and sell information to the highest bidder.

Psi Wand: Electronic device that amplifies psionic abilities.

Psionics: Special mental abilities common among Dahl and related sub-species.

Regalis: Capital city and seat of government of the Imperium, located on the planet Aldorus.

Sarkan ("Red Dahl"): A race of Dahl with bright red skin. Opposed to the Dahl's cooperation with the Imperium, they assist the Magna Supremacy.

Singing Lantern, The: An ancient Dahlvish artifact originally used to communicate psionically over long distances.

Sous-Sol, Le ("The Basement"): A bar located in Ashetown at the corner of Marlowe and Vine.

Sprite: Floating, mobile version of the Naiad. Appears as a liquid-filled orb with mechanical arms underneath.

Sylph: Race of fairy-like creatures found on Gwlad Ard'un.

Sylva (aka Woodland Dahl): A race of Dahl who prefer living close to nature. Female Sylvans have psionic abilities while males do not.

Technas Delphi: Ta Demona's homeworld, run by a female-centered theocracy called the Augmentors.

Technotown: A district on the planet Eudora Prime where electronics and other devices are sold.

Underdelve: An underground community on Eudora Prime, largely inhabited by non-humans.

Veber: One of the Five Families.

Wanderer: Freighter owned by Captain Ramus.

Warlock Industries: A mega-corporation operating throughout the Imperium, specializing in military hardware, advanced technology, and genetic experimentation.

West End: The richest district of Regalis. Also, the location of most Imperial government buildings.

Xeno: A non-human.

Xenotech: Alien, non-human technology.

ABOUT THE AUTHOR

W. (William) H. Mitchell was born in Omaha, NE and graduated from the University of Nebraska-Lincoln with a degree in English. He lives with his wife and cats outside of Kansas City.

Follow him on his website at WHMitchellFiction.com

www.ingramcontent.com/pod-product-compliance
Lightning Source LLC
Chambersburg PA
CBHW030817210726
48290CB00002B/639